MURDER in
BERKELEY
SQUARE

Also by Vanessa Riley:

The Lady Worthing Mysteries
Murder in Westminster
Murder in Drury Lane
Murder in Berkeley Square

The Rogues and Remarkable Women Romances
A Duke, the Lady, and a Baby
An Earl, the Girl, and a Toddler
A Duke, the Spy, an Artist, and a Lie

Betting Against the Duke Romances
A Gamble at Sunset
A Wager at Midnight

Historical Fiction
Island Queen
Sister Mother Warrior
Queen of Exiles

VANESSA RILEY

MURDER in BERKELEY SQUARE

KENSINGTON
PUBLISHING CORP.

www.kensingtonbooks.com

KENSINGTON BOOKS are published by

Kensington Publishing Corp.
900 Third Avenue
New York, NY 10022

All Kensington titles, imprints, and distributed lines are available at special quantity discounts for bulk purchases for sales promotion, premiums, fund-raising, educational, or institutional use.

Special book excerpts or customized printings can also be created to fit specific needs. For details, write or phone the office of the Kensington Special Sales Manager: Attn. Special Sales Department, Kensington Publishing Corp., 900 Third Avenue, New York, NY 10022. Phone: 1-800-221-2647.

The K with book logo Reg U.S. Pat. & TM Off.

Library of Congress Card Catalogue Number: 2024936514

ISBN: 978-1-4967-3868-4
First Kensington Hardcover Edition: October 2024

ISBN: 978-1-4967-3874-5 (ebook)

10 9 8 7 6 5 4 3 2 1

Printed in the United States of America

For the mystery lovers who love a twisty plot and a great feat of revenge.

For the Lady Worthings in the world making their way. Know your worth!

Cast of Characters

Character List	Alternate Names and Titles
Abigail Carrington Monroe	Lady Worthing Baroness Abbie
Stapleton Henderson	Commander Henderson Physician, Abbie's neighbor
Neil Vaughn	Godfather, Abbie's god-father Mr. Vaughn Uncle Vaughn, Florentina's uncle
Florentina Sewell	Miss Sewell Flo Abbie's cousin
Mrs. Smith	Abbie's housekeeper
Miss Bellows	Abbie's personal maid
Mr. Rogers	Abbie's butler
James Monroe	Lord Worthing Baron Abbie's husband

Character List	Alternate Names and Titles
Mr. Rawlins	Abbie's driver
John Carrington	Abbie's father Uncle Carrington, Florentina's uncle
Wilson Shaw	Mr. Shaw Abbie's solicitor Childhood friend
Dinah Carrington	Abbie's half sister
The Sewells	Florentina's parents Abbie's aunt (by blood), Abbie's uncle (by marriage) Vaughn's brother and sister-in-law
Lord Duncan	Charles Flowers The magistrate of London Neighbor in Berkeley Square
Benjamin Brooks	Barrister Neighbor in Berkeley Square
John Clayton	The Earl of Constock Neighbor in Berkeley Square

William Holston   Retired military man
                                    Neighbor in Berkeley
                                        Square

Frederick Talson   Retired physician
                                    Neighbor in Berkeley
                                        Square

Derrick Mayer   Financier
                                    Neighbor in Berkeley
                                        Square

Mr. Peters   Lord Duncan's valet

Mr. Villers   Lord Duncan's chef

Mary Edwards   Mrs. Edwards
                                    Human computer

Prologue

December 23, 1806
Thirty-Seven Berkeley Square

A chance to savor a fine meal while delighting in the tawdriest true crimes is an opportunity Benjamin Brooks will never forgo. Sitting in his study, he waits for the last of his servants to leave for Yuletide. Smiling to himself, ebullient, he picks up the tool that's going to be used to torment his foe, an old rebel's rhyme.

The parchment in his hands bears the lines of a hideous rhyme sung by the enslaved of Martinique when they're planning to attack their masters. He reads it, singing the threats aloud.

> *Stunned, seven little Grand-blancs mourn in sharp cliques. One slits his wrist. Now there were six.*
> *Hiding, six little Grand-blancs flee a buzzing hive. A bee stings one. Then there were five.*
> *Scared, five little Grand-blancs huddle and keep score. One gets cold. Then there were four.*

> *Running, four little* Grand-blancs *take weapons to flee. One twirls a sword. Then there were three.*
>
> *Forsaken, three little Grand-blancs gather rope and fight anew. One hangs himself, and then there were two.*
>
> *Trapped, two little Grand-blancs sitting in the sun. One got very warm, and then there was one.*
>
> *Guilty, one little Grand-blanc couldn't outrun. Closed his eyes forever. And there were none.*

The scheme to use this savage poetry to enrage and embarrass his friend, his rival Charles Flowers, the elevated Lord Duncan, makes Benjamin cackle.

Duncan hosts the men of Berkeley Square for what he calls the Night of Regrets. It's supposed be a merry dinner, but the event usually elicits dark confessions, but lately, it's been dull. No one trusts anyone, not like before. Duncan thinks that by inviting souls who don't live in the square, he'll get a different result.

Benjamin and his friend chatted last week about the next dinner. They concluded it would be another wasted evening, with Duncan droning on about some botched trial of a plantation owner from Martinique.

No one cares. Martinique is an ocean away. The man acts like no innocent person has ever been executed because the justice systems failed.

No, this poem, "The Rebel's Rhyme," from Martinique, will give the dinner more drama. How much he and Talson will laugh whenever someone at the dinner table thinks a neighbor is plotting his murder. Poor Duncan won't know what to do. Maybe the pressure will make him crumble, and he'll dare to talk honestly about dear Violet.

That's what he calls her, the woman over whom wars should've been fought. Benjamin drums his fingers on the desk, thinking about how Duncan often sounds like a minister trying to convict the men of Berkeley Square. The fellow who beat Benjamin out of being appointed as London's magistrate should have better sense.

Slam. The front door must've closed. Benjamin goes to his window, the one that offers a clear view of the plane trees in the middle of the square, as well as the rooftop of Duncan's house.

Snow covered, much like the ground, the house at Number Nine Berkeley Square puffs smoke curls out of chimneys. They blend into heavy gray clouds, which are becoming darker.

He should wonder about his servants making it safely to their homes and families, but the confirmed bachelor is interested only in meeting a fetching, desperate witness who wants to persuade Benjamin personally to avoid charging a friend with fraud. The crimes are heinous. The guilty might be punished with a death sentence. That notion should make this woman be very entertaining and convincing as she tries to persuade him in the remote inn at the edge of London, where they've chosen to meet.

Desperate women willing to do anything are his specialty. He looks back at the pile of witness statements on his desk and the ribbon-wrapped parchments bearing indictments and realizes he knows a lot of desperate people and a lot of lovely, lonely ladies.

He gapes, leeringly, at the life-size portrait of his favorite desperate woman. "Oh, Violet. I miss taunting Duncan about you. But tonight will make up for everything."

The portrait was painted right before she died, and he's sure it's a good likeness to the original. The joke of it makes many of the men of Berkeley Square scream with glee.

Then he sighs.

Life in Berkeley Square hasn't been exciting lately. Truthfully, it hasn't been the same since Violet died. The hand he played in her death he does regret.

And Duncan, he's never been the same. The man recently married and hasn't shown off the little heiress to anyone. Even nosy Talson hasn't met her at all.

Benjamin knows the old gossip will, even if he must manipulate his daughter to gain an introduction.

Pulling on his coat, he glances at the poem and decides to take only his invitation. If "The Rebel's Rhyme," as his expert calls it, falls out of his coat, it will give away the joke.

Grinning like a fool, Benjamin dances into his hall. The weather has made a few floorboards squeak as if he performs a bad jig. He laughs and stops in front of his mirror. Adjusting the long cravat, he reties it and admires greatly Mr. Peters's handiwork. Peters is Duncan's valet, but the man should be known as the valet to Berkeley Square since he's worked for many in the neighborhood.

This necktie was created as payment for some legal advice. White and gray stripes woven in the linen folds give it an air of elegance. After this dinner, if Peters finds himself out of work, Benjamin will hire him.

Snickering, Benjamin claps his hands. The secrets a man in Peters's position must know are limitless. Before the beginning of the New Year, he'll get Peters to disclose the names of the vendors Duncan has used to expand his house. Benjamin and his rival have the same floor plan. It should be illegal for Duncan to change his to outdo Benjamin.

It should be illegal for him to have anything Benjamin doesn't have.

His thoughts drift again to lovely Violet, and he wonders if Duncan has allowed his new wife to change his pink parlor. One step into the room is to be transported in time, and one could smell her violet cologne water and the vanilla sweetness of the beeswax candles lighting the sconces and the chandelier of the parlor.

He sighs and then chuckles, knowing that like all married

men, Duncan will come to heel. The new wife will rule him and his house. His neighbor to the far left, the Earl of Constock, is sadly led by his countess.

Peering again in the mirror, Benjamin says, "Handsome devil," to himself. He can be quite endearing when it suits him. And a devil when that suits, too.

Benjamin doesn't regret what he's done or what he's about to do. It will rock the inhabitants of Berkeley Square.

Stepping out his door, he takes his key from his pocket, then locks his front door. Stuffing his key into his purse, he makes his way down and steps into the freshly fallen snow. Maybe they will gamble at cards once all the jokes are done. Mr. Mayer, the gambling soul, should enjoy that, a chance to make a few coins before his empire crashes to the ground.

Staring at the flakes falling between the trees and dusting the top boughs, Benjamin traces a path through the middle of the square, the shortest way to get to Duncan's townhome.

A niggling feeling to stay home, drink wine, and reminisce with his stored letters calls to him. Yet the promise of Duncan's panic is too great.

The snow starts falling heavier. The wind blows, momentarily obscuring his view, but Benjamin keeps going until he's surrounded by trees. The snow is a little less deep here.

He wishes he'd left candles burning in his favorite window. The light would guide him to his home if the snowflakes become thicker.

Dusting flakes from his top hat, he sees a glimpse of Duncan's house. "Wreaths and candles are in each window. Like old times."

Shivering, he pulls tighter on his greatcoat and blows on his cold gloves. Benjamin hasn't turned himself around. Wandering out here in the cold could be the death of him.

A creaking noise sounds behind him.

He turns but sees nothing, not even his own tracks. He expected to see the Earl of Constock behind him. Given to practical jokes, he'd come early just to set them up in Duncan's house.

Well, he might be early to be away from Lady Constock.

She harps on him for being easily duped. The saucy thing is pretty and smart. Definitely doesn't take after Constock. She's a savvy thing like her father, but a woman can be only so clever.

Snickering, thinking himself devious, making plans to tease and taunt the countess, Benjamin presses forward.

Something clacks behind him.

He spins. For a moment, he sees a hunched shadow under a snowcapped plane tree.

A blink makes the image disappear.

" 'Tis the cold? Or is that you, you noisy fool? Talson, you know everything that goes on in our neighborhood. Come out. Let's go to Duncan's dinner together."

No answer.

"Holston? I know you've pinpointed the precise way to go from your military training. Come out."

Still no reply.

The cold must be playing tricks. Benjamin quickens his steps, but the walk, which should take no more than ten minutes, feels as if it's lasting forever.

Wiping sleet from his cheeks, he grumbles that the weather is worsening. Nonetheless Benjamin keeps heading toward the lights.

Crunch. Crunch.

This time, he's sure there are footfalls behind him.

Heavy but distant.

Swinging his purse, Benjamin rears back to strike, readying the silky thing laden with coins he swats . . . air. Nothing's there. Far on the other side of the square, a lone figure is plodding across the snow-covered pavement.

"Hurry on, Brooks," the man cries out. "Duncan has a new port. I'm not missing it. Constock will drink it all."

The voice belongs to Derrick Mayer. He's newest to the neighborhood. Nouveau riche, as Duncan's chef says, but the young man is proud of his quick rise to wealth. Benjamin has witnessed him floating about the streets in the finest carriages, entertaining investors. Last year he didn't speak of any regrets, but Benjamin knew he had them.

After talking recently to a few people who could write a great deal about his flaws, Benjamin knew a lot more about the financier. Maybe this year, Mayer will confess and lose those haughty airs.

"Hurry, sir!" Mayer says. "You know I love this weather!"

"Go on," Benjamin replies. "I'll be there soon enough."

"Suit yourself." The younger man sprints away. The next wind gust makes the falling snow obscure him.

Not to appear too anxious, Benjamin slows down.

It isn't the brightest idea to linger in snow and sleet, but he has a hearty constitution.

The little "Rebel's Rhyme" might make Mayer in a hurry to see Duncan. Letting some neighbors know about the lyrics might not've been the brightest thing. Talson couldn't help gossiping and tattling. Oh, this joke can't be ruined.

A ripping sound comes from behind.

Benjamin shuffles his feet and looks for a fallen branch. "Duncan? Constock? Is that you? You know I hate games."

No answer to his lie.

But Benjamin's heart pounds like a drum.

Something's there.

Someone has found out his secrets.

The snow crunches louder.

"I hate being late," he says, edging away, trying to appear unbothered.

Bam.

His fists strike a plane tree. Had it just planted itself in his path?

"They say King Henry VIII swung Anne Boleyn about these

trunks. They danced celebrating their adultery." This low grumbly voice is not imagined.

Benjamin was right. Someone has followed him.

When he turns, he sees nothing. "No, that was the plane trees of Greenwich, not here. This park isn't that old. Or so I hear. Constock, is that you?"

"You think the king regretted how things turned out? The deaths of the innocent people who put their trust in him?"

"The king beheaded women. That's not people." Nervous laughter tumbles from his chattering lips. "Duncan, is that you?"

The wind howls.

No answer.

It has to be Constock. This is one of his jokes. "Hey, friend. Let's go to Duncan's."

A dark outline comes closer. The build, the large silhouette . . . It has to be tall Constock.

"Fine. You always take a joke too far. That's why I hear Lady Constock enjoys calmer company."

Benjamin's words are bold, but he needs Constock to stop playing and just confront him about the rumors concerning his wife.

The figure stands away three feet, silent, clothed in black.

"Oh, goodness. Constock, you've become unhinged." Benjamin backs up and avoids the trunk of the plane tree he's just boxed. "Let's go get a drink at Duncan's. You like a good drink, Constock?"

The figure moves, rushes toward him.

Benjamin runs dead ahead toward Nine Berkeley Square, Duncan's house.

He's blocked by a stupid bench. Turning, he holds out his hands, swings his purse, hoping to push the attacker away.

Coins, his key, fly everywhere from his ripped purse. A pain slices at Benjamin's wrist. Grabbing his hurt arm, he sees the wound is deep. Something has cut into his flesh.

He can't stop the pain, the blood.

After undoing his scarf, he wraps his hand. "This isn't funny. I'm wounded."

Dizzy, he tries to wrap the scarf tighter. Anything to staunch the flow.

The shadow towers over him, but that's not hard to do given Benjamin's five-foot-five height.

"You attacked me on purpose. You'll pay. I'm a barrister for the Crown."

The beast stands there, not saying anything.

As if the wind has gained a voice, Benjamin hears, " 'Stunned, seven little *Grand-blancs* mourn in sharp cliques. One slits his wrist. Now there were six.' "

That's "The Rebel's Rhyme." That's Benjamin's joke . . . not a joke.

His blood pumps faster. More of his life leaks onto the snow.

Gasping, Benjamin spins back to the lights. "I'll get to Duncan. He'll know what you did. The magistrate's house is . . ."

The sleet pelting Benjamin's face stings. Snow melts on his lashes. He can't find the lights. His heart lunges like a war cannon.

The bench. It is still blocking him. He'll sit and rest, then get to Duncan. "Berkeley Square. Neighbors everywhere. Fiend, you'll be caught."

The dark figure says nothing but shoves Benjamin onto the cold, snow-covered seat; then the apparition backs away.

Losing his strength, Benjamin can only bluster as he does in the Old Bailey's court. "You need to get me help. Then I'll be lenient, for you will be charged for this attack."

Nothing. No one answers.

Slumping, Benjamin coughs. Trying one last attempt to cajole the criminal as if he's a good juryman, he says, "I'm one of the king's barristers. I'm Benjamin Brooks. I can make this go away. I've made worse go away. Help me. I'll ensure you won't swing by the hangman's noose at Tyburn or rot in Newgate. You'll remain free. I have the power."

The wind answers with a howl.

His wrist feels on fire. Every bit of his skin is aflame. The pain . . .

Did the shadow head to the lights?

Has the fiend gone to Duncan's?

Or is the fiend Duncan? Could this be payment for Violet?

Benjamin tries to rise but doesn't have the strength.

The red trail along the bench looks like ice. Then it's gone, buried in snow.

In an odd way, Benjamin feels at peace. All is white, quite *blanc*. Right and peaceful. He merely wishes he could view the candles again.

That regret is the death of him.

Benjamin Brooks, barrister of His Majesty's courts, dips his head and dies.

Chapter 1

December 23, 1806
Two Greater Queen Street, Westminster

The *Sun* newspaper dropped from my fingertips.

The words *put to death* stung my chest. My parlor floor-boards moaned when I stepped backward. I sank onto the sofa cushions. In my favorite room in my Queen Street townhome, I glanced again at the fallen broadsheet—the white paper, the indigo ink—announcing the assassination of Hayti's new leader to all of London.

The editor made the death of Dessalines, the emperor of the first free Black nation, seem inconsequential, setting the story beneath a sentence about the royal family's church outing and a notice about the Prince of Orange's house.

What did foreign chaos mean to Britain?

What did the death of a leader, a hero smeared as a butcher, mean to abolition? I closed my eyes and imagined how conversations among the politicians would be turning in the smoke-filled rooms and men's studies across town.

Those in power . . . Did they welcome this?

Had they expected such chaos from a nation led by Black hands? Or had the powerful of Britain caused this downfall?

The noise, the creaking boards behind me, made me turn to see a friendly face.

"Lady Worthing," my butler said, "the weather is getting worse. Perhaps you should change your plans. Spend the Yuletide here in Westminster."

I stared at him, then at the pile of evil correspondence that he'd brought me earlier and that I'd thrown on the table—canceled invitations and a letter from my errant husband.

"Things do look terrible, Mr. Rogers. But it's a tradition I had before I married. I don't intend to be alone . . . to be here for Christmas."

With a quick glance out my window, I saw my lawn was white. "I love the way crystals form on glass. I love the new glass."

"Ma'am, it would be no problem."

"Being without these windows during the summer made me appreciate how the panes look like waves of trapped water."

Rogers looked at me, knowing my rambles were the latest way I coped with the world.

"Ma'am, the weather?"

"If my plans are forced to change, yours will not, Mr. Rogers. You will be with your family."

My butler sort of smiled.

I turned back to my window and counted the icicles hanging from the roof. "Cold and lovely out there. Mr. Henderson has been out with his dogs this morning. Quite nice to see a man dedicated to the things he's chosen to care about."

I bit my lip. That sounded a bit too bitter. "Any news of Lord Duncan returning from his wedding trip with his new bride?"

"None, ma'am, but I doubt he'd rush back from Scotland in this weather."

"What man would?" Mrs. Smith's voice was loud as she came into my parlor. "Any man with a bride half his age should be content and not inclined to rush anything."

Mr. Rogers gave her the frowning eyes, as if it was not obvious to everyone that my husband, twice my years, had never rushed anything but our wedding night.

"Mrs. Smith, please." My butler tugged on his dark mantle, then made his posture more erect. "I'm trying to convince Lady Worthing to spend the holiday here. You see how bad the weather is."

Her fingers picked up James's open letter from the table. "Oh. Oh, yes. You should stay if the master will return for Christmas."

I turned from the two of them and let them sort out their cautious looks while I went to the window. My husband was not coming home. I didn't know when I'd see him again unless I agreed to his newest request.

Swatting the curtain tie, I steadied myself. I was done with James's games. "The conditions outside will make travel more difficult, but I refuse to quit my plans. I think it's time to consider all that I want and what is owed to me."

The squeaking of the floor between them sounded harried.

I parted the drapes fully. "The snow's been higher."

"But you've prudently stayed in." Mr. Rogers stood before the pile of correspondence on the polished ivory table. By the squeamish look the two exchanged, they'd read James's letter.

"Ma'am," Mr. Rogers said, "you haven't spent a proper Christmas here. It's very kind of you to allow the staff to take leave, but we will stay and serve you."

Proper? You mean waiting here, crying my eyes out, expecting James, only to get a note and Teacup, the runt of some litter.

I now suspected the gift was truly from Rogers or Vaughn, my godfather.

I pulled my hands together like I was going to pray, but my only wish was not to yell. "No. Sir. Ma'am. It's a tradition that my father has upheld. All his employees are home with their families for Yuletide."

"But, madam, we—"

"Am I not Lady Worthing, Mr. Rogers? Do you not work for me?"

Eyes big at my harsh tone, Mrs. Smith said, "Yes, ma'am. We both work for Lady Worthing."

My butler stepped forward as if he were in an executioner's line. "In the master's absence, you've led us well. No one questions your authority, but Lord Worthing wouldn't want you unsafe. The roads are unsafe."

My jaw trembled. My insides felt kicked in. "He's in Australia. That's where his sloop is docked. I'm certain he's not thinking of my safety. I mean, he understands I can make my own decisions."

Mrs. Smith had begun to busy herself with dusting in my yellow parlor. Then she picked up the *Sun* newspaper. Her finger circled the horrible article about treachery in Hayti, and she peered at Rogers.

Then I realized they'd read that, too.

I turned away and went to my fireplace and stood in the glorious heat. My cranberry carriage gown glowed, as did each of the silver buttons that lined the front of the gown from hem to collar.

"Lady Worthing." Mrs. Smith's voice sounded distant. "Let's pray your husband returns soon. Once he's here, he could use his old military connections to determine if the report about Emperor Dessalines is false."

James no longer cared or pretended to care about what interested me. He was on the other side of the world, frolicking or fidgeting or mucking . . . yes, mucking about.

And why give him something to do so that in *absentee husband logic*, finding out about Hayti would be some grand gesture? Breathing, not screaming, definitely not sobbing, I walked to the sofa and sat and forced my lips to lift into an appropriate happy smile. "Lord Worthing is busy. He's in the midst of some sort of discovery. No one shall interrupt him. He'll not be back, not for a while."

Solemn faced, Mrs. Smith hummed the nursery rhyme "Arthur o'Bower."

> *Arthur o'Bower has broken his band,*
> *He comes roaring up the land.*
> *King of Scots with all his power*
> *Cannot turn Arthur of the Bower.*

Why was she humming this?

Why would she do this, hum what we'd all be singing if the nursery on the third floor had a purpose? Did that nursery rhyme mean she agreed with the despicable ultimatum my wayward husband had issued?

Rogers's slow retreating steps renewed the floor's squeaking. The soft squeals from the odd-sized slats beneath his black slippers was oddly comforting. The noise sounded louder and longer in winter. His head craned up, and he stopped at the threshold. "Command the staff to stay. Turn with your power, Lady Worthing. It's getting so bad that everyone should stay."

Was that it? Did fear make people stay? Was being a placeholder for whoever had James's heart worth being here?

"For Yuletide, I'd rather not be here, and that's settled." My tone was low, barely audible above the noise my chestnut boot heels made as I paced in front of the fireplace. "My godfather and my friend Mr. Shaw will be joining Miss Sewell and me at her parents' house. I refuse to have you and the others away from your families. The sooner the hired driver arrives, the sooner my cousin and I depart, the sooner everyone in my household can leave to be with their families. As a matter of urgency, start dismissing them now."

He bit his lip, looking both fatherly and like a minister in his black coat. "Well, Miss Bellows is looking forward to Cheapside."

My personal maid had no family. She'd be content here or wherever there was lively conversation. Her love of the festivities and food that my other family, the Jamaican side, made for the holidays was a grand enticement.

Last year she and I and Mr. Rogers stayed at Queen Street, waiting for James. The day after Christmas, my godfather came and got us. We'd missed everything.

"You have your orders, sir."

Mr. Rogers bowed and left.

Mrs. Smith folded her arms about her gray uniform; then she offered me a smile. "Miss Bellows is packing her things. I think she's very eager to have a good Christmas with the Sewells."

At my aunt's kitchen table, there would be no limit on laughter. And there was a greater chance of catching Vaughn or Wilson Shaw and persuading them to use their connection to see if there was any merit to the nasty article written about the assassination.

"If the new driver is able to make it here, you'll have your way, Lady Worthing. I think everything will look different after the holidays. I think the New Year will be even better."

"If? Please tell me you found someone reliable. Mr. Rawlins has already had an accident in this weather. We don't need another one."

Mrs. Smith began to leave but stopped short of the door and said, "Rawlins's arm will heal up, and he'll be back to racin' you around in that odd carriage of yours."

My housekeeper's voice spun the guilt swirling in my gut. Yesterday my driver had gone out in this weather to pick up presents and to drop trunks at the Sewells' residence in Cheapside. On his way back, my light yellow bounder had slid off the road. Rawlins had hurt himself but had still managed to get out of the ditch and get back to Queen Street before collapsing.

"He's hurt because of me. Say it, Mrs. Smith."

"I know you're upset about Mr. Rawlins, ma'am, but he's going to be fine. He's as stubborn as you about completing a task."

Lifting my chin, I tried to seem confident. It was a losing activity. "Go hurry my cousin and maid. The jarvey you hired will have to be here soon, or we'll need to start walking."

Her olive face darkened at the cheeks. She looked . . . guilty. "He canceled this morning. So, I took the liberty of asking your neighbor to drop you all to Cheapside."

My eyes felt as if they'd popped and exploded in my skull. "You did what?"

"He's still light on staff. I check on him, Lady Worthing. Miss Mary asked me to. His sister is spending Christmas abroad, traveling with that Mayfair aunt and uncle."

"The Mathews?"

"Yes. They've traveled a lot since their ward's death. They needed to be away, Miss Henderson said. Her brother didn't want to go." Mrs. Smith's face seemed a little sheepish. "It's his first Yuletide since returning from war. And now with you leaving . . . I don't think it's right for him to be alone."

Mrs. Smith had a rigid nature for protocol, a sharp tongue, but a mysterious large heart for military men. Her father was a free Blackamoor who'd served on several navy frigates for king and country.

"So is that what's behind Mr. Rogers wanting me to stay? Lord Worthing's handpicked person to watch over me is waiting next door?"

"No. No, ma'am. Mr. Henderson has had a lot of loss this year."

"And misery loves company, Mrs. Smith?"

She dipped her head. "Our veterans. When they return and everything has changed, it can be difficult. And you are at your best when you're distracted."

The old me, who fussed with the man next door over dogs, would wonder why my neighbor's welfare was supposed to be my concern. The current me, who knew I was his keeper as much as he was mine, stayed silent.

The curmudgeon Commander Henderson, Stapleton Henderson, was a decent human being, and he'd become a friend.

Stapleton, unlike my husband, was here and honorable and, upon occasion, more helpful than I cared to admit.

"I thought since you don't hate him anymore, Lady Worthing, he'd be a guest here at your Christmas table. But you're not staying at Two Greater Queen Street."

"Bah, humbug! I don't want to be here, eating in the drawing room, beneath my husband's portrait, pretending this life is enough. I have family in Cheapside, who make me feel that simple Abigail Carrington is enough."

My hand covered my mouth. I didn't want an outburst. "Sorry."

She sighed and half curtsied. I supposed that was protocol for when your employer acted like a toddler.

Then she said, "Firstly, there's never been anything simple or plain about you. And your name, ma'am, is Abigail Carrington Monroe. You should be proud. You are a lady of the ton."

Did that mean I was supposed to act like those scandalous peers? Intrigues and dalliances were not me. "I wish you'd told me that you were entangling Mr. Henderson. When we arrive in Cheapside, I'll ask my aunt if he, too, may come to dinner."

"Ma'am, he seems very happy to oblige. He has an errand that he said meshes perfectly with this outing. And he was more delighted when I asked him to keep Teacup."

"What? How indebted am I going to be to Mr. Henderson?"

"Your aunt—she sneezes somethin' awful around pets. Did you forget?"

As if he'd heard his name, my boy bounced in, stopping every few feet to chase the squeaks from the floorboards.

After scooping him up in my arms, I held him close, like he was going away.

"Lady Worthing, you know he'll be happier over there with the bigger dogs and the quiet floors. The rascal seems quite spooked some days."

I nuzzled him against my neck. "I wasn't thinking. It would be wrong to bring him, but Christmas without my boy . . ."

I saw hope in her eyes that I'd change my mind about going out. Wind rattled my windows.

Everything seemed to be against me. Holding to my resolve, my fire, I thanked her. "Mrs. Smith, you think of everything."

"Well, seems Mr. Henderson will have custody of the three dogs for Christmas. That will make his Christmas bright. I know he'll enjoy the trouble."

"Trouble? No. No." Shaking her finger at me, Florentina bounded into my parlor. "None of that, Abbie. You promised."

I looked at her, wondering how there could be anything but trouble with a philandering, absent husband, three playful dogs, and a too-helpful neighbor minding my Teacup.

My housekeeper left my parlor, scooting past my cousin, who had donned her early Christmas present, a dark chocolate carriage dress that I'd had lined with bone buttons. Dark hair pulled up high, she looked lovely and fretful.

"Abbie, we're supposed to make it through the holidays alive and unbothered."

"We are alive and well. We just have to get to Cheapside."

Her frown deepened. "Oh, I forgot about Teacup. You can't bring him. My mom—"

"It's been taken care of." Cooing at my little terrier, like he was the baby my husband hoped *I'd* have, I shook my doggone head. "Mrs. Smith has everything arranged. My boy is spending Christmas with Mr. Henderson."

Florentina scowled at his name. Her full lips drew closer to her nose before easing. My cousin had done that frowning and giving me odd looks these past months.

When she sank onto the sofa, with her arms crossed, I prepared for her to turn into a sleuth and interrogate me. "Abbie, tell me the truth. I see the weather outside. We waited too long to leave. Now we'll have to spend Christmas here with the dogs and the neighbor."

"Flo, I'm determined to spend my holiday in Cheapside. Nothing will deter me, us."

The tense expression on her face did not ease. She leaned back, adjusting the soft blue wool baby blanket about her, fluttering the hem across her heavy black boots. She was every inch a refined and elegant mathematician.

"Then what's the trouble, Abbie?" She raised a palm in the air as if to stop me from speaking. "Maybe I don't want to know. As long as you keep to your promise, I'm fine."

"Of course, Flo."

"Yes. No investigations. No secret abolition meetings. No pushing for legislations. No running for our lives. Nothing but family and joy."

"I didn't promise any of that. And we've never run for our lives, Florentina. In all my investigations, only I have run. Henderson and me. Well. Mostly, we walked away for our lives, but one mustn't be so picky."

The scowl returned. Then she said, "The odds are increasing that the next mystery you stumble upon will have us doing just that, running and ruining these new boots."

Mrs. Smith returned. "Mr. Henderson's groom has said his carriage is on its way. And to be aware that he has to make a stop at Berkeley Square on the way. Then off to Cheapside."

My housekeeper left the room; my cousin leaned back on the pillows, with her arms folded. "I'm having a premonition, Abbie."

"What? You have visions, too?"

"Yes," Florentina said. "I'm feeling that you're doing this again, finding something to force us to spend time with your neighbor, and all three of us will have to run for our lives."

"That would be new, Flo, the three of us doing something together."

"Abbie, you're making fun."

"I'm doing nothing but trying to get us to Cheapside. The weather is no better. Rawlins had an accident, and you know how careful he is. Stapleton's big carriage will handle the snow and ice much better than my yellow bounder."

"Oh, it's Stapleton now." She tapped her short boot. "Why the neighbor? How could you ask him?"

"As I said, I didn't. Mrs. Smith did. He is also going to take care of Teacup to spare your mother."

As if the little fellow knew we were talking about him, the fuzzy brown thing went to Florentina and begged like he smelled bacon. With everyone using my next-door neighbor's dog-handling trick, she might have some in her hands.

My cousin picked him up, rubbed his back. "Oh, you are adorable, but my mama will be ill if she sees you."

After giving my boy kisses, she turned to me. "So what will you owe Mr. Hendersom for the ride and the doggie companion services?"

Wishing I could say nothing, I decided to get Florentina to sacrifice something. "I want to invite him for Christmas dinner. I'd like for him not to be alone on Christmas."

Her gaze whipped over me. That frown on her countenance reminded me not of my aunt's, but of Mama's.

Then my vision darkened. It was night. Stapleton and Florentina were in trouble. I could save only one. Or thought I had only one choice. My brow sweated. I couldn't move. I couldn't—

"Dinner? Abigail, I'll ask. It shouldn't be bad to have him at my parents' house, deepening his connection to you."

"Yes. It's not . . . I'm—"

"Hey." She set down Teacup and came closer, then pulled me into a needed hug. "You're shaking."

"Maybe. Shouldn't have to run away to . . ."

"Hey. Are you thinking about Rawlins?" She held me tighter. "You can't blame yourself for his accident. This weather is causing problems everywhere. It's early winter. Mr. Rogers said the ice on the roads looks black like tar. That's what's causing havoc, not you."

Black and havoc and a peril-filled world. What was to become of us all?

"Abbie, please. Say what's wrong."

How could I tell her that she and my neighbor might be endangered because of me or something I'd done?

"Abigail Carrington Monroe, you can tell me anything."

When in doubt, I talked of what I knew was a true threat to our world. "Hayti. It's in chaos again. A report is in the *Sun* that Emperor Dessalines has been killed. I'm hoping it's rubbish."

She mouthed the emperor's name. Then closed her eyes. "False reports happen. Hayti, the free nation, is far from Britain's borders. News can get confused, misreported. If Lord Worthing were here, he could find—"

"He's not." My tone started low, like water beginning to boil. Heated to fast bubbles, steam. I stepped away from her embrace. "I'm on my own to figure out things. And I'm not without resources. Mr. Vaughn or even Mr. Shaw knows things. Lady Worthing can be very resourceful, too."

"That she can be."

"Mr. Henderson, ma'am," Rogers said from the threshhold.

Stapleton waved away my butler and stopped him from taking his heavy gray mantle and the hunting hat curling about his ears. He stepped around my butler and offered us a bow.

Teacup bounded to him.

After patting my dog, he entered my parlor, lightly planting his boots, as if he'd memorized which boards creaked, to avoid making noise. "We need to get started, ladies. With my brief appointment at Berkeley Square, we must head out before conditions worsen."

Handsome, staring with his fiery indigo eyes, taking in my parlor, me, this retired military man might be able to gather answers on Dessalines, too. With James refusing to return to England, the soldier he chose to look after me might be the answer to many problems that my husband created.

Chapter 2

Two Greater Queen Street

After a near teary goodbye to my Teacup, I left him in Mrs. Smith's arms and proceeded with my party out of my house and onto Greater Queen Street. Florentina, Miss Bellows, and I climbed into Stapleton's carriage.

Sitting back in the spacious compartment, I couldn't help but admire the carriage's heavy frame, the way it felt settled on the road. Maybe there was a way to improve my sleek little bounder without making it sluggish.

"Fretting about Teacup already, Lady Worthing?" Stapleton said as he stretched on the seat, as if to make a show of how roomy his carriage was while ferrying four people. "I assure you the little terrier will be in good spirits. I asked your house-keeper to give him to my man-of-all-work before she heads out. Teacup will be in great company with my greyhounds. There's choice cuts of pork belly bacon curing for them."

His tone teased. I found it comforting, as I had had to leave my little guy. "It's very kind of you to take in my formerly wayward dog for a day or two. Make sure Silvereye and Santisma are on their best behavior."

"To be sure." He chuckled, knowing full well my terrier had once been the terror. "He's learned to do as the hand that feeds him has instructed. And don't fear, because Steuben, my man-of-all-work, is very good with dogs and has no history of criminality. Hopefully, I'll return to Teacup and see even more manners."

"More?" Gawking, I crossed my arms. "He's sensitive. He's—"

"Stop." Florentina glared at me, at Stapleton. "You two talk like these pets are children."

"Teacup is my baby. The closest thing I have to a child." All that I wanted with an absent husband.

"You two bicker like a couple. The dogs are your young ones, yours and his. And you're arranging custodial visits like Uncle Carrington and Aunt once did."

How could she compare Stapleton and me to my parents? We were neither—neither married, neither in love, nor victims of a love destroyed.

"She's joking, Lady Worthing." Stapleton pushed closer to the window, increasing the distance between himself and me. "But Miss Sewell must understand that these dogs are family, and I begrudgingly love a dog with a horrible name as much she cares for my greyhounds."

My maid giggled. "You both are proud dog lovers. Of course, they'd treat their pets like family."

"Yes. Lovers," Florentina said. "I forgot that this is or can be."

The unspoken accusation hurt. She knew me.

She had been there when I accepted James's proposal. She'd been my bridesmaid when I married. My cousin knew how I felt, how committed I was to being a proper wife.

And if Florentina would take the time to get to know Stapleton, she'd find him loyal and admirable. Nothing untoward had transpired between us.

I watched him to see if he'd noted her tone. His gaze flicked from me to the frosted window. Our friendship, our unique understanding of one another, had grown. That was something to admire.

Nothing to be ashamed of.

Yet my cousin frowned more deeply. Her disapproval saddened me to the depths of my soul. Wilson Shaw shamelessly flirted with me and her. He was our friend. My cousin never reacted upset to Wilson showing me attention.

Did she want Stapleton and me to be enemies again?

Tonight, when it was the two of us with glasses of champagne, our favorite cheeses, and a stolen slice of black cake, I'd ask.

For now, I'd use my resources on a more dire matter, the assassination. "Mr. Henderson, I presume you've seen the papers, heard the rumor of the death of Hayti's leader."

His brow furrowed; his countenance became dour. "No. I haven't." He drummed his knees. "Been a little preoccupied with Mary and putting affairs in order."

"Affairs?" Florentina tossed me a saucy look. "Perhaps, I'm fretting over the wrong things."

If Stapleton hadn't caught on to her snide attitude before, that surely was a big hint.

His eyes cut to her, then back to me. "Unrest again in the Caribbean? Too soon. Nelson had tried . . ." Stapleton's mouth snapped shut. He tugged off his well-worn onyx gloves and put them in his pocket.

It hadn't been fourteen months since his commander died. Not quite a year since the admiral was laid to rest at St. Paul's. Luckily, our route to Cheapside should take us nowhere near the cathedral, but I wondered if Stapleton, like me, had been part of the long line of those who had gone to pay respects.

Florentina, maybe realizing she'd overstepped, looked a little repentant. Her voice softened. "You think it's true, Mr. Henderson? General Dessalines, the man who freed a nation from enslavement—"

"Emperor Jacques I is or was his title," he corrected. Stapleton turned again to the window. His gaze seemed pinned there. "Hayti's remained volatile a year out from its revolution. Anything is possible. Though I had heard there was jealousy among his lieutenants—"

"You are saying one his men turned against him?" Miss Bellows sounded so innocent, but rivalries could be lethal.

He shrugged. "Could be, but I wonder if foreign influences are at play."

Florentina closed her eyes. "No."

Mine were open, and I absorbed Stapleton's words, the damning truth those in that the outside world who rooted for disaster might want harm to come again to the free Black nation.

"This is terrible," my cousin said. "How can progress—"

The carriage slid to the left.

Miss Bellows rolled against Florentina. I banged into Stapleton. An arm wrapped about my middle, keeping me from falling to the floor.

"Oh dear." My maid righted herself and clung to the seat back. "Hope we don't flip like your bounder, ma'am."

Florentina gawked at me, and I realized that I hadn't moved. I still sat so close to Stapleton, and his arm remained about me.

Inching away from his warm, heavy coat, I thanked him, then moved farther away.

"My pleasure to shepherd you three to your destination in my solid Berlin. Worthing's light bounder is a travesty. This is four times heavier, and it is buffeted in this carriage. Can't imagine what that carriage would be doing."

"The yellow bounder belongs to Lady Worthing. And it won't be going anywhere for quite some time." Miss Bellows tugged a slipping blanket up onto her and Florentina's laps. "Mr. Rawlins, either. Poor dear. His arm, that elbow. It's all mighty sore."

Feeling guiltier, I decided to steer the conversation to something safer. "Mr. Henderson, let me thank you again for taking in Teacup. I hope Mrs. Smith didn't make me seem so desperate. My aunt, Mrs. Sewell, sneezes all the time when dogs are near."

"A proud woman desperate? Never. And to your credit, your housekeeper is a skilled negotiator."

A funny feeling swirled in my stomach, like I owed him something. "What did my housekeeper promise?"

His mouth opened, then slowly closed, his lips curling, as if he savored something. "An apple tart with the finest cream. Something to enjoy in my study for the holidays."

That sensation of having to choose deepened. And the thought of a friend enjoying a dessert alone made me rethink abandoning Westminster and Stapleton.

His gaze met mine. A smile appeared for a moment.

"You seem very obliging to my cousin." Florentina folded her arms. With her brow rising, she said, "Your promise to your friend Lord Worthing to look after his *wife* is something you take very seriously. Admirable to care so much for what is your friend's responsibility."

Now I wanted to choke, but I took comfort in the fact that she didn't have her finger lifted, pointing at him.

"The baron is more than a friend," he said. "He's a fellow comrade in arms. Worthing and I served under Admiral Nelson for many years. The baron confided in me the hardships a wife must bear during a husband's extended absence. I'm glad that we neighbors are no longer enemies."

This felt true on Stapleton's part, but it also made me re-examine James's motive, particularly in light of his latest demand. He knew my godfather was here to help me. The versatile Wilson Shaw, who managed my husband's money and now mine, was also available to assist me. I hadn't needed my neighbor's help until a murderer ventured along our adjoining lawns and both Stapleton and I were in need of alibis.

"Service to the navy is enough to obligate you to a stranger. That's so admirable." Miss Bellows's cheeks dimpled. "Just so nice in a world lacking kindness."

When she said, "Lord Worthing is such a decent man. Insightful, too, knowing that two dog lovers would eventually get along," I wanted to groan.

Florentina did and then looked up to the ceiling.

"Those old arguments with Mr. Henderson seem so silly." There, I did it. I said something inane that didn't expose my fury at James, the alleged decent husband who'd sent his wife an indecent proposal.

The carriage jostled again.

Holding on to the seat, I feared for the driver leading the horses. I feared for my cousin and maid. I feared for my neighbor, who looked more and more guilty, as if it had been his choice, not mine, to have us on the roads.

Bang. The wheels hit the ground again.

My insides jittered. "Perhaps the horses will slip less, and the carriage will be steadier, the closer we come to town."

Stapleton shook his head. "Ladies, we may have to turn around. The snow is falling harder, and the wind has picked up. We might get stuck. Bond Street is definitely less traveled."

Out the window, I could see the shuttered doors of the many shops. "The proprietors must be unhappy, having to close early so close to Christmas."

The carriage slid again. Stapleton's driver slowed down but kept us moving.

"We're passing Buckingham House and the guard gate." Stapleton's voice was calm, even, and smooth. He may have wanted to appear unruffled, but with his palms fastened to the seat, the white of his knuckles exposed his nervous apprehension. This adventure was going to get worse.

I could fake calm airs, too. "You think the sovereign is here or at Windsor?"

"The paper said he was in town, ma'am."

Miss Bellows had retrieved the paper this morning. Of course, she'd read it and learned about our sovereign's church attendance and the assassination.

"Abigail," my cousin said, "this is foolhardy. We should've left earlier or waited until this weather got better. Christmas Day all might be well."

"And miss the days of feasting? The songs about the pianoforte and Aunt's black cake? Black cake, Florentina. Molasses and rum, the fermented cherries. We sneak a piece on Christmas Eve. It's our tradition, cousin. I won't miss it again."

"A burnt cake, you say?" Stapleton's dark eyes glittered. "A great deal of fuss for that. Traditions are important."

"No, silly." Miss Bellows drew her arms deeper into her dark gray coat. "Black cake. Dark rum fruited cake, which the mistress loves. And Mrs. Sewell buries it in the yard for months to seal in the flavor."

Couldn't deny my maid's enthusiasm or her love of rum, which had arisen from a lifetime of service to immigrant households, but the intricacies of preparing the luxurious cake must sound nonsensical to a British-born gentleman.

Our host didn't seem confused or horrified. Then his gaze left mine, and he peered out the frosted window. His hands, especially his knuckles, grew whiter, like they were in the snow. "It's understandable to go to great lengths for good cake. All good things, actually. I think I requested the wrong dessert from Mrs. Smith."

The back wheels shifted, and that feeling of being airborne made my stomach lurch.

When my guts and the carriage landed, I was ready to admit defeat. "Take us back to Queen Street." I said with my head bowed, wanting to be with my dog.

Being with Teacup and my fireplace had to be better, even if it was my last holiday in the house, the house that James would put in my name if I surrendered to his crazy request.

"Unfortunately, Lady Worthing," Stapleton said, "it's too dangerous to do anything but go forward. Sometimes, we have to finish things, no matter what."

The ominous sound of his words drifted beyond the weather.

This was bad.

None of us should be here.

Luckily, I hadn't seen my death in my dreams. I'd just had the odd vision of choosing between my cousin and my neighbor.

"We're almost to Berkeley Square," he said. "We'll have to seek refuge there."

Florentina leaned forward. "That is your stop?"

Stapleton's serious, sour scowl made my heart race. "Yes. I have an invitation to dine there. I was hoping to get out of it. Now I suppose we shall all have to be guests."

"Sorry." My voice was soft, but the attentive man heard me and offered another brief smile.

He always seemed to notice me—weak me, indifferent me, stubborn me and, hopefully, mostly strong me.

"The weather tests us all, Lady Worthing." He appeared calm, very assured. The man sat erect, fumbling with his silver great-coat buttons.

The back end of the carriage shifted and slid, then steadied itself.

How well he hid his fear of us overturning, but those white knuckles again latched on to the seat said it all.

"Ladies, I'm confident we'll make it to Berkeley Square. In the morning we'll try again."

His tone impressed Miss Bellows, who began to grin again. Florentina and I were in our twenties, and Miss Bellows had fifteen or more years on us. Nonethless, the bubbly expression on my maid's oval face could pass for a schoolgirl's. "Sounds like an adventure. Will we all find room at an inn?"

That was a very true question. Not everyone would take in a man and three women. Not everyone would want to help at least two of us in this carriage.

Gawking at the back window, my cousin seemed unconvinced. "Mr. Henderson, would things have been easier if we'd gone straight to my parents in Cheapside?"

"It's a longer way, with no safe place to stop."

Had he read my thoughts?

If he had, then he'd know my sadness. We were close to a new year, and not many things had changed. Abolition on a wider scale hadn't taken hold. Though new politicians had risen and made rousing speeches, the politics of freedom remained stuck.

"You believe your *appointment . . .*" Not looking at him, Florentina threw her head back on the seat. "They'll not mind you bringing a crowd into their abode and disturbing the intimacy of the gathering?"

"Intimate? I think not. I waited too long to decline dinner. And I had hoped the need to escort you ladies across town would provide a proper excuse to avoid staying. So much for offering my apologies and escaping."

Wait a minute.

From a stop for an appointment, changing now to a meal—such progress. Why did the bachelor wish to hide how he spent his evening?

With a hand falling to her hip, Florentina reared back in her seat. "I suppose my cousin is lucky that you don't mind taking the time to dote on her."

"And her friends. It's all of you, Miss Sewell." His unbothered tone quickened, turning to the annoyed fast way of speaking, something that had marked our early acquaintance. "I suppose it's wrong to gain something for being helpful."

"Perhaps gain a little guilt," I said. "And now we're all entangled. I suppose *she'll* be upset, what with three additional women to add to her dinner."

"She?" he asked, his eyebrows rising. Pink bloomed in his cheeks. "It's a *he*, Lady Worthing, an acquaintance of yours. Lord Duncan."

Blinking, I gaped, and it took a few seconds to utter something that wasn't nonsense. "I didn't . . . I wasn't aware that you'd begun socializing with him."

The pelting of ice on the carriage roof grew louder. The pace of the horses slowed.

"Is that wrong, Lady Worthing?"

"No, not at all."

I'd solved cases for Duncan. I'd proved James innocent of an embezzlement scheme, one that almost had him hung. I'd solved many mysteries for the magistrate, but he'd never invited me to his home.

My heart beat with jealousy. I heard the rhythm in my ears until I asked, almost yelling, "Is it much farther?"

Stapleton leaned forward and peered out the window. "We've half a mile before we turn onto Hill Street. The mews for Berkeley Square is there. We can be dropped at Duncan's house, and it won't be far for my driver to take the horse team to shelter."

"Oh, we're not to stay in the mews while you enjoy the invitation to the magistrate's house." Florentina sighed. "Well, I suppose it's warm in there. That's something."

She must be feeling the same way as I, angry at being overlooked.

"Of course you're to come to the main house." He chuckled. "Nothing else will do for Lady Worthing's party. Duncan's not a fool. But his friends might be."

"His friends?" Florentina and I said this at the same time.

"Four or five, I think. He invited me to come to his dinner and discuss medical aspects with his neighbors."

"Medical aspects? Of what?" I asked, and it might have been my imagination, but Stapleton seemed to take a hard swallow.

Then he said, "Of murder. The dinner is some ritual thing he holds annually for his friends."

Feeling like I'd been slapped across my cold cheeks, I sat back, absorbing the fact that the magistrate, with his pretense of possessing forward thinking, had invited my neighbor to speak on the crimes we'd solved. For the work that all of us—Florentina and I and our resources and my neighbor—had performed, Duncan was going to credit a single person, Stapleton Henderson.

"It's a men's meeting, Abigail. Apparently, he does it every year. He calls it the Night of Regrets."

"And you're invited." Florentina stretched in her seat, then righted her onyx bonnet with orange feathers. "Why are men gathering to talk of such gruesome things? Aren't cards and brandy enough?"

Stapleton put a hand to his mouth and seemed to hold in a laugh. As the carriage wriggled, he straightened. "I wouldn't know, Miss Sewell. I hadn't intended to stay."

With her rosy cheeks glowing, Miss Bellows said, "Now we'll all have to be there. And at Berkeley Square. That's a nice neighborhood. And the park the homes surround is so beautiful, full of trees and benches to sit on and take it all in."

"It's shelter for us all," he said. "That's all that we can hope for. And so much for getting out of this dinner."

Steam fled his nostrils as it might an angry dragon's. "At least I'll have you and Miss Sewell to help explain the circumstances of any of the murders he wishes to discuss." Something in his eyes didn't quite look as aggrieved as his tone suggested he was.

Stapleton wasn't a wizard or a god who controlled the weather, but whatever boredom he thought he'd endure while attending the dinner alone was gone.

My neighbor had three women willing to be held captive with him at Duncan's all-male party.

Chapter 3

The Lane of Berkeley Square

Stapleton's carriage passed Hill Street and slid into Berkeley Square.

It seemed as if we'd keep going right into the house at the corner, but we did stop at the largest house in the center of the lane.

It took a moment for me to breathe again.

Then I stopped when no one came outside. A footman should come to greet us.

"This is Number Nine. Lord Duncan's house." Stapleton pulled on his gloves. "Let me go apprise the magistrate of our circumstances."

Miss Bellows reached for him. "Shouldn't we wait, sir? There should be a proper greeting for my mistress."

"When I spoke with Lord Duncan a month ago, he explained that this dinner has very little staff. He lets everyone go but one or two servants. I think it quite nice to do so for Christmas."

Florentina sat back. Her parents kept a full staff through Christmas, but they had a lot of guests. The servants would then be more at ease from Boxing Day to the New Year.

But did anything make up for not being with family on Christmas?

Stapleton bounded out of the carriage and trekked up the snow-covered steps. The house was typical of the ones lining the square. This one had a palatial front, with two columns supporting a modest portico.

"Lord Duncan must've lived here quite a while." Florentina cupped her hand and looked out the glass. "His house stands at the center on this side of Berkeley Square."

It looked to be the biggest, and it surely had one of the best views of the park.

A shiver went through me as I looked at the trees weighed down with snow and ice and the ends of a bench, which would make for a perfect place to view the park.

Peering out the other side of the carriage, I counted windows and noted a large one, the curtains of which were open. The window held a fir garland and lit candles.

I could smell the fresh evergreen and I point to the lights. "It's all lovely. This is what Christmas is all about—snow and greenery. Remember when Dinah and I strung similar decorations throughout my father's firm?"

"Yes," Florentina said, "I remember. And I recall how she whined when you got to light the candles. I'm glad Carrington and Ewan didn't burn to the ground."

Sighing with deflated lungs, I decided not to ask Florentina which one of us—my sister or I—she thought would set flames to Papa's practice.

"Is that Lansdowne House to the left?" Miss Bellows pointed to a residence set back away from the square, with large chimneys puffing smoke. "That must be it. The lovely gardens are covered. I hope the gardener knows how to care for the plantings."

"There's probably an orangery. All the big homes have

them." Florentina held her neck, as if her crown was weighed down by a headache.

"Cousin, you're not the least bit curious as to what the interior of the magistrate's house looks like?"

Shaking her head, she sat up straight. "Why be curious when we have not been afforded a proper invitation?"

"He'll not refuse us, Flo. The weather—"

"That's not what I mean, Abbie. He lets you play mystagogue and be clever. It makes him look good to the public, but this is his private home. We're not welcome. He doesn't consider us his equals. Just Mr. Henderson."

"Until recently, Lord Duncan was a widowed man. It would not be right to invite women." At first, Miss Bellows looked at us with wide, innocent eyes. Then she clicked her tongue and tossed us a saucy look. "And it's men, dears. When do they ever look at any woman as an equal?"

My dear maid had brought up valid reasons for why Florentina and I might be excluded. Yet it didn't actually matter. I nodded, adjusted my bisque bonnet with the ruby-red trim, and sat quietly. I prepared my face to hold steady, to show no emotion when Stapleton returned with an excuse as to why there was no room in the magistrate's house for us, just like there were no seats for us at his table.

Drawn to looking at the snow falling on the trees and covering more of the bench, I startled when Stapleton tapped on the window.

He tossed open the door. "Lord Duncan requests all of you to come inside."

I blinked, recovered, and offered my cousin a smile. She didn't have to know that for a moment, I had doubted the magistrate's humanity.

"Good," I said. "It's getting a little cold out here."

"I assure you, it's very warm inside." He stuck his arm inside. "It's very slick, ladies. I'll escort you one by one. Miss Sewell, ready?"

She took his extended hand, and he helped her descend.

From the back window, I watched the hem of her carriage gown flutter beneath her emerald coat. The darkness blended with his greatcoat, then almost swallowed them up as they both swayed and nearly fell.

The wind picked up again. The snow came down heavier.

I sat back from the cold window and watched as the lone portmanteau Florentina kept with her this week at my home was being taken into the house. "Looks like we made it before we had to face the full rage of the storm."

"Don't fret, ma'am. I'll figure out how to care for us tonight, but I wish we had one of your trunks. You should look your best in a place like this."

I didn't know how to respond to her. My head was in a hundred different places as she listed the things I didn't have with me. Rawlins had dropped it all off in Cheapside. Oh, how happy I was when Stapleton came back for my maid. I needed a moment alone.

When they left, easing their way across the ice and snow, I listened to the bitter wind whipping the roof.

The neighing of the horses told me they were suffering. They, and the driver, needed to get to shelter.

Pushing my bonnet higher, I stepped out and called to the driver, "Go on to the mews. Stay warm."

He nodded and started away. I hoped he made it without incident.

Standing in the cold, with a little ice falling on my collar, I became transfixed by the park. I was drawn to it.

"Lady Worthing," Stapleton yelled from the top of the steps. He wasn't alone. Miss Bellows and a tall, well-dressed Black-amoor man stood there, too.

They went inside as Stapleton ran toward me. That was dangerous. He could slip and fall on the ice.

Yet I couldn't move. My attention went back to the park. Something drew me there.

Stapleton was a few feet away when I heard him yell, "Abigail. You should've stayed inside the carriage until I came for you."

I couldn't answer.

"Abigail?" His tone was lower. "Are you cold? Are you well?"

He stood next to me. His boots slid a little as he held his arm out to me. "Come on. Let's go inside."

Something about his wrist being slightly exposed, dangling, made me nervous. I couldn't move.

"Woman, are you all right? Too jostled from our ride? Or are you cold? Disorientation can set in quickly in this weather. Do I need to carry you inside?"

"Fine." I snapped to attention and clasped his hand. "I'm just fine."

He took a step and kept my arm close to his side, then began pointing out icy patches on the drive as if I hadn't become stiff with fear.

When we reached the top step, Miss Bellows came back outside. "Look at the park, ma'am. The trees and snow."

"Is she always like that?" Stapleton's warm breath felt good on my cold ear. "So enthusiastic?"

"Unfortunately, yes."

"Ma'am. Lady Worthing. Look at how the snow bends the boughs."

Still holding my arm, Stapleton murmured, "Let's humor her. She may calm down. The last thing we need is excitable women. This is a hallowed men's night for Duncan."

The man with the silent footfalls and the increasingly sarcastic voice angled me toward the oblong park as if we were performing a reel. He was smooth, or maybe the ice beneath my boots made the turn graceful . . . like that of a dancer.

"It's beautiful," he said in a breathy, wistful tone. "I almost wish St. James's Park was closer to our houses, so we could have such a view."

I agreed with his sentiment. Up here, the whole of Berkeley Square could be seen, even the rooftop of the houses on the opposite side of the square. One looked somewhat similar to the magistrate's. "Berkeley Square is hauntingly beautiful in the sleet and snow."

"And look, ma'am. Someone has taken the time to build a snowman. There on the bench. You can see the scarf and boots under the bench."

"What is she talking about? Surely, she's seen snow, Lady Worthing . . . a snowman . . ." His voice died off.

Then I saw what they saw—boots, a scarf, even a few shiny items scattered about, like from a dumped purse.

"Ladies, go inside."

"Sir, we should investigate." I freed myself from his arms and eased down to the lower step. "I think we should look at the snowman now."

"You know"—Miss Bellows came down to my step—"that doesn't look like a snowman."

The wind whipped.

The snowman fell over. More of the scarf was exposed.

Everything in me felt fiery hot and freezing at the same time.

"Go inside, Lady Worthing." Stapleton went down another step. "Get warm. I'll take care—"

I heard nothing else.

I started running.

As if they had a map, my boots launched me down the stairs and avoided the slippery ice patches across the drive. I ran faster when I came to the park.

Sprinting ahead of someone calling my name, I couldn't stop, not until I reached the bench. "Sir, can I help you?"

The figure didn't answer. He didn't move.

My breath came in gushes. I came closer and brushed snow from his hat.

More fell from his brow.

"Abigail! Stop."

It was a little late, because I'd started the covering of snow to fall away. A frozen face, with eyes wide open, glared at me.

I leapt backward and tripped over a solid chunk of ice and fell.

My purse spilled. My bonnet rolled away. After grasping my purse, I snatched up a key and some coins.

Stapleton bent over me, his hand sinking toward me. "Grab me, Abigail. I'm not going anywhere." Then he cursed.

I gawked at him, then followed his eyes to the snow, the red snow. It was all over me.

Stapleton's eyes grew big. "Abigail. Your arm."

My palm sank deeper into the snow. Things shifted and melted beneath me.

My boots, my kid gloves became scarlet, bloody scarlet.

My heart raced. "He didn't freeze to death. He bled."

Lightheaded, I felt my world spin. I struggled to fill my lungs, but they'd become ice.

The next thing I knew, Stapleton had me up in his arms and was carrying me away from the dead man in Berkeley Square.

Chapter 4

Nine Berkeley Square

My mouth possessed the most terrible taste. Through my lashes I saw two unfamiliar faces. Then I heard Florentina's voice.

"She should be awake by now. What have you given Lady Worthing?"

I relaxed again until a spoonful of fire was shoved down my throat.

Eyes starting to open, I focused on the medallions and moldings on the ceiling. I coughed, and the rawness of my mouth and throat returned. "Have I swallowed fire?"

"No. But good-quality brandy." An older man sat in a chair beside me. He was quite close, and his breath smelled of the poison he'd been feeding me. "Needed to get your body temperature up fast. Brandy warms everyone."

I rose up a little. "Are you a physician?"

"Retired, but don't let the silver whiskers scare you. I still know quite a lot. Though some of the young bucks of the ton will tell you differently."

"Well, I don't spend much time with bucks *or* the ton," I said. "I don't have many conversations with bucks to compare, sir." Repeating myself. My wits were scattered.

"I bet you don't, and I'm sure that is a shame." He lifted a half-empty glass in what looked like a toast, and then he held it to my lips. "Lady Worthing will prove to be as interesting as you claimed, Miss Sewell. But we'll answer the questions you surely have after you take another sip."

"Do it, Abbie. I'm convinced it won't hurt you or your condition."

"No, I think nothing will help the condition of being impulsive. I think I will always have that gift."

The old physician pushed the goblet to me again. "I insist. Another swig will do you just fine."

Moving his hand away, I sat fully upright on the pink floral sofa. My coat was gone. The sleeves of my cranberry carriage gown were damp but without stains. I was grateful the nightmare I'd fallen into had ceased for the moment.

"Take your time, Abigail. You had us all filled with fear."

Florentina's voice—like a crystal ready to shatter—made me scared. Again, I checked my arms, my wrists, even my neck to see if I had bled like that man in the square.

Drinking from the goblet he'd tried to give me, the old man stood. "Maybe we should orient her, Miss Sewell."

"Yes. Lady Worthing, you are inside Lord Duncan's home," she said. Her voice sounded louder, as if I'd lost my hearing. Had I?

"This is Number Nine Berkeley Square," the physician said, "My home is Number Eleven. I'm on the corner, the far corner. Go directly through the trees, and then go that way." He fisted his hand about his cane and made what looked like a left turn.

I concentrated less on him and studied the room. It seemed fine, tastefully done, with pastel pink–papered walls. The large window that I'd seen from the drive was here in this room. The greenery and the lit candles proved it.

"The writing desk by the window . . . It's beautiful. " I said, "I can't imagine how nice it would be to write my letters there."

"His wife—the first one, Mrs. Flowers—did love that." The physician's eyes became misty. "Yes. Charles Flowers, or Lord Duncan, as Miss Sewell calls him, has done pretty well for himself. Well, I know he at least married well the first time."

The way he peered over his spectacles gave me the feeling he wanted me to give an opinion. I doubted that he truly wanted my thoughts. I surmised that he wanted to gauge what I knew.

"You met her, his first wife? Of course you did." My cousin seemed very jittery. "You said you were neighbors."

"Yes. She was a dear friend of my daughter. I acted as a father to many girls, with their own going to war in America or the Caribbean." He sniffled and snorted, then said, "Some, under my influence, married well."

Though he looked very willing to gossip or give us his unsolicited opinions, I decided I didn't want to play. Or, more so, the ache in my head decided.

Sitting up a little straighter, I was more interested in not losing my breakfast. Nonetheless, I was curious about the man feeding me poison. "And you are who, sir? I would like to know to whom to offer my gratitude."

"Talson. Frederick Talson. Some call me 'the father of the square.' And my daughters are my only connections. One's a duchess, and the other a countess. We can't have everything."

That was a humblebrag. Why was he trying so hard to impress us?

He came closer to me with the goblet. Its wine scent burnt my nose. "Ready for another sip, Lady Worthing?"

"No, sir. I'm not."

"You should be. Death can be quite a shock." He drew the goblet to his lips and downed some of the brown liquid. "Then you get used to it."

Florentina folded her arms. Her brown gown looked sweet, without wrinkles as she paced. She finally settled near the fireplace. Oddly, above the mantel hung a set of crossed silver swords.

"Weapons? Very strange for such a feminine room." I covered my lips with my palm. The fuzziness in my mind or the drink might have made me very talkative.

"Ah, you like shiny things? That's a pair of Viking swords. I repaired them for Mrs. Flowers. They are from her clan. They can be traced back to the Norse explorer, Leif Eriksson."

"Oh. Her clan," Florentina said. "She's related to Norsemen who first sailed to the Americas."

"The land mass, yes. And Eriksson and his men carried these swords, made strong by being wrapped in fine silver. Go look, Lady Worthing. Let's see how your balance is."

Talson helped me stand. The pride in his tone had made me believe he wanted to show off his handwork. Or perhaps he would delight in seeing me toddle across the room and fall.

Barefoot, I traversed the room, concentrating on the slapping sound of my soles on the polished pine floor. Soon I stood at the mantel, luxuriating in the radiating heat from the flames and taking in the silver masterpieces. They were beautiful, with all different types of filigree, thin and thick, wrapped around the hilt.

"Mr. Talson, has Lady Worthing shown any of those signs you discussed with Mr. Henderson?"

"She has good balance, but let's keep observing. You learn so much by watching and listening."

Why were they talking like I'd gone mad? Had I . . . gone mad?

It took everything in me to keep myself from running out of the room to find Stapleton. He'd tell me truthfully if I'd succumbed to my mother's madness. Well, that was what people called the worst of her visions and her decision to divorce my father.

Stapleton would be blunt and brutally honest. I could count on that lack of sensitivity.

The gentleman kept eyeing me and sipping the brandy.

No longer wishing to be studied like an exhibit at a gallery or a loon in Bedlam, I turned back with a hand on my hip. Buttons jingling on my sleeves, I said, "I'm alert. I can answer questions. If I suffer from anything at all, it's embarrassment."

"Nothing to be embarrassed about, young lady. You saw death up close. That's not an experience for women."

Before I could challenge the jaded statement, nausea struck. Images of the bench, the body, and the shed blood filled my head. What were the man's lifeless eyes staring at? What were his eyes trying to tell me?

Easing to me, as if she didn't want the floor to squeak, Florentina said, "Abigail, please sit. Let me help you return to the sofa."

"My coat . . ." The things I thought I remembered gathering. "Where are my things? Have I ruined everything?"

"Things? You're fretting over your coat and bonnet?" She grasped my hands. The fretful look distorted her classic features, making her appear drawn. and anxious. My chest stung anew. "Sorry, Flo."

"Your maid is soaking everything, ridding them of stains. We thought you were bleeding. When you fell, did you hit your head? Are you in pain?" Her speech was fast. I could see her thoughts racing.

"No. I don't think so." I clasped her hand to my bosom. Hopefully, she could feel that scared heart inside me pumping. "I'm better. But you thought I was dying?"

"There was so much blood . . . red, like paint all over you. We checked but found no lacerations, but you do have lovely ankles." Talson winked at me. "Delicate but nicely thick, with a bit of muscle."

Why did I want to toss a blanket over myself? And why did this man have to grin like a dirty old sailor who'd say lewd things to ladies walking near the Thames?

"I'm feeling better, Florentina. Truly."

Slowly, with my cousin in tow, I went back to the floral sofa, taking my time as I passed under a large chandelier made of crystal stars. It twinkled and shimmered. The smell of vanilla and honey was strongest underneath it.

When I sank onto the cushions, the scent of sweet powdery violet wafted through the air. This wasn't my imagination, was it? Perhaps it was an effect of the concoction the old man had fed me.

"She'll be fine, Miss Sewell, " said Talson who'd taken a seat on a frail little chair. The chair's patina and the shape of the legs matched those of the writing desk. Sitting back, he said, "Looks like you ladies will be trapped with us. No one is going anywhere."

"Mr. Henderson's driver?"

"The mews is like another house. He and the horses will be well. It's snowing too hard for him to try to walk back here."

Florentina ran to the window. The window sheers were still wide open, showing the heavily falling flakes. "It has to stop. We can't be trapped here."

Talson chuckled. "No man here can change the weather. But I do hope the gentlemen hurry."

"Hurry where?" I leaned forward as new panic shivered down my spine. "You just said no one can go anywhere."

For the first time, the old man frowned. "They are all out there with Benjamin Brooks. Trying to figure out what happened before they move the body." He shook his head. "He's been murdered on the Night of Regrets."

I peered at the windowpane, cold and freezing with ice, and wished I could see the bench and the body once again.

Chapter 5

The Pink Parlor, Nine Berkeley Square

Sitting on the sofa, I repeated the name of the victim, Mr. Benjamin Brooks. Mr. Talson, "the father of Berkeley Square," as he called himself, told my cousin and I about knowing Brooks since the man was a child.

"Precocious," he said. "Always a good student."

"Sir, tell us more about Mr. Brooks as an adult and neighor." Florentina patted the edge of the sofa. "He also lives in the square?"

Talson twirled his silver cane, which had a handle similar to those of the swords but was made with a finer filigree, the thinnest silverwork I'd seen. "Benjamin Brooks, a barrister for the king, was one of the finest legal minds I know." Talson choked up a little.

"Smarter than Lord Duncan?"

It took a moment before he responded. "Yes, Lady Worthing. It is possible." He laughed, then sobered. "Benjamin Brooks was a legal scholar, probably one of the brightest London has ever seen."

"Who would want such a bright light dimmed, Mr. Talson?"

My question shook him from his reverie. He frowned. "A great many. He handled high-profile trials. Many men he made swing at Tyburn. Didn't your husband escape that fate?"

The practice of keeping my face blank proved to be my saving grace. I waited at least five painful seconds before I responded. "I don't think he was ever meant to be charged with any capital—"

"You mean a bloody crime to be punished by the Bloody Code. Brooks excelled in the Bloody Code. He loved having men hang." He folded his arm and supported his chin. "Hanging isn't truly bloody, is it?"

Florentina gasped. "Mr. Talson, please. My cousin is recovering, and you're mocking a man who was brutally murdered."

Talson's face shifted, probably one of the many he possessed. "You are right. The men, as you will see tonight, will be cordial, but the competitive, even haughty nature of us all cannot be avoided."

"At least you're honest about it," Florentina said.

Then I asked about motives. "Mr. Talson, was Mr. Brooks receiving threats?"

"When was he or Charles not? Barristers don't make many friends. There is always a disgruntled party, an angry family member wanting to exact revenge. It's no wonder Charles keeps the new Lady Duncan away from town."

Maybe the perceived slight wasn't one at all. Hard to be invited to dinner if the wife was never here.

"You've come from your house to this dinner? A full evening for men?"

"Yes, Lady Worthing. Men must have society, too. Charles calls it the Night of Regrets." With both hands on the hook of his cane, he leaned forward. "You look as if you are regretting getting up too soon. Feeling dizzy again?"

Shaking my head at him could have nauseous implications. "I am feeling better, but you were telling us about Benjamin Brooks."

"And who are all the men outside with Mr. Henderson and Lord Duncan?" Florentina had peered again through the window. I wondered what she could have seen with the snow falling so heavily.

"Oh yes. Benjamin Brooks was a confirmed bachelor. He took interest in my daughter once, but she married John Clayton, the Earl of Constock."

The door to the parlor opened. The tall Blackamoor gentleman we'd seen earlier on the steps of Number Nine Berkeley Square stepped inside, or rather actually limped across the threshold.

"Madame looks to have recovered." His voice was a strong, deep baritone.

"Oh good, Mr. Peters is here," Talson said. "The valet is vital to the next part of the story."

If looks could kill, Talson would be a dead man. Mr. Peters's glare had fiery darts. "You're not gossiping about me. You know I hate that."

Talson waved his hands. "Now calm down. I was just going to mention retired army colonel William Holston. Holston was part of the Ninety-Ninth Regiment of Foot, which you ladies can appreciate. They battled in the West Indies. But Peters's part is that they served together in the old Americas. They fought the good fight at Valley Forge."

"Miserable war," Peters said. "Got nothing but gout from it."

Waving his cane, Talson laughed. "You gained your freedom from your masters in America. That's something for a man from Martinique. The horrors you'd face if you were caught being disloyal . . ."

Mr. Talson needed to take care: his needling was angering the valet.

Mr. Peters grumbled something in French under his breath.

"*Grand blanc*, did you say?" Florentina asked the man, but he didn't answer.

The fellow slammed the tray he held in his hands onto the tea table. "Gingerbread cake from the chef. Mr. Villers heard of your collapse, young lady. The man believes food solves all ills."

"When you meet Mr. Holston, you'll see he believes that, too." Talson puffed up his cheeks and splayed his hands about an imaginary belly.

Peters murmured something, and by the look of my cousin's wide eyes, she heard it and understood.

Slowly, the valet turned and walked to the door. "As we are short staffed, Lord Duncan has me helping everyone now, including your maid." He left, but his parting words were clear. "Can't wait to retire and leave the square."

The door closed shy of a slam.

I turned to Talson for an explanation.

He dimpled. "The man has been ready to retire for a while, but money's been an issue. The gentleman has worked for all of us, even Brooks, to make a little extra. But I fear his finances aren't quite what he thought they'd be."

So Talson's gossip was not only of the neighbors but of the staff, too. I didn't want to hear any more. The sweet ginger and clove smell of the cake enticed me, but not enough for me to risk my stomach's rejection.

I rose from the sofa, walked toward the window, and stopped at the writing desk. It was pretty and without a hint of dust along the surface, on the edges of the tiny drawers along the top, or on the rim of the single large drawer underneath. I wanted to look at the bench outside, but I couldn't. Instead, I searched the tops of the trees.

Talson walked over. He barely used the cane, which meant it

was more for show, a piece to be talked about. "It's still coming down, but you can make out Mr. Brooks's house. It's right on the other side, directly through the trees. Number Thirty-Seven." He pointed straight ahead with his cane. "You can't see mine, but I am to the left, on the corner."

"With you living the closest to Mr. Brooks, did you see who visited him today?"

"Lady Worthing," my cousin said in her most formal voice, "I think you should refrain from asking questions and should continue to sit. You've had a terrible shock. You're not the fainting kind." Her tone with me was like when we were small and I'd been caught doing something naughty.

"Dear Florentina, I'm much better. You needn't be so concerned."

"Would you take advice from Commander Henderson? He insisted that you rest."

"Oh, Miss Sewell"—Talson clapped his hands at my cousin—"was that the handsome bloke who almost refused to let her out of his arms?"

Stapleton. The man was dear and had grown as overprotective as my godfather. Somehow on a day I discovered a body, it didn't seem so bad to have someone caring for my welfare.

"Mr. Talson, you've drunk all the restoratives," I said. "Would you mind getting a little more? I want to be ready for our conversation on Mr. Brooks. I do look forward to learning everything about him and who you think murdered him."

"Um." He hesitated.

I put my hand to my head in dramatic fashion. "Please, sir."

"Yes, Lady Worthing. I'll be right back."

He left the room, and I motioned to Florentina to close the door. When the soft thud sounded, I rushed to her. "Tell me what is wrong or what it is I don't know."

"Are you ready to confess, Abbie?" She walked across the squeakless wide planks to stand behind the beautiful pink floral sofa. This room and the decor might've been in fashion years ago. Somehow, it seemed even more fragile, like all could crumble with my cousin looking madder than a hornet.

"You can tell me anything," she said. "Abbie, hurry, before the gossiping man returns."

"What do you want me to say, Florentina? That I'm a fool? That I'm weak and I fainted in front of Stapleton and a house full of men? So much for earning anyone's respect."

"You fainted because you fell into a pool of frozen blood. You found another dead body, Abbie. Does that seem like a normal occurrence for you?"

She stood opposite me on the other side of the sofa. The wall behind her acted like a frame made of plaster frieze.

With her light baby blue shawl, she could be the subject of a painting, a sprite of justice. "You've been acting so odd, Abbie. But I figured it out. You can tell me that you are with child and that Lord Worthing's not happy with the situation, particularly since he's been away."

If Florentina had slapped me, I wouldn't be more stunned. "What?"

"You're pregnant."

My mouth dropped open. I truly wasn't the fainting type, but this hit me hard.

"Abbie, admit it. Then I will help you. We all will."

"No." I shook my head.

"No, you don't want help? Don't be silly. You will need me."

I rounded the edge of the sofa. "I'm not with child. Being in that condition would require my husband's presence. He's not been around for many months. His most recent letter indicates it will be many more before we are in the same room."

For a moment, she looked relieved. Then that fearful look returned. "Pregnancy doesn't require a husband, just a willing partner. I'm sure you've found one. You're pregnant, and we all know who the father is."

My lungs stung again. I couldn't be more shocked.

Mortified and hurt, I stared at my cousin in disbelief. "After all the heartache and brokenness that infidelity has cost my family, do you actually think I'd entertain such a thing? How can you be so cruel?"

"I'm sorry, Abbie, but since the burglary of your house, I've noticed how entangled you've become with Mr. Henderson. I see the attachment. I think your affections are drifting."

"Because we're not at each other's throats, we have to be lovers?"

"You used to talk about James. Now you talk about the neighbor or his sister or something that draws you more deeply into his sphere. Soon there will be no separating you."

"Flo, he loves Teacup. I'm attached to his greyhounds. And lest we forget, they patrol my property, in search of unseen dangers." Then I decided to let her know where my new peace came from. "Stapleton's concern is a blessing. And it's more than I can say about my husband. He's made it plain that he doesn't care what I do. James never cared for me, not the way I did for him."

"Abbie, couples fight. You must've misunderstood—"

"There's nothing to misconstrue." I clapped my mouth shut, trying to contain my fury, but it got the better of me. "James doesn't want a marriage, not a true one. He wants the lie. He wants me to have affairs. He doesn't care if I have a child that's not his. In fact, he wishes it to be that way. I can be secure with a false heir if he never returns."

Florentina looked faint, but she had asked for this fight. I would finish it.

"James has written with an ultimatum. He wants me with child. He doesn't care by whom. He'd probably prefer it be Stapleton's, his handpicked choice to protect me. But Commander Stapleton Henderson is honorable. And I have no intentions of living a lie. When we get to Cheapside, I will get Mr. Vaughn to get me out of this marriage. I will divorce."

"Abbie, I'm so—"

"Stop. I don't want to hear any of it. You've accused me of

being the worst kind of person. What you should have called me was a failure. I've tried to make a difference and failed at the basics. I failed at being Lady Worthing."

There were tears in her dark eyes. It ate at me to see her cry, but at least she finally felt the burden that James had dropped upon my shoulders. I looked up at the ornate molding crowning this beautiful pink room and let the tension drain from my neck. It did feel better to have said this out loud. "Now that you know, you can stop being mean to Mr. Henderson. It's not his care that's the problem. It is the lack of my husband's."

With a hand over her mouth, my cousin rushed over to me. "When you fainted . . . you could not see how Mr. Henderson carried you. He cradled you and almost refused to set you down. He cares for you, Abbie, deeply."

"Why are you crying? I forgive you. How many wrong-headed conclusions have I come up with? I was wrong about him for a long time. My neighbor is a good man, but more importantly, he's honorable, and he respects me."

Tears dribbled down her cheeks. "Blood was on your arm . . . I thought you'd been shot. The fear in his face confirmed my worst nightmares. I didn't want you gone, not without me telling you how much I love you. You're the sister I never had. I was jealous that your last moments were with him, not me."

The choice?

Was that what my dreams were about? I drew her into my arms. "Hey, Flo. I'm all right. No friend or man could ever replace you. You're so important. My life doesn't work without you."

She gripped me tighter. "I've been jealous. My work for the navy has been so demanding. I'm away crunching figures with Mrs. Edwards, and he's always around. You two are sharing secrets. I feel left out."

I wanted to ask why that had to mean Stapleton and I were engaged in an affair. Instead, I held her tighter. "Florentina, I tell you secrets, too. And now you know one I couldn't fathom speaking aloud to anyone but you or Mr. Vaughn."

Putting my hands to her wet cheeks, I said, "Look at me. Our lives are always changing, but there will never be a day I don't need you. We've changed so much. So much has been lost, except us. You've always accepted me. You're my sister. We've chosen to love, to bond, to build. No one will ever come between us."

She wiped at the water running down my face. "I'm sorry."

"We tell each other everything." *Well, almost everything.* "Mr. Henderson witnessed me faint and probably thought that whatever drained the life out of that poor man in the snow had gotten to me. I'm embarrassed but fine."

"But I'm not, Abbie. We're always being drawn to death, and your neighbor is always at the center of it, too. I'm frightened. The attack on your house this summer cannot be forgotten. We are vulnerable. I don't know what I'd do without you."

"Florentina, a man in Berkeley Square was murdered. The killer is probably long gone."

"Or close by." She stepped back. Her head twisted from side to side. "The killer might still be in this neighborhood, trapped by the weather, too. He might even be here. You heard Mr. Talson. There's a lot of competition and envy here. While you were lying on the sofa in here, I heard Mr. Mayer, another of Lord Duncan's guests, arguing with Mr. Peters."

"About what?"

"I'm not sure," she said, "but Peters called him a *Grand-blanc*, and the valet didn't seem to be congratulating him on a success."

That was odd, a servant having words with a visitor.

She brushed at tears along my jaw. "I can't lose you or watch you suffer. That's why it pains me to say this. I think you should get on the next boat as soon as possible. Sail to Lord Worthing. What he's requested is foolish. He's surely said it to test you."

Why did she refuse to understand?

Must I say aloud that this marriage of convenience was merely a reward for clearing James's name so that Mr. Brooks or Lord Duncan or some other barrister wouldn't have the pleasure of hanging him for embezzlement?

"All my girlish hopes are dead, Flo." I went to the writing desk and started opening the drawers of the desk. "I will find some paper. I will write my terms for Mr. Vaughn."

"Abbie, you know you need to go to Lord Worthing. Bring him back. Or go explore the world together."

I snapped a drawer of feather pens shut and opened another with pink stationery. In gilded letters, it read ANNA VIOLET FLOWERS. "A reconciliation will prove very difficult when this marriage is nothing. Our marriage is a financial transaction. There is no love, no mutual desire, and now I know there is no respect."

She started to come to me but then stopped and sank onto the pink sofa. "But you truly care for your husband. Or are you looking for an excuse because your affections have drifted? Was I right on that?"

"Worthing has drifted. He sees his lover daily. His guilt wishes for my desires to drift. He is perfectly serious in requesting that I'm to be unfaithful."

Her head fell back, eyes bulging. "Abbie . . . I'm—"

I clutched a piece of the beautiful pink paper and wrinkled it in my fist. "I thought his letter last summer would be a divorce settlement. I wrote him again. I begged him to come back. He requested this sham."

"Oh, Abbie. I'm so—"

"No. No pity. I don't want to think of him right now. Nothing of my predicament. There are far too many other things happening in the world of greater significance than my marital woes. A man has died a horrible death. I have paper. And here's a pencil. I can do something that has nothing to do with James."

Throat clogging, flooding with hurt, I stopped talking and

merely tried to breathe so I'd not cry. I went and grabbed the writing chair and lifted the fragile thing. After putting it in front of the desk, I sank onto it and made a list of suspects in the murder of Benjamin Brooks.

Lady Worthing's List

Murdered: Mr. Brooks
Suspects: Unclear

Men attending the Night of Regrets:
Charles Flowers, Lord Duncan
Stapleton Henderson
Mr. Frederick Talson
Lord Constock
Mr. Holston
Mr. Mayer

Servants working the Night of Regrets:
Mr. Peters
Mr. Villers

Women stuck at Nine Berkeley Square:
Miss Bellows
Florentina Sewell
Abigail Monroe, Lady Worthing

Chapter 6

The Pink Parlor, Nine Berkeley Square

Sitting in the pink parlor, I put down my pencil. My list had names, but none I could clearly determine as suspects. Other than knowing where Brooks was killed, I had no idea of time of death, let alone motives. I wished I could figure out how long he had been on that bench.

After examining my notes, I folded the paper and put it and the pencil in my pocket.

"Do you feel better, Abbie?" My cousin's voice sounded soft, hesitant.

"Yes, but I am fretful about the men being outside so long. The weather is not improving."

"Meant having written your note," she said. "Making lists about murder. That is your favorite thing."

I nodded and then made sure all the desk drawers which I'd searched were closed and again looked untouched. "This room may not have been used since the late Mrs. Flowers's death. I don't want to seem as if I've taken liberties."

"Abigail, don't withdraw." My cousin came to my side. "I was careless in my words, but Uncle Vaughn will know what to do."

"He will figure out how to implement what I want this time." If left to him, my godfather would resolve things in terms of status and power. "I need peace. I need a world which I've built that won't be upset by politics or whim. I want to be whole and sane when I look in the mirror."

Florentina's soft eyes probed mine, but I had nothing more to say. I'd never honor James's request. And even if our marriage vows meant nothing to him, I had meant them when I said them in St. George's and when I let him into my bed.

I pushed past her and went over to the window. "Let's see if the men, those non-fainting souls, have discovered our culprit."

After wiping at the fogged glass, I saw Stapleton and Duncan draping a sheet-covered figure on the ground.

The door began to open, and I turned quickly at the noise.

Mr. Talson had returned with a bottle under one arm and mugs in his pockets. "Oh, Lady Worthing. Please stay away from the window. I'm of no stature to help you up off the floor."

Juggling the bottle, his cane, and his attitude, he looked very strong to me. "I'll be no more trouble."

He laughed as Florentina and I met him at the tea table. As we sat on the sofa, he poured us each a mug then eased to the close chair. "Why do I feel as if you will be a lot of trouble for as long as we are stuck here?"

"Tell me more of Mr. Brooks, your longtime neighbor, the man I discovered. And of the others who are outside with Mr. Henderson and Lord Duncan. I presume they are Lord Constock, Mr. Mayer, and Mr. Holston."

"I didn't say who was out there, but I see you are good at figuring things out."

I'd merely guessed, but I gazed at him like it had been some feat of deduction. "Tell us about these men who've come to Lord Duncan's Night of Regrets."

He sipped on his brandy. "Charles has mentioned you, Lady Worthing. He said you were very smart."

After picking up a mug, I took a quick sip.

Florentina did, too.

The brandy was as bad and as strong as before.

"We are all longtime neighbors. I've known Charles Flowers and Benjamin Brooks since the beginning, when they trained at Lincoln's Inn. They were up-and-coming men from good families. With daughters, it's important to know men to recommend."

"But they were rivals?" Florentina looked at me and put her mug back down on the table. "How can you drink this?"

"Very easily, young lady. And yes, the two were always trying to outdo one another. They even secured property here about the same time."

I wasn't actually drinking this swill made from brandy but pretending to and pressed Talson to tell us more. "Is that why the houses are on the opposite sides of the square?"

"Yes. That's why the chief rivals houses are directly along opposing sides. The rest of us are spectators. " The rise of his thick, bushy eyebrows indicated he'd remembered something surprising or humorous, but he kept whatever it was to himself. "Well, Charles and Benjamin have been competing forever. Why not war over who has the highest chimney on the square?"

"That seems odd, arguing about who can blow more hot air." Florentina lifted her mug again and sniffed it, then set it down. She sat back on the sofa with folded arms. "But your house is closer to Brooks's. That's what you said before. Does that mean you saw him often?"

His nose wrinkled. "Not much lately. But we all come together, as neighbors should, for things like this. I guess we will all gather after this storm to lay Brooks to rest."

Talson became quiet, distracted or perhaps lost in reverie. We let him have his moment.

But as soon as he touched the bottle to refill his mug, I readied myself to ask the next series of questions.

"I do try to keep abreast of everything happening in Berkeley Square." He sighed. "This place won't be the same without Brooks."

"Was he beloved?" I asked.

"Are any of us?" The old man laughed. "He was hated by almost everyone but was respected. You don't amass as much power in the courts as Brooks had without people admiring that."

His gaze went above the mantel toward the crossed swords.

For some reason, I thought it was significant. I changed from the question I was going to ask about Brooks's last trial to one about the owner of the swords. "Did Mr. Brooks know Mrs. Flowers?"

Mug in hand, Talson shot up, panicked. He went to the window. "You are clever, or I'm too sentimental in this room."

He drank his brandy. "Brooks was in love with her. He tried to pursue her up to the wedding, maybe beyond. The night she died, in early labor, I think he was here pestering her. Don't know how Duncan ever forgave him. Maybe he didn't."

Florentina glanced at me. We had our first suspect in the death of Mr. Brooks: the magistrate of London.

From the window, the old man intoned, "The Earl of Constock also had problems with Brooks. I think he felt he was trying to corrupt his wife."

That was a rushed confession on a subject we weren't conversing about. I decided to play along. "How do you know this?" I asked this question and waited to gauge how much gossip the man consumed.

"The lean man drinks too much," Talson said. "He can't hold his drink. And once he's lost his sobriety, he'll tell you everything, even the location of his safe. That's unlike William Holston, our military man of Berkeley. He could outdrink a mule."

"That's not good. It must make his countess fretful."

Talson turned away from the window and nodded. "You understand the situation completely. Worthing's not a drinker, is he?"

"No more than the next military man." My full smile stayed bright, not exposing that even as James's wife, I knew very little about him. I join him at the window. "Speaking of men who serve in the armed forces, tell us about Mr. Holston."

"He served as a colonel in the East Indies. At Valley Forge he was a captain." Talson pointed me to the window glass, then began cleaning his spectacles. "He's the rotund gentleman walking back to the house. He will get out of lifting everything, even his friend Brooks's body."

I made a mental note that Holston was the only man that Talson had actually claimed was Brooks's friend. Perhaps a casual reference meaning nothing. "And the young man? I thought I saw one."

"Ah, Mayer. He's the handsome one." He turned to my cousin. "Miss Sewell, you are the only unmarried woman here. Take note. He's single and wealthy, though no one can say exactly how much money he's made. But he does spend a fair amount of time courting heiresses from the merchant classes and those sent here from the West Indies by their wealthy fathers in order to attend school. Would that be how you came to London? I detect a slight accent."

"You hear my mother and aunts in me. I was born in Cheapside. I'm as English as you." Florentina didn't demur. I loved that about her. I might be mad at her, but I was as proud of who she was as I was of my own upbringing.

The sly old man chuckled, but it was nasty to allude that Mr. Mayer was a fortune hunter.

Turning my attention back to the murder victim, I wanted to establish how long he'd been out in the snow. "When did you arrive at Lord Duncan's home, Mr. Talson?"

"Been here for a few hours. I came early, thinking the weather would get worse." He lifted up his cane. "I was right."

"Did you see anything unusual?"

"No, Lady Worthing, but if I had"—he unhooked something on his cane, and the bottom dropped away, exposing the long blade of a sword—"I'm prepared for pickpockets and thieves."

He bent slowly and retrieved the rodlike casing of his cane and again sheathed his sword. His gaze fell upon the top of the desk. "Fingerprints. Lady Worthing, Charles is very particular about people touching things in here."

He took a handkerchief and wiped at the drawer I had opened. "There. Now it looks untouched."

"Why is that?" Florentina glanced down at the table and picked up our mugs. "Is the parlor used?"

"No. The room is very much an homage to his late wife. It was her favorite room. He's never made a change to it. It even smells of her cologne water, violets."

The man looked very sad. It may have been the second bit of truth that he had shared. "Whatever trouble Brooks ran into, it must've been early."

"What time did you say you say you arrived, Mr. Talson?"

"I didn't, Lady Worthing. But I will state for whatever notes you are making that I arrived at about two. The snow was lighter then, but the air was cold."

I glanced over at the clock on the mantel. The hands said it was about six o'clock.

Lighter snow would mean that Talson, or any of the other arriving men, might have seen the attack or even the man dying on the bench. The murder had to have happened after two. "What did you do while waiting for dinner, which I'm assuming will start at seven or eight?"

"Seven. Seven on the dot. Charles made improvements to his house. He enclosed his orangery. It's now entirely made of glass windows. He set up steam-heat pipes to keep it warm."

Head leaning to the side, my cousin asked, "You spent time with hot air?"

"Hot air in pipes, Miss Sewell."

At least it wasn't one of Florentina's typical math jokes, but I was sure she would soon be running survival or guilty ratios.

Wait, did she do a calculation to predict that I was pregnant? I offered her a snide look, which made her back go up.

"Charles and I spent a lovely afternoon inspecting his gadgets." He looked at me over the rim of his mug. "Deep in the house, with pipes making noise, we missed Brooks asking for help. I feel bad about that."

I gazed out the window. Why hadn't they moved the body? "What is the delay? They must be cold."

Talson shrugged. "Maybe they are memorializing him now."

"And you don't want to do that, Mr. Talson?"

"I will in my own way." He went to the mantel and nudged the clock an inch to the right, then moved the base of a candlestick so that it was equidistant to centerline of the crossing swords, and matching the position of the candlestick to the right. "There. Perfect symmetry above the fireplace. If only lives could be so orderly."

It was obvious Talson had had ill will toward Brooks. But was it enough to compel him to murder or help with a murder?

Lady Worthing's List

Murdered: Mr. Brooks
Suspects: Lord Constock
    Mr. Talson

Chapter 7

The Pink Parlor, Nine Berkeley Square

Florentina held both our mugs as she sat on the sofa. I assumed she was afraid to set them down. She said, "Mr. Talson, if the men take any longer, you, as a physician, should go get them. This can't be good for their health."

"Wave your sword at them," I said, offering the man a good ribbing. "I'm sure they will listen."

He glanced at me through his spectacles. "An old bull knows better than to get in the way of young ones. When you learn the gossip about here, you'll understand my meaning."

The door opened, and Mr. Peters walked in. He had a tray in his hand. Acting like a footman, though not dressed as one, he went to Florentina and took the mugs, then took Talson's bottle.

The classic cut of his coat, the rich emerald wool, and the intricately tied cravat spoke of elegance.

"Mr. Peters," my cousin said, "I thought you went to rest that leg of yours."

The fellow winced, shifting his weight in his shiny slippers. "You should make me a cane like that for when I retire. I would like to walk down Bond Street with such an elegant cane."

Though he was requesting a gift, Mr. Peters again sounded angry. With his salt-and-pepper hair—not powdered and worn about one and a half inches high—he looked very distinguished. Distinguished and disgruntled.

"You're acting as the main server tonight?" I asked. "Does that mean you will be in the kitchen, helping the chef?"

Peters sighed as if his soul was tired. "Yes. Lord Duncan insists. He always insists. I've been working with him since he started having this Night of Regrets."

What an odd name for a dinner, I thought. "How long ago was that, sir?"

He looked at me, and I knew he was digging deeply to find patience. "This is the sixth year. He's done a Night of Regrets every year, right before Christmas, since his wife died."

Talson's smirk appeared. "It is good of you to volunteer—"

"There is no volunteerin'." Peters coughed. The island accent that had appeared faded when he added, "When it comes to this night, Lord Duncan knows how I feel about being here and serving these guests. But the gentleman's a good employer, and my wages are superb, so I persevere. I'm here, in his service, until I can leave."

He pulled a cloth from his pocket and dusted everything that we could've possibly touched. Then the brusque man went to the door. "Enjoy your evening here, ladies. Hopefully, it will pass quickly and you'll be on your way, as I will be on my way to my celebrations."

"Sir, wait," I said. "Do you hate it here that much? Or is it the pain in your leg? It's obvious you're limping. And traversing the steps and the marble, going back and forth to the kitchen, must be terrible."

He smiled for a moment. "If that is the least of my troubles, then I'll survive."

Mr. Talson eyed the valet. "You complain a great deal. But I know Charles compensates you well. That's why you work for him."

"One could say I'm bonded to him. Or I found my other employers deplorable." Mr. Peters looked about the parlor. "I'm fond of many things and memories, but that doesn't change my not wanting to be here. It's bad for my health. I'm ready for change."

"You sound tired, Mr. Peters." I leaned forward a little. "I will try not to be much more of a bother."

"Gentlewomen like you or the late Mrs. Flowers are never the problem. The grands . . . the grand gentlemen always competing or looking for gossip or to be amused at someone's suffering, that is the problem."

"Mr. Peters." Florentina caught his attention when he was almost out the door. "You almost sound as if it's dangerous to be here."

One eyebrow went up, as if he was sending us a signal. Then he left.

The door closed with a bang.

Florentina rose, went to the window and checked outside. "The snow keeps falling. We're trapped. And we've been warned."

Talson sort of laughed. "Oh, don't mind Peters. He's much more agreeable when he's merely dealing with tailcoats and waistcoats. He also makes the most stylish cravats."

Studying him, I began a leading statement. "I suppose he's a trusted servant to Lord Duncan and therefore allowed liberties. Peters must be a good sport as well as, willingly performing duties that should be a footman's or a butler's."

"Actually, he worked for Mr. Holston before. They had some sort of falling-out, and Duncan took the opportunity to hire him. You see, we at Berkeley Square live in each other's pockets."

Talson shifted to the window again and peered out. "And then there were just three men. Mayer is outside with Duncan and Henderson. The earl and Holston must have come inside to get warm. Or to gossip."

Conscious of touching things, I returned to the desk again. I had stationery in my pocket and was a little worried that the disappearance of these pages would be noticed. "This room has been left exactly like the first Mrs. Flowers left it?"

"Yes. Before Flowers's ascension and becoming Lord Duncan, Anna Violet died in childbirth. The babe, too. Such a peril-filled thing you women endure. I think of her always, happily writing her letters in this room." Talson lowered his hand as if to tap the writing desk, but he stopped himself. "She loved this room so."

That was indeed sad to know, that Lord Duncan had lost his wife and a child. "Such losses are unimaginable. At least he's found love again."

"Love? If you call it that."

His chuckling was odd, slightly unhinged. But most marriages were business transactions with the hope of happiness.

Still feeling very otherworldly from fainting and the brandy cure, I'd settled on a plan. Until I could get to Cheapside and I could talk with Vaughn to figure out how to resolve my conflict with James, I was here with a mystery. "Mr. Brooks . . . Did he marry? Does he have children, who must be told of his demise?"

Mr. Talson pulled a flask from his pocket. "No wife. No by-blows that I know of."

Florentina started her pacing again. "And you two were close associates?"

"I'm his neighbor, miss. I'm retired. I have plenty of time to see who comes and goes. You can say I'm the keeper of the af-fairs."

"As a physician, do you have any idea how Brooks died?" I asked. "I didn't see a wound."

For the first time, the arrogant physician looked uneasy. "I don't know."

"Was he shot? Was he stabbed in the middle? There's quite a lot of blood in the snow. That didn't come from the air. And it is so cold. One would think a slow draining wound would freeze."

"Lady Worthing, I don't know. But I suspect that's why the men are still out there looking." He took a handkerchief and wiped at his mouth. "I'm sure we'll know shortly."

He turned away from us and again peered out the window. "And then there were two. Only Charles and Mr. Henderson are still out there."

I folded my arms, frustrated at his humor and at the fact that his stance blocked me from seeing out the window. "For a man who has his eyes on the square, you seem less certain of things."

"In this circumstance, that is true. I do know Brooks was quite frozen. He'd been seated on that bench for a while."

Talson checked his flask and put it to his lips. It was empty.

Florentina pointed to the door. "I should've stopped Mr. Peters. My mug was full. Waste not, want not."

"Shameful," he said. "There's an older saying, I believe from the fifteen hundreds. 'Willful waste makes woeful want.'"

"Mine's shorter by a word, but the sentiment is the same."

He glared at her. "Do you like old sayings or poems?"

"Well, yes, I do," she said. "Please don't say anything droll, like you don't expect women to read."

"No, Miss Sewell, but it's not something I often talk to women about." He adjusted his grip on his cane. "I've recently been sent an old poem. I'll have to show you. For it seems you both will be guests tonight. Since we are stuck here, it might add a little levity to the evening for such fair spirits to join us."

Participating in this Night of Regrets might help illuminate whether any of the men here had an interest in Benjamin Brooks dying.

"Brooks was a picky man, always high-strung," Talson said without any prompting. "I wonder if he wanted to die in what he wore to the dinner."

That was an odd notion for the talkative man to entertain. He leaned again on the silver cane that converted to a sword. It was a finely polished cane, with an ivory lion's head carved on the false shaft.

"You carry a defensive weapon," I said. "Were you or any of the men under attack?"

"No, but Brooks did have enemies. What man upholding the law doesn't? Then there is Mr. Mayer. Many are rubbed the wrong way by a man who likes to show off his money."

This complaint coming from the man with the silver cane was laughable, but I kept that to myself.

"If I say Brooks was a good man, does that place me lower on your list of suspects, Lady Worthing?"

I offered him a smile. "You are on the list. Everyone is, until they have a clear alibi or until someone has been proven guilty."

Florentina winced. I supposed it was wrong to accuse a man of murder, especially if he was the murderer.

"I'm going outside to see what is taking so long." He drew closer to the door. "For what it is worth, ladies, Brooks was a good egg, but he was also finicky and at times peculiar. He was given to dark moods when he felt he had lost something. And he never liked the rules Charles set for this dinner, but he never missed one."

"What rules?" Now my tone sounded pitchy, like that of a parrot. "Do tell."

"Oh, you'll find out tonight if Charles and the other gentlemen let you play."

Then we had to play. Florentina and I would have to press for Lord Duncan to invite us.

Florentina had moved to the window. I hadn't noticed her

do that and wondered if she'd picked up Stapleton's quiet footfalls. "The men are ging back out, sir. The others have rejoined Lord Duncan and Mr. Henderson. They're lifting the body together."

"Then I should go offer moral support. You ladies stay in here." He tapped his nose. "We've never had women participate in a Night of Regrets. It could be fun. I wonder what things you two will say."

Talson slowly pounded to the door. "I'll ask if Duncan will give you both seats at the table. Some of the others will resist, but I think it right that the woman who found Brooks should take his place."

The fellow left.

Florentina shook her head. "Abigail, I'm not sure if I want a seat at this table. Hearing the lewd things that men regret shall probably be disturbing."

"Agreed. But we need to know more about the men who've been invited here. One of them is a murderer. I can feel it."

"No possibility, Abbie, that Benjamin Brooks's death was an accident?"

"Being caught in the snow and dying from the cold can be an accident. Losing all the life that courses through the veins is the result of an act of violence."

"It still doesn't have to be murder. It could have been self-inflicted. Mr. Talson said the barrister had moods."

Suicide.

That was a possibility, but it just didn't feel right.

My thoughts were interrupted by the knocking of front doors and the pounding of boots. That had to be the men trudging into the hall with the body. I turned toward the parlor door. The noise called to me.

Florentina approached me and wrapped her arms about me. "No. No going out of this room until Mr. Henderson comes for us. I promised him."

Given that she didn't seem to want to get along with Staple-

ton, whom she'd accused of being a cad, I found it odd and en-
couraging that they could bargain with each other.

"We're stuck in here, Abbie. Let's make the best of things."

Like my cousin, I wasn't partial to participating in men's secret affairs, nor did I like the thought of dining beside a killer
passing dinner rolls.

Yet this notion of a Night of Regrets, of hearing dark truths,
was as intriguing as the circumstances of Benjamin Brooks's
death.

Chapter 8

The Hall, Nine Berkeley Square

With my ear to the door of the parlor, I listened to the men in Duncan's hall.

"Shouldn't we straighten Brooks out?" The voice was a little nasal. The fellow might have become sick, standing in the cold so long.

"We can't, not until Brooks warms up, but that will mean his body is not preserved for the coroner." This was Lord Duncan. His tone was businesslike. He hardly sounded like a man either mourning or overjoyed at the demise of a rival.

"Abbie." My cousin waved to get my attention. "Get away from the door. You will be caught."

I wanted to say she fretted too much, but she was right. Eavesdropping was risky. But how else was I to know what they had discovered or had decided to do with Brooks?

"Good Lord. You can't leave him on the marble floor with just a sheet." That voice belonged to Mr. Peters. "I'm done,

Lord Duncan. I will do no more. You shoulda left him there. You know you can't stand him. Now you're dirtyin' your floors."

After cracking the door open, I peeked out and saw the valet mumbling and climbing the steps to the upper level. He was limping more. The fellow seemed in great pain, but his scowl at the men, living and dead, was fierce.

"Well," Talson said, "the angry valet is right."

"About Duncan hating Brooks?" asked the largest man in height and girth. He had a dignified chin, and his back and neck were aligned like a flagpole. "We all know that. I didn't care for the braggart that much, either."

Talson covered his eyes for a moment. "Not talking about feelings. Just facts. We can't leave him here in the hall. He will melt. The odor will be foul. There are weak women among us. I'd suggest the orangery, but it's way too warm."

Bristling at Talson's sentiment, and the fact that no one had corrected him, I had to calm down. Fretting caused noise. I'd be discovered listening, and what would that do to all these men's perceptions of women?

"The orangery is warm? Well, well, there is a bright spot." The lean man with the light voice moved from his position closest to the grand stairs, which Peters had taken. He headed down toward a corridor that surely led to the back of the house. "I'm going there to get warm . . ." His voice trailed off.

"The cellar is cold, and access can be controlled," Stapleton said. "Duncan, that's the best place to keep him."

"Access?" The large man took off his wet gloves. "Who'd want to see Brooks now? It's not like he can help with anything."

"There's probably clues all over Brooks to determine who killed him or how he was killed." The nervous voice belonged to the youngest man in the group. That had to be Mr. Mayer. He was blond and dashing, so I understood why Talson assumed ladies would have him in their sights.

"We've hesitated enough." Lord Duncan sounded darker, more disturbed.

I widened the crack I'd been peering through to view Brooks and all the men.

"Sacrebleu! It is true what Mr. Peters said. One of you killed the barrister."

"Mr. Villers, back to the kitchen," Lord Duncan said. "I am handling this."

"But you hated him the most."

"Mr. Villers, please." Duncan sighed. Steam seemed to be released from his red nostrils. "Back to the kitchen, sir. Lest you have a confession for us."

The patter of slippers beating a retreat sounded. I thought that Villers was going down the same corridor the lean man had chosen.

"The orangery and the kitchen, Flo, are toward the back of the house, along the corridor," I whispered to my cousin.

She shook her head and made angry gestures suggesting I flee from the door.

When I tried to open the door a wee bit more, Florentina caught my arm. "No, Abbie."

"I need to see what these men are doing."

"There's a bloody dead man in the hall," she said. "You already saw him and fainted."

"Need to see the body again. I need to face my fears."

"No, Abbie. This is about handling a man's body with dignity, not your need to know something or to prove yourself."

She steered me toward the sofa. "We are going to wait until we are given the signal to come out of this room. Have you forgotten that we've intruded on a house of men on an evening meant only for men?"

While I summarily dismissed the notion that I was weak and that a gruesome crime scene could throw me into distress, I did not lose sight of the fact that the Night of Regrets was designed exclusively for men. "They may have discovered something important. I want the truth unfiltered or not sanitized."

Her hold on my arm didn't slacken. "Oh, Mr. Henderson will tell you anything you wish to know. That will give you the convenient permission to consult him in private later."

"I'm not Teacup. I don't need to be tethered." I yanked my arm free. "I won't leave the room, but I need you to stop being so quick to think less of my neighbor."

Her head tilted. "It's not him. He seems to be your very polite champion. It's your failing to notice his increasing sentiment. Abbie, he likes you a great deal. You just told me how you will not break your vows. Then why do you keep putting yourself at risk of being the kind of woman you despise?"

As if she'd tossed me down a cold well, I stopped moving, stopped resisting. She was right.

Knowing that my neighbor was close by helped me sleep better. Understanding he did have my best interest at heart warmed my hurting soul. "I need allies, Flo. *We* need them. Whether it's the fight for abolition or even the wish to survive the scrutiny at a dinner for men, we require allies."

"Allies or someone to pine for you the way James won't?"

That was too much. Stapleton was not James, and I didn't want him to be. I'd come to respect him too much to believe he was weak minded or *pining*.

Insulted and affronted for him, I flounced away and left her bereft of a denial.

Her lip trembled. She mouthed the words *no* and *sorry*.

At the threshold, I turned away from her fully. Once a thing was said, it was impossible to forget. Or forgive.

In defiance, I opened the door just a hair's width more and listened to the debating men.

"Holston, calm down," Talson said.

"No. I will not." responded the largest man, who had the best posture. "I have a point. We should bring in the bench, too."

"Not this again." That was the youngest fellow, Mr. Mayer, talking.

"Brooks was in a struggle. The contents of the man's purse went everywhere." Mr. Holston was animated and was pointing back toward the front door. "I think we are leaving critical evidence behind. I'd have my troops cordon off the area."

"You've had no one to order around for years. And I don't think Brooks cares that you brought him inside and left *his* bench. By the way, the bench belongs to us all, all the residents of Berkeley Square. And I remember picking the design." Talson's remark solicited loud groans from the others.

"I'm done." Mr. Mayer flung up his hands. "Between the jokes, the gore, and the indecision, I've had my fill. I'm going to join Constock in the orangery. I know he's in there, warm and probably with a drink."

He had started heading down the corridor when Talson stopped him. "The earl is trapped here like the rest of us. You'll have plenty of time over the next few days to convince him of another risky investment. Stay and help Henderson take Brooks to the basement."

"Rigor mortis has set in." That was Stapleton's voice. I couldn't see him. "The cold cellar will slow the decay," he continued. "That's the best way to preserve evidence."

Holston stepped closer to the sheet-covered victim. "We need to keep everything intact for the coroner and give the man some dignity."

"No coroner is going to come today, tomorrow, or maybe a few days." Lord Duncan's meaning rang clear. Everyone was stuck here. "The weather conditions are deteriorating. No one's going anywhere, either."

Someone coughed. Words exchanged were made inaudible.

The magistrate took charge again. "Mr. Henderson's analysis shall stand. He has worked with me on other homicides. And I agree with him. This was no accident. I don't believe Brooks would commit suicide."

"Are you sure?" Talson's tone was less snide, but it made someone groan. "A man alone, with no family to endure the holidays with, is sad. Who knows how desperation and melancholy can make a man harm himself?"

I'd heard enough. After pressing the door shut, I took a slow breath and turned back to my cousin.

Frowning, she patted the pillow beside her. "Did you get caught eavesdropping?"

"No, Florentina. I did not. I am beginning to excel at all sneaky ways."

"Oh, I don't want to be here. I want to be in Cheapside, with black cake and songs."

My cousin was miserable and right. "We're going to get out of here."

"Abbie, not for days. And if those men caught you listening, you'd prove right every disparaging notion they have about women."

"Does it matter? Whatever we do, there is always suspicion. Right now, I am more intrigued about someone murdered two days before Christmas."

She came over to me and brushed my shoulder. "At least we're stuck together."

"Is that still fine? Us, Flo?"

"Yes. All tantrums are done. I will share you with Mr. Henderson as long as he keeps us and Miss Bellows alive and gets us to my mother's."

"Mathematician, riddle me this. What are the odds that the killer is still here, is one of Lord Duncan's guests?"

"Same odds that the murderer is Lord Duncan. One in six."

"You're counting Mr. Henderson? He was with us."

Florentina counted on her fingers. She may have carried a one in the air for drama. Then my cousin nodded. "Well, it would be the first time he wasn't personally involved."

"Flo, you said no more tantrums."

She gaped at me. "I'm merely reminding you that the murders in Drury Lane and the one in Westminster had connections to your neighbor. And we came here first because Mr. Henderson was invited to Berkeley Square." She clapped her hands. "Connection number three."

"I'm just as connected to each of those murders. Soon you'll be saying that someone will die wherever the two of us go."

She cocked her head to the side as if I'd just stated a fact. "Abbie, Mr. Brooks might not've been found for days if not for you. Was it a vision?"

"Miss Bellows saw what she thought was a snowman. I just knew it wasn't. I took off running. Wasn't wise. I could've fallen or made Stapleton fall chasing me."

Before her lips frowned, I decided to remind her about strays and adding people to our inner circle. "Remember the last time we saw a scarf in the snow?"

"Wilson?" Her face softened. "I remember. Poor lad was kicked out by his father. We found him. Together with Uncle Vaughn, we saved him." She hung her head. "He's family now. I'll give Mr. Henderson more of a chance. And I choose to believe you, Abbie."

Florentina embraced me. We were on the same side again.

She sighed long and heavy. "If Mr. Henderson believes Brooks's death to be a murder, then it probably is."

"Then we agree. Since we are stuck here, we might as well be useful."

"Let's live and get black cake. That sounds like a better plan, Abbie."

The masculine voices grew loud again. The men must've returned from taking the barrister to the cellar.

"Gentlemen, go into the dining room," Duncan said. "Our dinner will start soon."

"We can't possibly think of going on." Holston's tone was loud. "The Night of Regrets should be canceled."

"Well, Brooks died trying to come to the Night of Regrets," Talson replied. "It's a shame. To not go on with it is to not honor him. In principle, we should have it and include Lady Worthing and Miss Sewell."

Well, maybe the man wasn't so bad or so arrogant if he championed our attendance.

"The ladies should be spared the coarse talk," Stapleton said. "I was reluctant to come. I'm not sure it's—"

Florentina kept me from clawing the door open.

"Why must his overprotective nature kick in now?"

"Abbie, he's trying to protect us. He's spent time in the cold with them. I think we can lean into his judgment. And he didn't want to attend at all. I think that he deserves more credit."

I stopped struggling. My cousin was right. And it pained me.

Lady Worthing's List

Murdered: Mr. Brooks
Suspects: Lord Constock
Mr. Talson
Lord Duncan

Chapter 9

The Pink Parlor, Nine Berkeley Square

The door to the parlor opened fully. For one moment, I could see into the empty hall—no bickering men stood about, no body, just gleaming marble.

Silent and stone faced, Lord Duncan, Mr. Talson, and Stapleton came into the parlor.

"Miss Sewell," Duncan said as he entered, "Lady Worthing. Welcome, ladies, to my home. I wish it were under better circumstances."

"See, sir," the old physician said. "See, Mr. Henderson, I told you she was just fine."

"I can see that." Stapleton looked guilty, not in a I-killed-Brooks kind of way, but in a I-droned-on-manly-and-foolishly kind of manner. "You shouldn't be on your feet, Lady Worthing."

"Maybe you should carry her about the room. Or maybe you should, Duncan. Practice for seeing the new bride."

"Don't mention Lady Duncan even in jest, Talson." The magistrate's tone matched Stapleton's gaze, fiery.

Wanting to ease the tension, I stepped closer to Stapleton. "It was a momentary shock, Mr. Henderson. I'm recovered and ready to participate in helping solve this crime."

Duncan shook his head. "Nothing to solve until the weather clears. The thief who did this has to be long gone."

"A thief?" That sounded odd and hadn't been mentioned at all in the hall. "Sirs, are any valuables missing?"

"It's hard to tell. The contents of his purse were scattered. Anything could be gone or stuck in the snow." Stapleton glared at me like I could read his stiff look or obscure thoughts.

If he wanted me to stop asking questions, he should say his wish aloud. Alas, the man knew me well enough to realize how hard it was for me to quit searching for answers.

"The weather has made things difficult." The magistrate's typically straight posture sagged. He needed the military man's assistance. Lord Duncan wore a tired, sullen expression. He looked like he'd aged decades since I last saw him, and that was a few weeks ago.

He moved from us to the writing desk near the window. The man pushed the chair back into place, an inch from where I had put it. Then he hovered over it, as if he had to be certain he'd succeeded in putting it in place.

Duncan then walked up to the window. The wind whipped, rattling the grand glass. "This used to be a casement window. My wife hated the draft caused by the hinges to the side. This sash window was an improvement for her. Three panes wide, two panes high on top. The same on the bottom. She'd count them."

"He's not talking about the new one." Talson's whisper grated.

Lord Duncan must've heard and snapped out of the reverie

into which he'd fallen. He turned and faced us. "A tragedy has happened here in front of my home."

"Thank you for taking us in," I said, hoping to lighten the tension in the room.

"I'm glad you are safe. It was quite a scare seeing you covered in blood." Duncan turned again and looked out the window. Though snow was coming down and darkness had begun to fall, one could see the top of the bench.

"Benjamin Brooks was a good barrister for the Crown. He was our long-term neighbor, Talson. I cannot believe this happened, and right in front of my house."

"I'll play Benjamin's part tonight, during the dinner," Talson said. "I'll do my best to honor him and scoff at the same tale of Martinique you tell every year."

"Martinique, yes. The trial where the innocent person was killed because no one would tell the truth, not to the jury or to anyone who mattered." Duncan's gaze never left the window. "I guess this will be the last year for that. This would've been the last Night of Regrets."

"The last, Charles?" Talson sounded hurt.

"I don't think you all took it as seriously as I intended it." Duncan rotated to face us. "But we shall go on with our Night of Regrets just to remember Benjamin Brooks."

He turned to me. "I'll have a meal sent upstairs for you, Lady Worthing, for you and your party. Henderson, this will be an unusual evening for— "

"We won't be joining, Lord Duncan?" My tone wasn't low or shameful, but all the men and my cousin looked at me as if I'd shouted insults.

"Regretfully, Lady Worthing," Lord Duncan said, "it's a tradition. No women."

Talson stepped forward and leaned on his cane. "Well, their attendance would liven things up."

"Liveliness was never the point, Talson." Lord Duncan folded his arms, as he often did when reviewing evidence. "The dinner was always to be a place for honest confessions."

"Oh, right," Talson said. "The Night of Regrets is for men. As charming as you may be, Lady Worthing, et alia, you'll have to occupy yourself with reading or something."

There wasn't much I could say, if I could persuade my mouth to work.

The old man pivoted to Stapleton. "Will you join us, or will you be upstairs guarding the women?"

With his eyes on me, my neighbor nodded. "I've not been too eager to participate. Excluding Lady Worthing and Miss Sewell does not make me more ready to participate. Given the circumstances, I don't think it well to separate us. Pray let us all stay together."

Talson chuckled, as if Stapleton had made a funny inquiry, but Duncan seemed oblivious as he stared at the writing desk.

And he looked . . . acted guilty.

My pulse raced.

Could what I heard be true? Could Lord Duncan have orchestrated Brooks's death?

"Lady Worthing," he said as his eyes drifted, "Nine Berkeley Square has known better days."

"It's a fine house, sir." My response was low, even humble. How else did I absorb this humiliation on top of the other when I fainted? "Built in the sixteen hundreds?"

"Yes." He turned and touched the grand molding that framed the window. "It's an old house. Been here for over a hundred years. The builder Inigo Jones designed it." He moved to the door and pointed at the marble inlays that were between the oak boards. "There are touches of his genius everywhere."

"But not in the modern window." Then Talson lost his smirk. "This is the one room that will never change. Not even the new mistress has that power."

Duncan offered a begrudging shrug, then returned to my spot by the sofa. "You have no stockings?"

"Miss Bellows is cleaning those and my cousin's boots." I'd been walking around so much, I'd forgotten about them. "Yes. I suppose that is another reason to eat in a guest room, lack of proper attire."

"I will have Mr. Peters bring you a sumptuous meal upstairs."

"The valet will continue to act as a footman? I don't think I need an angry man bringing me food. Let Mr. Villers know that I'll send Miss Bellows."

"Lord Duncan, if it is a matter of too many women at your table," Florentina said, "I could dine upstairs with Miss Bellows. If you had to make an exception, a lady of her stature should be given this license. I'm sure by now everything is dry."

"It's not too many women." Stapleton balled his fists behind his back. "It's women in general. Again, I'd like no part of this obvious segregation."

"Oh, how noble." Talson picked up his cane and waved it at Stapleton. "No. You must participate. But don't fret about the ladies. You've insured that your room is next door to them. Perhaps Mr. Villers can send dessert by you. How does that sound?"

My neighbor's gaze turned into a flowing volcano. If I didn't know him to be benevolent—well, mostly benevolent—I'd fear for Mr. Talson.

"I'm concerned for Lady Worthing and Miss Sewell and Miss Bellows's safety," Stapleton replied. "They weren't supposed to be here. I should've insisted that we all stayed in Westminster to avoid being stranded by the storm. Their discomfort is my fault, as is any slight their presence precipitates."

I looked at him—at his stiff shoulders, ramrod straight back—and saw the military man fighting for us.

It was endearing, but I wished I could assure him that none of this was his fault.

He wasn't one of those confused sorts like my father, like James. Those men shouldered nothing. They kept nothing—no love, no blame . . . no Abigail.

Stapleton leaned over me. His heavy sigh, I almost felt it on my brow. It saddened me so much that I yielded.

"I'm perfectly happy having my meal upstairs with my ladies." That sounded kind of queenly, but I meant it. "I understand completely. And it will be safer, with a potential killer on the loose."

"My wife is in Scotland. When she returns in the New Year, she will have you over for tea." Duncan's words . . . Did he mean them to be some sort of consolation?

Scotland had a rebel queen who would remain a threat until death. I hoped that was not either Lady Duncan's position or mine. "My maid, Miss Bellows . . . Where is she? I don't want her stowed away in the servants' quarters."

"She's upstairs, in the room Lord Duncan provided." Florentina shifted her stance. She looked anxious to flee the parlor. "Let's go to her now."

"Lady Worthing," Duncan said, "this is not exactly how I wished to invite you to my home. An invitation is overdue."

"Of course, my lord." I held his gaze and hoped my countenance didn't show my doubts.

In public, we were social.

At my house in Westminster, in the theater of Drury Lane, he'd solicited my advice, heard me out, and even used my logic to indict the guilty.

For all his belief in my value to his investigations, he'd never invited me to the place where he lived.

No. He had invited my neighbor.

For a man wanting to be a progressive magistrate, perhaps Lord Duncan was still a man of his times.

Swallowing hard, pushing the slights deeper into my soul, I agreed with Florentina. "Thank you, sir. But these events have been upsetting, and I'm a little tired. Perhaps we ladies should retire now and let you have at the Night of Regrets business. Mr. Henderson, please join them. Let's not slight our host."

Stapleton cut his eyes to me. "Are you sure? I'd like to ask the other guests to see if they mind a woman attending the dinner."

Rubbing at my neck, sensing the return of a headache, I decided to retreat. "Miss Sewell, lead me to these rooms."

I joined her near the doorway, then turned again in the magistrate's direction. "Lord Duncan, thank you for your hospitality, and I offer my deepest sympathies. I understand that Mr. Brooks was your longtime neighbor and friend and rival."

Stapleton smiled slightly, acknowledging the obvious. I might've conceded to dinner, but I hadn't given up my position on the murder investigation.

The magistrate's anguished eyes lifted. "I've known Benjamin Brooks for a long time. We were rivals always. Our rise at Lincoln's Inn started at the same time. Our first cases as barristers were days apart. Many times we met each other as adversaries in the courts."

"Yes. And you two even had similar tastes, in houses and such." Talson straightened.

Duncan's face flushed. "I beg your pardon."

Talson guffawed. "Brooks's house. It was also constructed by Inigo Jones. It's an exact match to yours, minus your improvements."

There was something more than houses implied. I made a note to myself to inquire with the gossipy Talson about what other tastes Duncan and Brooks shared.

"Lady Worthing, Miss Sewell," the magistrate said, "my chef and Mr. Peters are the only servants remaining in the house. Your needs—"

"Do not have worries, sir. We shall manage," I replied, interrupting him.

"Henderson," he said, "in thirty minutes, we gather in the drawing room. Traditionally, men gather to talk of regrets. Under the circumstances, we will also memorialize Brooks. You seemed hesitant to attend, but I insist you come. Actually, I insist that you and Talson join me now. Our other neighbors, Constock, Holston, and Mayer, are probably already in the dining room, having drinks."

Stapleton nodded. "Let me have a moment to address my neighbors and see them to their room. Then I will join you."

Talson moved with Duncan from the parlor back into the grand hall.

The open parlor door framed the reflection of the high chandelier on the pinkish-gray marble.

"We should hurry," Talson said. "Constock might drain all your brandy. I don't know how he stores such rich liquors and stays fit. Unless it's a corset. I think he was going to ask for Mr. Peters's advice on advancing and remaining in fashion."

"I'm sure my valet has opinions."

Before the parlor door closed, Duncan stepped back to the threshold. "It's obvious that we will be snowed in at least until tomorrow. Everyone will join together for dinner tomorrow."

The man didn't need to fear my hurt feelings. Lord Duncan needed to survive an inquest, where a group of men would determine who was guilty of the murder of his rival, whose brutalized body was found on a bench near where the magistrate lived.

Chapter 10

The Pink Parlor, Nine Berkeley Square

After crossing the parlor at a hastened pace, Florentina closed the door behind the magistrate and his gossiping neighbor and leaned against it. "Odds tell me, Mr. Henderson, that you have a reason for wanting to avoid the dinner."

I looked at Stapleton. "I must agree, sir. Tell us what you've discovered."

Stapleton glanced at us, then turned to the fireplace. He still wore his greatcoat and gloves.

The look on his countenance was as if he'd just remembered that he was cold.

He stooped low, close to the flames. "Swords in here? Very odd."

"Mr. Henderson." Florentina folded her arms. "You were telling us what you've learned."

"Oh, yes." Patting his hands toward the flames, he said,

"Benjamin Brooks was callously murdered. 'Twas no accident. No suicide. Intentional slaughter."

He ripped his gloves off with his teeth. His poor fingers looked very red. The man could barely bend them.

Knowing that he must be in pain, I rushed to him and rubbed my palms about his.

Florentina coughed.

But instead of being embarrassed for being overly familiar, I chastised her. "Come here and help me get his fingers warm. The man was out in this snowstorm the longest. Frostbite."

She shrugged, then came toward us. Holding her arms out like she'd hug him, she moved to the side, dumped coal onto the embers, and stoked the fire. "There. My part."

Stapleton's smile flickered, then dimmed. "I appreciate your concern, ladies, but you both are in jeopardy. We all are."

"What?" She leaned on the ornately carved side of the mantel. "Then what are we to do?"

"Well, we shouldn't antagonize anyone but me." Stapleton glanced in my direction. "We don't know what we are dealing with."

"Wait." I dropped his hands. "What are you implying, sir? That I will cause trouble?"

"Abigail, not every man, particularly the ones here, is comfortable with a direct and assertive female." He blew on his pinkish fingertips. They'd turned dark like the papered walls. "Someone here is dastardly. One of these men viciously killed Benjamin Brooks."

I waited for him to say he was joking, but the man barely ever did. Florentina jabbed the logs harder with the wrought-iron poker.

"What did you find out?" I asked.

"Abigail, it's not what I learned. It's what I saw. No one truly cared that he'd bled to death."

Stapleton removed his coat and dropped it next to his drying boots. The ebony collar covered my toes. It felt thick and cold. I knew it was not enough to have kept him sufficiently warm.

"Why did you stay outside so long?" I asked. "The others came inside."

"Forgot. I'm used to standing post in the worst weather and watching over the fallen until they can be dealt with. I couldn't move." His lovely eyes were darker than I'd ever seen them, almost pitch black.

I didn't have to wonder what he'd witnessed. I had seen it. Brooks had been lifeless under the snow; all his life force had painted the snow.

"Is that all your thoughts? We're in danger. And you, the man who directed us here, have nothing else to say?" Florentina said. "Well, Mr. Henderson, tell us the rest of your thoughts."

"I have many, Miss Sewell, but I doubt they'd be of interest to you or our baroness."

Our? Was I communal property?

"My first and only concern is to get you ladies securely sequestered before I join this farce of regrets," he added.

Perhaps expecting a different answer, she bristled. "Why hadn't you mentioned that you were being initiated into a gang of old men? Ones who've come together to brag and pretend to feel remorse about something they've done and gotten away with."

"Miss Sewell, I was at sea a long time. I need to be better acquainted with society. But nothing of this invitation did I want. I tried to get out of it, but the magistrate insisted. Taking you all to Cheapside was my last way to get out of this dinner without slighting Duncan."

She put a hand to her ear. "Hark. I hear no one here willing to tell them that this whole evening is wrong."

I released a muffled laugh. Florentina was upset and on a tirade.

"So now you've no choice but to join these merry men," she remarked.

"I wasn't trying to be inducted." Stapleton picked up his coat and stared at my bare feet. "We need to get you stockings."

"Miss Bellows has been cleaning the stains I returned with. Hopefully, everything is dry by now."

He tossed his coat over his arm. "Ladies, I apologize again, but let's get you upstairs and sequestered. I must make sure that all of you leave this place unscathed."

"But who will protect you, Stapleton?"

"Abigail, I can handle myself."

For a moment, I closed my eyes. I saw Brooks's body, his position on the bench. "Ruby snow, the red wetness on my coat and stockings, my boots. How do we keep you safe from all that?"

Florentina stepped between us and went toward the door. "It could have been a thief. He could be long gone. We just have to take care for the night. We will be out of here tomorrow." She turned back to me. "Christmas Eve, Abbie. We will be free."

I wanted to believe her, but I doubted I'd be able to solve a murder in just one night. "And you are positive that Brooks's wound or wounds that made him bleed weren't self-inflicted?"

"I don't but the slit to Brooks's wrist . . ." He dropped his head into his now normal-colored hands. "A scalpel is not something an ordinary thief would have."

"But a retired physician might."

His brow scrunched.

"Not you, Stapleton. Mr. Talson is also a physician."

My neighbor shook his head. "Mr. Talson talks a great deal. I don't see him being that skilled or steady."

Now it was my turn to look up at him for an explanation.

"The cut to his wrist was deep, thin. One could barely see it except for the blood. Cut right through the veins. Brooks was dead in minutes," he revealed.

He bowed his head for a moment, then glanced at me. "It could not have been self-inflicted. I would have expected to see a gaping wound if Brooks had done it to himself. He was bleeding fast, so he couldn't have traveled any distance greater than a few feet."

I searched his countenance for a bit of hope, for something that indicated nothing more nefarious than a robbery gone awry was underfoot.

None. And I didn't need to turn to Florentina and her calculate odds that my mentor had played no part in his neighbor's demise.

"Ladies, something very sharp and thin cut through his arm. It went to the bone. I've never seen anything like it."

A flash of light, a sparkle of memory made me see Brooks again. Snow covered his face, his eyes were open, and he had a scowl. "He saw who did this to him. He died knowing his killer."

"The odds that this mysterious death is a murder are a hundred percent?" Florentina started counting on her fingers again. "No five percent margin of error?"

"This wasn't an annuity or an income. It was a life, and a miserable one, from the remarks I've overheard." Stapleton's tone, while low, showed his frustration had begun to build. "Brooks's purse was cut, too. Money was found all over. We've kept what we found, and put it with his body. Sorry, Miss Sewell. He was no victim of theft."

Before I could console her, my cousin started pacing. "Since he's a barrister," she said, "isn't it more likely this was done by some criminal seeking revenge, not by a guest or a neighbor currently in the magistrate's home? We're safe. That is a possibility, Mr. Henderson?"

His mouth opened and closed. Then he offered the conflicted look I knew so well, the one where he was trying to be gentle as he explained the cold truth. "Anything is possible, Miss Sewell. I'll give you your five percent, but honestly, I don't know."

He sounded tired and not annoyingly confident. His hands had come back to peach. No frostbite. That was good.

His eyes locked with mine; my breathing hitched. I knew how I had been affected by seeing Brooks. I wondered what finding this body before Christmas might do to a retired commander who'd seen a lot of death during his military service.

"Stapleton, you're probably still very cold. Perhaps you should beg off and . . . retire. It's been a long day," I said.

A half smile showed on his face.

Then it disappeared when a crash sounded.

Screaming.

I ran toward the door. "That's Miss Bellows! She's in trouble."

Stapleton grabbed my hand, stopped me, and tossed his coat into my arms. "Keep this and stay put. You, too, Miss Sewell."

He flew into the hall, with us on his heels. I wasn't letting him go alone, and I had to get to my maid.

Men crowded around the center of the hall, blocking the view of something or someone.

After going to Stapleton's right, I saw Miss Bellows shrieking at the top of the landing.

Stapleton pushed through the ring of gentlemen and exposed the worst.

His boots stopped about a foot or two away from the bleeding Mr. Peters. Duncan's valet lay on the marble floor of the hall with his skull split open.

Lady Worthing's List

Suspicious Attack: Mr. Peters
Murdered: Mr. Brooks
Suspects: Lord Duncan
Lord Constock
Mr. Talson

Chapter 11

The Upper Level, Nine Berkeley Square

Barefoot in the hall of Nine Berkeley Square, I watched Stapleton attend Mr. Peters, hoping for a miracle. He searched for a pulse. With every passing second, it became clearer to everyone that the valet was no longer alive.

Stapleton pulled a handkerchief from his pocket and covered Peters's face, covering the split in the valet's skull.

Numb. I stood transfixed, my cousin burying her face into my shoulder.

Lord Duncan rushed down the stairs. "What the devil?"

His foot pounded the last tread. "Good God, no!"

Stapleton stood erect, shaking his head. "Dead."

With his goblet dripping wine, the Earl of Constock stepped close and wafted his hand. "That smell. It's laudanum. Did the man bathe in it?"

Miss Bellows began yelling again. "Oh. No!"

Duncan bowed his chin and said a prayer. Then, as if he'd

just noticed me, he ground his teeth and said, "Lady Worthing, Miss Sewell, go upstairs. Gather your yelping maid and be sequestered. The men need to handle this."

I wanted to comfort Miss Bellows, but I also wanted to help.

The vein throbbing on Duncan's temple announced his spent patience.

"Yes, my lord," I said. I took Florentina's hand and started moving.

Miss Bellows kept screaming.

Clinging to Stapleton's coat and Florentina's hand, I walked around the body. My bare feet flapped around the pool of red; then I headed up the stairs. I took my time, making sure my footing was solid, watching the men surround Mr. Peters.

"Sheets," Mayer said. "Someone get sheets. My guest room is straight ahead. Take mine."

Snapping out of her reverie, Florentina moved faster, taking the treads two at time. She reached the top of the stairs before me. "I'll get them."

She flung open the door to the first room and returned with an arm full of bedclothes. "Here are some."

"Toss them down, Miss Sewell." Stapleton opened his arms.

She dropped them over the banister.

When he caught them, he said, "Now lock yourselves into your guest room."

All the men—the earl, the military man, the young man, the old gossip, Duncan, and Stapleton—had gathered around the fallen valet.

"Oh, Abbie." Florentina took my hand and led me to my bawling Miss Bellows.

I grabbed her, then rocked her until she calmed down. Yet I kept looking over her shoulder to the scene below.

Mr. Peters, the man we'd seen about half an hour ago, was dead.

Duncan and Mayer were on one side, Holston and Stapleton

on the other, and they each held a corner of the sheet in which they intended to cover the dead man. Slowly, under the whisper of a Psalm, they piled linen on Peters.

Part of his pressed tailcoat escaped. One polished slipper poked out.

How did this happen? Did this confirm there was a killer in their midst?

Pushing me again, Florentina made me and Miss Bellows move until we were in front of a bedchamber door at the end of the corridor. "Inside, ladies. Let's try to follow instructions."

Miss Bellows kept sobbing, but I heard her say, "Poor man. He didn't want to be here."

"The door's stuck." Florentina jiggled the door latch.

I stopped paying attention to her and the woman crying on my shoulder. I heard everything below, as the high ceiling made the hall a theater.

"Could he have taken too much laudanum for his gout?" Duncan said.

"Why do you have the man working if he's suffering from gout?" Constock pointed his finger at the magistrate. "You caused this."

Shaking his head, Mr. Talson tapped his cane. "Not Duncan. What happened?"

"Mr. Peters fell," Lord Duncan said.

Talson pushed through the men and bent low. I presumed he felt for a pulse, but that was unnecessary. Maybe that was what shock did. The fellow needed proof the valet he'd chatted with earlier in the pink parlor was no longer alive.

Stapleton helped Talson stand up. He told the old physician, "Mr. Peters died upon impact, when his skull hit the marble floor. A bone in his neck is dislodged. I suspect that is broken, too."

Duncan turned his back to the men. His face pointed to the parlor. "He's been with me a long time. Anna adored him."

"With me longer." The stout fellow said this. "We served together. Peters was a man to count upon when things went awry."

The man with the goblet snorted. "I thought he was a gift of some sort. You know, came along with the wife as part of her dowry. The first Mrs. Flowers, she was one of those heiresses from Martinique, with a father owning quite a number of plantations."

"Leave the gossip about my family alone, Constock." Duncan's voice was raw. It was the angriest tone I'd ever heard from him. "Your family is not exactly on the right side of history when it comes to plantations. Or shall we call them habitations?"

"Well, at least I'm not whining about losses in Hayti like Holston."

With his fist raised and ready to pound the earl's chest, Duncan said, "Constock, this isn't the time for one of your sotted jokes. I need—"

"Gentlemen," Mr. Mayer said, "we still have an audience. Unless you all wish to show the ladies that we'll fight over anything, including poor Mr. Peters's body, I suggest we rein in these tempers."

The magistrate's gaze turned to us on the landing. "Lady Worthing, Miss Sewell, please take your maid into your bedchamber." His voice shook. "Lock your door! We gentlemen have to search. I'm not convinced that this was an accident. Someone who means me ill may have found their way into my home. That can be the only explanation for this chaos."

"The door is stuck," Florentina said. "I don't know why it won't open."

"The key, ma'am. You need it. It's in my apron." Miss Bellows dipped into her pocket and pulled out a brass key.

I wanted to take it, but I felt my fingers would burn. Why was I having such a reaction?

Florentina snatched it. "I'll have the door open in a moment."

It would be wrong of me to ask her to take her time in order for me to gather my wits, for Miss Bellows to settle, for me to catch another second of everything happening below.

Before any one of those things happened, Florentina opened the door. She let us inside, but she looked frightened. With her fists up, ready to attack, she went around the bedchamber, searching for a fiend.

Truthfully, I'd never stop being scared.

Someone in this house was on a killing spree.

The bedchamber Lord Duncan arranged for us was very pleasant. Not pink, like the parlor below, the walls were a muted blue skirted with brown burnished paneling that ran from the floor to chair height.

Florentina's portmanteau which must have been brought to the bedchamber earlier sat next to a gold-colored chaise. She'd have a change of outfits, even a robe if she chose to sleep.

"Poor Mr. Peters." Miss Bellows wept anew. "I should've helped him."

I rubbed her arms, as if my warmth could rid her of fear. "Tell us what happened, dear. What did you see?"

Miss Bellows wiped at her eyes. "I just came out to get more linen. Mr. Peters was just standing there on the upper landing. He said nothing when I requested sheets or blankets. I thought maybe he was ignoring me. He'd been so upset earlier. I asked again. Then I saw him fall. The marble floor done him in."

"He just fell?" Too busy testing the lock, Florentina didn't look at us. "The railing along the landing is high, Abbie. Well above my thigh. The tallish man wouldn't just trip." She stopped, put her hands to her hips. "Miss Bellows, are you sure you didn't see someone push him?"

"I don't remember seeing anyone." Miss Bellows started crying again. "I wish I could've helped him."

"If you could've, you would have. Everything will be all right." I let these comforting lies flow from my lips and kept talking. "Lord Duncan and Mr. Henderson will deal with this situation."

"Abbie," Florentina said as she slid the lock bar in place for the sixth time, "this can't be a coincidence. Two men who knew Lord Duncan are both dead."

Our eyes locked. "Duncan," she whispered.

With a nod, I motioned to Florentina what I couldn't say, not with my maid still in the throes of shock, that I'd begun to doubt Lord Duncan's innocence.

"Figuring things out is imperative, Flo. It might stop another murder from happening. I don't think waiting for the men to solve this whilst we women wait upstairs is the right approach."

"You have that feeling, too, that the danger is not done? Abbie, what are you not saying?"

Over Miss Bellows's head, I again nodded and then mouthed, "We are in danger."

Eyes getting big, Florentina used hand signals and whispers to convey that we were cooked gooses and should've been in Cheapside, eating goose and black cake.

"Poor Mr. Peters," Miss Bellows sobbed. "He was about to retire. He was going to buy a house in Cheapside. He wanted to live there, even set up a warehouse."

How did she know this? When did she have this conversation? "I need you to calm down, dear. Then take your time and tell us everything," I said.

She nodded as I eased her onto the gold-colored chaise by the window. I draped Stapleton's coat over her.

As she sniffled and wiped her eyes with her handkerchief, I took a moment to note how differently this room was styled as compared to the pink parlor. This décor was more modern, with an Egyptian-style sitting chair placed beside a vanity with shiny brass knobs. The bed, with its high gnarled posts, could be from any year. This décor was neither sedate nor frozen in time like the parlor's. This room had been allowed to change.

"Now, my dear, take a deep breath." I commanded gently as

I watched Florentina bend down and peek under the bed and shake the mattress.

"I'll try," Miss Bellows said, but she kept shivering.

Fresh from searching the closet, Florentina brought me my dried stockings. "Here. Before you catch a cold." She handed them to me. "Please, Miss Bellows, start with what made you scream."

Miss Bellows sniffled and peered toward the door. "I came out of this room to go ask for another blanket. I know how you, Miss Sewell, like a lot of blankets, ma'am." She fluttered the wool coat on her like butterfly wings. "See, this is thick. Those blankets on the bed look very thin."

"Focus please, dear." Drawing her attention back to me, I patted her hand. "You came out of the room. Did you hear any noise or commotion before you entered the corridor?"

"None. And these floors are in good condition. Nothing squeaks like the ones in your parlor."

I sighed. Knowing this was how she spoke on a calm day, I offered her a smile. "What happened next, dear?"

"I saw Mr. Peters standing by the stairs. He was sort of leaning. I asked about the linens. He said nothing. I asked again, and he just sort of tipped over."

Florentina came closer to us. "Just fell? No one was around. No one pushed him?"

"No, Miss Sewell." Miss Bellows lifted her forearm straight up, then lowered it, her elbow staying fixed like a pivot. "He just tipped over like a book falling off a shelf."

That was odd. Well, a health attack or palsy could have happened. Those things could come on suddenly. "He made no sound? Nothing to indicate distress?"

"No, Lady Worthing." Her breathing settled. "Not a peep, ma'am. Just fell."

Florentina paced faster. From the footboard to the open closet, where my cleaned coat hung, she traipsed back and forth. "Peters merely stood there. Could he not have noticed you?"

Miss Bellows sat up straight. "Many people don't. That's why I relished working for the Carringtons and now their daughter. Lady Worthing, you always let me know I'm seen."

Clasping her hand, my tan one upon hers, I acknowledged that not being seen or heard was common for all women, no matter their station. "Let's discuss your first interaction with the valet. Was there any indication of a condition or of him being hard of hearing? You might remember something that could help us puzzle this out."

Miss Bellows started to tear up again. "At first, he was kind. So happy."

"Happy?" I said.

Florentina shrugged. "Kind? There's not another Mr. Peters?"

"I know that's what I thought," Miss Bellows insisted. "Then the young man arrived, and they chatted. Then Mr. Peters was completely different."

"After one conversation with Mr. Mayer," I said, "the valet changed?"

"Yes, ma'am. He became pompous and angry. I didn't like his tone. When I was cleaning your coat, Peters made it sound as if women being here ruined things. He was very rude, and I—" She bit her lip.

"Please go on," I said. "We won't judge you. We're here to help."

She looked at me, then at my cousin, then returned my gaze.

Her eyes were redder. "He kept complaining about being here, about having to serve everyone. Mr. Peters said things used to be good until the magistrate's first wife died. Then Berkeley Square changed."

Miss Bellows put up a finger, as if to indicate something important. "Mr. Peters refused to see how lucky he was to be employed and paid extra for working so close to the holidays. The man mocked me. And I wished he'd been hit on the head for his foul attitude."

Miss Bellows drew her hands away and put them on her reddening cheeks. She sat up straight, Stapleton's coat falling. "I
did it. I caused this. I must've put a root on him, like your
mother used to talk about."

Mama? A root?

My mother's talk of old-world magic and hexes was foolishness. But then, so was the belief in visions, the horrible trait
that she and Papa had both passed down to me—Jamaican and
Scottish havoc. But Miss Bellows, the poor soul, was a solid
woman from old London. "Roots are Jamaican or are from
Africa or the West Indies. I'm no expert, but you have to be
taught such things to learn to manifest them."

"Oh." Her sobbing eased as I held her again, merely to keep
her from looking at Florentina, who did a miserable job of trying not to laugh.

"Miss Bellows, you can't wish harm on someone," I said. "If
that were the case, Mr. Henderson would've been endangered
after our first argument."

Florentina rolled her eyes. "Well, time certainly changes
everything."

"It's good to be open minded. And at least we know that of
the men gathered here, Mr. Henderson was the one least likely
to be involved with these deaths."

My cousin shrugged. She had to agree with my logic, but I
wished I could be as confident about Lord Duncan. If something untoward had happened to Mr. Peters, the magistrate had
to be considered a suspect. Wasn't he on this landing or coming
from a room up here when we were gathering below?

"Miss Bellows," I said, "I know this is difficult, but I need
you to be sure about what you saw or heard or even smelled
when you left this room."

My maid turned beet red. She grasped my collar. "Then I'm
the next to die. That's how it always happens. Don't let me die,
ma'am. Don't let me die before I've a chance to live."

Florentina dug into her pocket, found a fresh lacy hand-kerchief, and handed it to her. "No one's going to get you, Miss Bellows. Remember, invisibility is our cloak. It will protect us."

And I intended to use mine to root out the killer in our midst. I needed to take another look at Mr. Brooks's body. If these two deaths were related, then a clue might be on his person that would connect the incidents. Being invisible to haughty men might help me escape to the cold cellar without being caught.

After a dozen swipes to her cheeks and a couple of blows to her nose, Miss Bellows settled down. "I'll wash this hand-kerchief, Miss Sewell. Like my lady's coat, I'll have it fresh and new."

My cousin nodded, but I saw her adding on her fingertips. "A valet and one of the Crown's barristers have died, hours apart."

I sat on the edge of the chaise and began pulling on my white woolen stockings. "Go on, Florentina. Tell me the odds of two men acquainted with Lord Duncan dying in or near his house on the same day. You're the numbers girl."

"It's more than zero," she said, "but I was counting the likelihood of us living and getting to my parents' house for a slice of our favorite cake. The odds are low if Mr. Shaw beats us to Cheapside." Florentina moved to the bed and sank upon it. "This is not how I expected to spend my days before Christmas."

It wasn't my idea, either.

Nonetheless, it was better than being stuck in Westminster with nothing to do but think about James and his ridiculous request. Why would a proud man want his wife to cheat on him? There were easier ways for a peer to pursue a divorce.

Could he not have children? Why not just say that, rather than hiding his condition in adultery?

Shaking my head, I focused on the situation at hand. "We'll stay in here together. I, for one, am not hungry. We'll let the men sort through things downstairs."

Miss Bellows rose. "But, ma'am. There's a lot to clean down there. Except for the chef, there are no other domestics on the premises. I could—"

"Nonsense." I shook my head. "We are the only women in this house. Haven't you heard? We are too fragile to help. I, for one, proved how easy it is to get upset and faint. No, we shall stay here. Cleaning up death is men's work."

Covering a brief chortle before becoming serious, Florentina folded her arms and went again to the window. She brushed back the curtains, revealing more snow. Leaving in the morning or even in a few days began to seem impossible.

However, staying a moment longer without knowing if our host or one of his guests was a murderer was equally torture.

Lady Worthing's List

Suspicious Death: Mr. Peters
Murdered: Mr. Brooks
Suspects: Lord Duncan
Lord Constock
Mr. Talson

Chapter 12

A knock on the door made my heart race.

Over Miss Bellows's shoulder, I peeked at Florentina, who stared back at me.

I wasn't ready to let in a killer. Nor was I willing to wait for the murderer to become enraged and kick in the door.

"Coming. Who is it?" I said. I slowly walked to the door after picking up the iron poker from the fireplace. I stood still, looking at the lock. "Please answer."

"Your neighbor, Lady Worthing. Let me come to you."

Stapleton. Thank goodness. I didn't want to see another soul, especially not Lord Duncan.

Breathing easier, I slid back the lock and opened the door.

The relief at seeing him uninjured and whole dissipated as soon as he pounded inside the room. His face, blank and ashen, foretold danger.

My pulse jittered. I felt my blood throbbing within my veins. "Another person has died?"

"No." He blinked and scanned the room. "No, not yet."

"Stapleton, what do you mean, not yet?"

After stepping around me, he closed the door and thrust the lock into place. Then he put a hand to his neck and rubbed the muscles. "I'll just say it. I don't think Mr. Peters's death was an accident."

I was afraid the physician was going to say that. "Laudanum poisoning?"

"No, but he was sotted with it." With his back to all of us, he went to the window. "But I saw no signs of him being forced to drink. No stains on his cravat or clothes. No bruising on his neck or arms, so his consumption had to have been intentional."

"The taste of laudanum is awful." The fowl brew Talson had given me contained hints of it and brandy. "It's so strong and bitter. How could one want to drink it?"

His head dipped. "Talson just argued that with enough honey, it can be pleasant. Apparently, Mr. Peters helped out with the bees the new Lady Duncan likes to keep. There would be plenty of honey."

"What are you saying, Stapleton?"

"Mr. Holston kept talking about how bad Peters's gout was." Head still lowered, he turned around and faced us. "They both kept insinuating that it was an accident done by the valet's own hands. The man I met when I first arrived seemed jovial. He was looking forward to tonight."

"Jovial?" Florentina gaped at me.

I probably did the same at her. "The man we met was anything but jovial. Something definitely happened."

I made a note to myself to talk with Mr. Mayer, as he might know why there was a change. "How is Lord Duncan taking Peters's death?"

"As well as can be expected. Two deaths in one day, and he at least cared for one of the men." Stapleton Henderson was a person of logic. He was slow to anger. I'd never seen him acting irrational. His leap to Duncan's guilt in the death of Brooks was a measured one.

I swallowed the lumps beginning to lodge in my throat. "Did he confess? Did the magistrate admit to killing Brooks? Or wanting the valet injured?"

"No one admitted to anything, Abigail. But I smelled laudanum on Mr. Peters and Duncan. On the former, the scent was heavy, like he'd bathed in it. On the latter, it was faint, like he'd spilled some on his clothes."

As in the drops that would have leaked on Duncan if he'd tried to feed the medicine to Peters. "You said he was sad about his valet's death."

"You can be sad about having to kill someone." The way his scowl deepened concerned me.

"That's circumstantial," Florentina said. "Looks. Drops of medicine. All of this could be innocent."

"It could be, Miss Sewell." Stapleton pulled the curtains open and peered down. "You have a view of the park, where this all began."

After folding his coat, Miss Bellows handed it back to him. "We must hope that all can be resolved."

"We can all hope that these are clues which are designed to cast aspersions on Duncan's innocence." I wanted to look at my list again, reviewing the suspects. "Someone is trying to incriminate him."

"I agree," Stapleton said, "but that would mean there's an active killer in this house."

He still had faith in Lord Duncan, sort of.

"The laudanum." He adjusted the lines of his coat along the seams. "While laudanum may have contributed to Peters being intoxicated, it wasn't the cause of his death. The fall onto solid marble from the top of the stairs and directly bashing one's skull would be lethal. It was lethal to Mr. Peters."

Stapleton put his coat down on the chaise; then he started to walk in circles. He was winding himself up. His emotions seemed more frazzled.

And did I hear a footfall?

After going to him, I clasped his shoulders. "You're disturbed, sir."

"And you need shoes. Where are your boots?"

"Here they are." Miss Bellows pulled cleaned white calf boots out of the closet. "They were badly . . . stained."

The pause, the memory of how they had become stained.

Stapleton clasped my shoulders. "Are you well?"

"Haunted. It was haunting. I'm attached to it."

"Like a vision, Abigail?"

"Worse than that. No vision. But I'm drawn to it. The images. It's like I'm . . . supposed to remember something."

He made me sit. His focus on me seemed to make him steady again. "Put those boots on before you fall. I can't stand to think of another person falling."

"Then you drink some water. Florentina, get him some."

She looked at me like I'd talked foolishness, but she went to the blue pitcher on the chest of drawers near the closet. After pouring a glass, she brought it to him. "Here." Then she pulled it back. "Laudanum could be in the pitcher. How long has this been here?"

"I filled it myself from the pump room," Miss Bellows said. "I met the chef. Very intense man, that Mr. Villers. He's made a lot of food for dinner tonight."

My cousin sighed and gave Stapleton the glass.

"Thank you for caring, Miss Sewell." He drank like he had been in a desert. "This helps. That smell. Laudanum takes me back to the ships, to trying to save lives at sea. I administered so much of the drug to numb pain. It also allowed a man to die with some peace."

He closed his eyes, and I wondered what he'd seen. What images did he suppress? They had to be worse than my momentary visit with Brooks.

Filling his chest, making it rise, he puffed up his patterned tailcoat. His cuffs were soiled. I wondered about the state of his gloves.

Stapleton tightened his fist about the glass. "Abigail, don't stare at me. I'm not in shock. And Miss Sewell has been so kind as not to mention that this is my fault."

"I'm polite, sir."

"Miss Sewell, you would be right to say it again. It's my fault that we are here in Berkeley Square. We won't be able to leave until Christmas. That is two more days in which you will be at risk."

"Unless we solve the mystery," I remarked. "We have to, for there's a killer in Berkeley Square."

Florentina scowled. "You love distractions, but are you sure being here is better than fighting snowdrifts?"

"Staying warm or alive? That's an awful choice, Flo."

My quip made Stapleton gape at me. His eyes looked hurt in some inexplicable way.

"I'm not blaming you, sir—"

Florentina interrupted me. "She's not blaming you. And I do wonder what other things you've forgotten to tell us, like you forgot to mention the Night of Regrets."

Wishing she'd be more at ease, I drew on one boot and then the other. "It doesn't matter now. We are here. We will make the best of this. And we will stay well."

"Doesn't matter," Flo said, "until we find out what else someone has forgotten to say."

"Don't be so dour, Miss Sewell. Of course, ma'am's right. We will leave soon and have a good Christmas," Miss Bellows declared. "Lady Worthing is a woman of her word. She promised. This Christmas will be better than all of them."

Forcing a smile, I kept my gaze on Stapleton, not on Miss Bellows or my cousin. He could see through my show of confidence or lack of it. My maid, a woman who had worked in the Carrington home, knew how important the holidays were and how broken promises ruined everything.

And I tried not to think about the fact that my neighbor did have a habit of forgetting to mention damning facts.

Miss Bellows helped me fasten my left boot. It was always easier to do the right, given that I was right-handed. Sitting on the chaise, I watched Stapleton pace, struggle, then stop.

"There is something I haven't mentioned," he said as my cousin's brow rose.

Before she started gloating, he said, "Brooks. Though I never met him, I knew of him. I had no opinion of him, but my father did. At one point, Mr. Brooks looked into charging him for fraud. Nothing came of it, but my father was embittered. With Lord Duncan's personal invitation to me, he'd mentioned Brooks was attending. I'd not wanted to attend, and upon hearing the barrister's name, I had absolutely no desire to be at Berkeley Square. The weather prevented me from sending regrets sooner."

"You had a personal connection to Brooks." Florentina rolled her eyes. "Why am I not surprised?"

"I'm surprised." I folded my arms. "To avenge a grievance against your family, you came to confront him."

"No, Abigail. I never intended to be here more than a few minutes. The worsening weather and a little luck put us here, as opposed to trying to find a stable or mews and hoping for admittance and heat. Attempting to get you safely to Cheapside, I've brought you to a Christmas fiasco."

"Sorry, Mr. Henderson." Florentina took his glass and refilled it. "I'm just frustrated. I shouldn't take my displeasure out on you."

"It's easy to do, to be displeased with the stranger in your midst. It will take time to become used to me being around you all." Stapleton's words sounded strange, a cross between contrition and a gloat.

Yet the look between the two—Flo glaring at him, wanting to be right and Stapleton, stone-faced sober looking at her, then glancing at me accepting his faults but not wavering—gave me additional pause. But we had a mystery to solve. "Do you think that Mr. Brooks was aware of your attendance?"

"I'm sure Duncan mentioned it. I'm also sure the barrister would've delighted in telling everyone tales of my father. I didn't want to spend an evening like that."

"Aside from sweet Mary, and the aunt- and uncle-like pair in Mayfair, you rarely speak of family."

"Abigail, we have more in common than most, including difficult relations. My father died the year before I returned. Like with my late wife, there was no easing the situation. Now the disagreements no longer matter."

Stapleton appeared to be quite resolved. I envied that. Both my father and James were alive. I did wish to fix each matter, but no choice was easy. Neither situation could be changed without me being less authentic.

Why be less of me, less of the woman I was becoming, just to have peace or the regard of someone who simply wasn't worthy?

"Wise words. I'm glad that you have found peace. I intend to have every moment of kindness and honesty that I deserve, once we determine the killer among us."

His lips smacked on the side of the glass. "That sounds like true wisdom."

Florentina leaned against the gnarled bedpost. "Next time,

I'll just invite you directly, Mr. Henderson. Then I'll be assured we'll be in Cheapside on time to enjoy the best celebration."

Stapleton clapped, then put his hands to his side. "That is an invitation I will accept without reservation. On my word of honor, I will get you all safely there as soon as we are able to leave here. For now, the wintry storm won't relent. It's even too dangerous for Duncan's neighbors to return to their houses in the square. Everyone is stuck here."

Flinging back the curtains, Miss Bellows exposed frosted panes. With her sleeve, she wiped at one until a little patch warmed, then cleared. The circle showed a steady flow of fluffy flakes, seemingly worse than when Florentina and I looked out from the pink parlor. This was the same view, just from higher up. In the daylight, I could probably see more of Mr. Brooks's house.

The cold clouded the glass again, blocking the view, and Miss Bellows said, "I will go down and bring you back something to eat. That is, if it's tidy enough to go down there."

My stomach rumbled as soon as she mentioned food, but it wasn't safe for us to be separated. "No, Miss Bellows, we can all go."

"Nonsense," she said with her innocent gaze. "I should go help him. Perhaps, I should even serve. There are at least . . . How many people are left?"

"Seven men, which includes the chef," Stapleton said. "Then three women, all of you."

"In a house this big, Lord Duncan sent everyone away." My cousin shook her head. "Someone as important as London's magistrate has put himself in a position of vulnerability for some crazy Night of Regrets."

"It's Yuletide, Flo. People should expect to be away from duty. My father, he . . . His solicitor firm allows his employees to enjoy time with loved ones. Because of that, Wilson Shaw is probably engaged with Aunt's tarts right now. We must hope to be freed and that our solicitor grows too full to eat all the desserts."

Florentina counted on her fingers. I refused to ask her calculation for the odds of all of us living or Wilson eating all the black cake. Instead, I turned to Stapleton, "Mr. Henderson, you've been around all these men. Who do you suspect?"

He looked up at the ceiling and rolled his shoulders. "You all know as much about them as I do. But there is one more thing I should mention." Stapleton bit his lip. "Yes, one more thing. Maybe two more things, starting with you. Abigail and Miss Sewell are now invited to dine with the men."

Eyes popping open wide, Florentina plopped down beside me. "I knew there was something else." She pointed her finger toward him. "And that's why any man here could be the murderer."

"Thanks for casting your doubts upon me again." Stapleton rolled his eyes. "That's usually Abigail's notion to suspect me and accuse me to my face."

"If I thought you were the killer," I said, "I wouldn't have let you in my room." I offered him a frown, or an upside-down smile, for I was grateful to have one male in this house of men that we could trust. "Our personal disagreements do not matter. I'm your alibi. You were beside me both times when a body was discovered."

The fire in his eyes was the only thing about his expression that showed emotion. Perhaps he couldn't read upside-down expressions of gratitude. "Yes. I was standing with you, Abigail."

Miss Bellows sat at the end of the chaise. "I'm fearful for the poor chef. I don't mind helping, ma'am. I don't want to remain up here alone."

Wanting to see all the suspects again, I was ready to accept this new invitation. "Only where absolutely needed, Miss Bellows. Nothing more."

I made my tone sound assured. Bluster was all I had in a house that wasn't mine, around men who, for the most part, could care less if I or my cousin or my maid was made uncomfortable. "Ladies, how can we not accept this invitation?"

Glowering, Stapleton rubbed at his chin, then dropped his arms to his sides, as if to relieve his tension.

"What is it you are not saying, sir? Can we be done with the revelations?" I asked.

"Let me guess this one, Abbie," Florentina said. "If you hadn't found Mr. Brooks earlier, I doubt if his body would have been discovered anytime soon. Is that it, Mr. Henderson?"

Stapleton gazed at my cousin and slowly dipped his head. "That is true, but the killer may have planned it to be so." He looked down at his boots. "Oh, and unless we figure out who has done this, I believe more deaths are coming."

Before I could ask what he meant by "more deaths," Florentina rose from the chaise and stormed toward him. "What do you mean, more? Aren't two enough?"

He shrugged and leaned against the wall right next to our roaring fireplace. Shoulders wrapped in the onyx dyed wool of his tailcoat contrasted with the bright white paint of the door molding and the muted blue paint above the chair rail.

The day had been trying, but this reticence made things worse. "Just say what it is, Stapleton. If we are to go to dinner with these men, we need to know what we are facing."

Stapleton reached into his pocket and pulled out a piece of decorated paper. "From the money spent on this invitation, you can see Lord Duncan went to a great deal of effort for his Night of Regrets."

"Regrets do cause problems, but not death, and definitely not two in one day." I took the fancy folded piece of dyed parchment paper, which looked ebony on the outside, with shiny gold lettering. "It's lovely. Lord Duncan spared no expense. I still do not see the problem."

"Before you open it, look at this. A tightly curled paper lay in the center of his palm. He put it in Florentina's hand. "Unfold it. Read it. I took this from Mr. Peters's pocket."

She sniffed it. "It smells of the bitter laudanum."

"Miss Sewell, you must read it before Abigail opens my invitation."

Taking her time, she unfurled the foolscap. "Braggin, eight little Grand-blancs think they own heaven . . ."

She looked at Stapleton, then at me.

Florentina dashed over to the brass wall sconce and stretched the curled paper again to catch the light. "I must've read that wrong."

My cousin recited the rhyme again, this time forcing an accent that sounded heavy, like her mother's Jamaican brogue. "Braggin', eight little Grand-blancs think they own heaven. One leaps high. Then there were seven."

With a sharp intake, Miss Bellows gasped. "Mr. Peters fell away. He fell."

Stapleton moved toward her as if to catch my maid if she fainted . . . like I did, but I intervened, stepping in front of him. After putting my hands on her shoulders, I gave her a little shake and then hugged her to offer my support. "You're strong, Miss Bellows. You're safe. It's an odd rhyme."

"It's an omen, ma'am. Mr. Peters's fell away, right over the banister." Her eyes were big like saucers. "It's an omen."

The beating of her heart became deafening. She grasped my wrists. "We need to get out of this house. We have to get out of here."

"She's right, Abbie." Florentina's cheeks had paled. "The lyrics are going to tell us how everyone will die."

Leaving Miss Bellows to Stapleton, I moved to my cousin. "Look at me. Dearest, you're not making sense. Between the two of us, you always make sense."

Her ice-cold fingers laced with mine. "When my mada . . .

my mother gets cheated at the market, she hums a tune instead of making a scene." Florentina swallowed hard. Her eyes began to leak. "The rebellions in Jamaica have songs that are war cries. The elders teach the children this rhyme to help them rise up and be fearless."

"What a horrible thing to teach babes." Miss Bellows face was red. "How is everyone supposed to get along when hate is taught in poems?"

"How indeed, Miss Bellows?" I drew a handkerchief from my pocket and wiped Florentina's tears. "Why would that poem be on Peters?"

"It's 'The Rebel's Rhyme,' and we must take it as a warning." My cousin sniffled. "The habitation owners—the plantation owners, as they call them here—spread violence at the first inkling of trouble. When the magistrate or any of those rich men downstairs see this poem, they'll want to put down the threat. We're the threat. They'll come for us."

"No, Miss Sewell." Stapleton stood erect. "That poem, or rather this stanza from it, was in his pocket. It's similar to the one I received in my invitation."

Similar? That made no sense. "Why would you be singled out?" I asked.

"He shrugged. Maybe it's used to initiate new participants into the Night of Regrets."

Upper-crust men were not above games. Antagonistic Mr. Talson would probably love to use this as a joke. "Has anyone else mentioned receiving 'The Rebel's Rhyme' or even a stanza from it?"

"No, Abigail. Not a one. But the day has been chaotic. It may come out during tonight's dinner."

"Nope." Florentina flopped onto the bed and lay flat, with her arms at her sides. "No, Abbie. I don't want to go and then be blamed."

"Miss Sewell, they can't blame you. If they received anything, it was delivered weeks ago. You were not supposed to be here. You cannot be at fault."

Lifting herself up, she looked at him with disbelief, like he'd proposed the wrong solution to a geometric proof. "A man looking for a party to blame will always blame someone who they think will be voiceless. In this house it's women. It's us."

"Miss Sewell, Miss Bellows, and even you, Abigail, none of you have received a stanza of the poem. You weren't even supposed to be here. You're not at risk."

"But you have received a stanza from the rhyme." I gaped at him. "You are in danger."

"Open the invitation now, Abigail."

Connected together—Stapleton and I—supported by his gaze, I knew he sensed my fear. I clutched his invitation and felt the lump inside it. After turning the folded parchment over to reveal the seal, I saw that the red wax must've grown warm in his pocket. I pried it off and opened the gilded invitation. Fancy cursive invited Stapleton Henderson to the Night of Regrets. Inside the last fold was a strip of foolscap, curled up similarly to the one Florentina held.

After unrolling it, I noted the similar ink, but this script was smooth, unhurried. I read it aloud: " 'Trapped, two little Grand-blancs sitting in the sun. One got very warm, and then there was one.' "

"That's a stanza near the end of the rhyme." Florentina sat up, tapped on her forehead as if to dislodge a frozen memory, then drew her arms together like she had chills. "Lord Duncan is holding this Night of Regrets. It's his dinner. His invitations. He's behind the threats."

"Two little Grand-blancs and then there was one. Mr. Henderson is the second to the last to die." Miss Bellows had whispered what we all must be thinking.

Well, at least it was obvious why Stapleton didn't want to attend the magistrate's dinner. Who would wish to do so when "The Rebel's Rhyme" predicted death?

The Rebel's Rhyme

*Braggin', eight little Grand-blancs think they own heaven.
One leaps high. Then there were seven.*
–Mr. Peters

Trapped, two little Grand-blancs sitting in the sun. One got very warm, and then there was one. –Mr. Stapleton Henderson

Chapter 13

Taking advantage of the silence now enveloping my guest room, I wrote down the two stanzas from "The Rebel's Rhyme." I hadn't heard it before, but my panicking cousin had.

She sank again on the bed, then turned her face from me.

Miss Bellows sat at the end of the chaise, tying and retying her apron strings.

Stapleton stood against the wall, watching me, not offering another word . . . or admitting something else he'd forgotten to mention.

This was so confusing. I decided to be brave and share what was puzzling me. "Why would Mr. Peters, a valet acting as a footman for the dinner, have a stanza from the West Indies rhyme in his pocket?"

"Was he in need of rebelling while working for Duncan?" Florentina's tone sounded mocking, but at least she was listening.

"Flo, Mr. Peters was mean to you?"

"No. More like indifferent."

"Miss Bellows," I said, "he was professional but agitated?"

"Yes, ma'am."

"And, Stapleton, you are sure Mr. Peters was in a genuinely good mood when you met him?"

His brows rose, as if he was questioning my need to question him, but Stapleton nodded. "Upbeat, looking forward to the dinner. He did become a little terse when I mentioned that you ladies were stranded with me. But still pleasant. Didn't see him again until he fell."

Stapleton rubbed at his neck, along muscles that looked tense. "Was he rude to you?"

"No, just terse, but you all met Mr. Peters while I was recovering. Something happened once Brooks was discovered." That seemed to make sense.

"Why would he have a stanza from 'The Rebel's Rhyme' in his possession? He wasn't a guest." Florentina rolled over and peered at Stapleton. "Did the other men have one, too, or was one merely given to you because you knew Brooks?"

A bell tinkled. The sound was light when it crept through the crack under the bedchamber door.

"Dinner will be served in the main dining room in twenty minutes." The shout had a French accent. "Do be prompt."

"That's Mr. Villers," Miss Bellows said. "As I said before, I met him earlier, when I went to the pump room. He's very proud of the food he's created for the evening."

"No more going anywhere unattended, Miss Bellows," Stapleton said. "It's not safe." He'd resumed his task of supporting the wall, his back fully above the chair rail.

My maid looked at me to see if I agreed, and I nodded. "Miss Bellows, we don't know what we are dealing with. We need to take precautions. Mr. Henderson is right."

Glaring at him, with her arms tucked under her head, Florentina said, "Then let's err on the side of caution and not go to dinner. That would be the safest option."

"In light of the circumstances, Duncan has decided it's best for you two ladies to join us. It would be awkward to decline now."

Maybe I was still learning the difference between what my neighbor said and didn't say, but I heard between his words that he had fought for Flo and me to have seats at the table.

"I don't want to go." My cousin closed her eyes. "I'm not hungry."

"But you should be," Miss Bellows said. "Mr. Villers has created quite a spread, and some sort of dish of cheese magic."

"What type of cheese thing?" While Flo's eyes remained shut, her tone had perked up. Her lust for milky goodness would be her undoing.

"Let me see." Miss Bellows tapped her lips. "It was a Cheshire cheese sauce made with Canary wine and, I think, finely ground mace. He says it is delicious, and he plans to serve it with crackers and freshly made toast."

"The fiend is diabolical." Florentina sat up, even putting her feet on the floor. "He knows how to coax us all down to dinner to die."

"Doesn't mean anything of the sort," I said. "Only that these men-only affairs offer fine cuisine." I wanted to say more, but my stomach made a noise. It had been hours since breakfast in Westminster. Death should've stolen my appetite. Unfortunately, a mystery and cheese ensured it raged. I guessed those two things were my weaknesses.

"We will garner suspicion if we don't go down. We must attend, Florentina. Up here, we could miss an important clue," I added.

"And they could blame me," Miss Bellows said. "I was on the landing with Mr. Peters. I've worked in Jamaican households. They could think I've heard of 'The Rebel's Rhyme,' that I pushed him to make him leap high."

"Miss Bellows," Stapleton asked as he came closer to us, "do you think so little of your fellow man that we'd put the blame on a conveniently placed woman?"

"In lieu of a convenient Blackamoor," Florentina said, "I'm sure the gossiping Talson will accept a maid's alleged guilt and tell everyone."

Her words, her truth, stung. I became winded and tired, because unfortunately, that would be the gossip. Then it would become *the truth*.

Stapleton closed his eyes for a moment. "I can't attest to what you have all experienced. The ton has turned against my sister for her youthful indiscretions. I sympathize."

Poor Mary. That was why she was holidaying with the Mathews, trying to live past the slights.

"I'll keep you all safe," he said. "It is still my fault that we are here. Unless I'm the mastermind of these crimes, you will all leave here unscathed."

"But you're the second to last to die." Miss Bellows's voice was high-pitched and clear. "You won't be around to save us."

"I'll be around." Stapleton looked at me. "I'm committed. I will not fail or abandon you."

My cheeks grew warm. Not sure why.

Or maybe I was. The commitment of a man to protect what he valued was intoxicating. And shamefully, the sentiment reminded me of Vaughn's commitment to my mother. My godfather would rather die than have a hair on her braided head be endangered.

"Flo, if the magistrate is behind this, he wasn't expecting us. We need to follow his plans. This is one time we must try to blend in."

Stapleton's gaze lowered, and he adjusted the buttons on his midnight-blue waistcoat. "I wouldn't know how you'd do that. But I'm at your disposal."

Miss Bellows's brow furrowed. "Lord Duncan has always seemed so nice."

Florentina counted her fingers. "His neighbor and his valet are dead, but his chef made a cheese dish."

"There's more than one, Miss Sewell." Miss Bellows rubbed her stomach. "And each are delicious."

My cousin's gut rumbled. "Blackguards."

"Ladies." Stapleton's voice was lower. He had stepped back again and was leaning against the wall. "I know it looks bad, but Duncan's not a killer."

"But he indicts people, and they die, ma'am. That would have been Lord Worthing's fate if not for you."

"What was that crime again, Abigail?" Stapleton was still actively serving in the navy when it all had occurred. Unlike him, the rest of London had known about it.

"Embezzlement." My tone was solemn, for it was a shameful thing to be accused of perpetrating. "Lord Worthing's whole ship's pay had gone missing. He regrettably served as the paymaster. It was his last commission. I proved that his friend, a solicitor who managed his personal funds and the ship investor's accounts, had taken the funds. The guilty man, a Mr. Teswick, committed suicide before being taken into custody."

That wasn't the first time I had used my gift of puzzling things out, but it was the most important.

"If Lord Duncan had listened to you sooner, he might've learned about Mr. Teswick. He might have stopped that suicide," Florentina said. "Lord Worthing putting all his assets to be managed by your father's firm improved your family's circumstances."

"He had a hard time living down the scandal, the lingering mistrust. Then he married me. That didn't help him much." With my smile in place, I sat still and offered no indication of how sad my circumstances had become. My reward, this marriage, had to have made James flee.

"Abigail, what did you say?" Stapleton glared at me. "I think you misspoke. Worthing was the lucky man for you to wish to be linked to him."

I gazed at the fireplace, feeling the wafting heat and imagining all the lies I'd been telling myself burn.

"Abigail?"

"Excuse me, sir. With Mr. Shaw's help, I traced the records, but we never understood why Teswick hated James enough to have him disgraced."

"You mean to have Lord Worthing killed," Miss Bellows corrected. "That's a little more than sullying a name, ma'am. Perhaps *this* murderer doesn't want to use the legal system. He's more direct."

I bit my lip and contained all the feelings that coursed through me. Then I focused on the important thing, the most pressing. "We must determine the order of events and if Brooks was the first murder victim."

"Abbie, you're trying to solve the mystery. Sometimes, it's not our business," Florentina stated. "Let's all stay up here and use our efforts to stay alive. Then we leave, alive, when the weather improves."

Stapleton perked up, straightening his shoulders. "Yes, staying alive is good. But not angering anyone who might have done the deed in the past few hours is better."

He was absolutely right about us attending the dinner.

Big and tall, seemingly able to defend himself, he seemed more concerned about us. "I'd rather you all be where I can see you, defend you if necessary."

I walked briskly, as if I would head out the door, but stopped beside Stapleton. "Did Brooks's body have his invitation?"

"I didn't check for one. Abigail, you want to see it?"

"We need to. If it has a stanza from the rhyme on it, then that will prove that his murder was orchestrated according to the rhyme. This evening was meant to kill Benjamin Brooks."

"That means you believe it to be Duncan." Florentina slid to the edge of the bed. "You actually think he did it."

"Dinner will allow us to see if anyone had more of a motive

than the man who planned the dinner. We need you to remember every line of 'The Rebel's Rhyme.'"

Her lips curled down into a frown. "But what if Mr. Peters was behind this but then couldn't go through with it . . . ? The guilt of killing Brooks, of wanting to kill more, might make a man want to take his own life."

"The barrister was brutally killed. But it was more than an act of rage," Stapleton said. "I still have no notion of what type of weapon could slice through flesh like that."

"If you ever thought to convince me that a random thief could be to blame, you are failing." My gut rumbled anew. "To the cheese. Then later to Brooks's body."

"Oh no, we're not going there, Abbie." Florentina stepped in front of me and flounced to the door. "I'd rather die from the tasty Cheshire cheese than from lurking in the cold cellar."

Staying here while all the men were dining in one location would give me ample opportunity to search Brooks . . . and not faint again. "Why intrude any further? Send up dinner. And we women won't interrupt Duncan's homage to the colonial system—rebellions and grand blanc passions."

"You would have me believe you'd not take the opportunity to interview the suspects?" Shaking his head, Stapleton looked fierce. "No, you're so intent on risking your life and your cousin's and maybe your maid's merely to go alone to see a dead man."

What he'd said was technically true, but I wouldn't give him the satisfaction. "No one will be hurt if all the men are in one place."

"Oh, Abigail." He folded his arms. "Are you still annoyed that I was invited to Duncan's party and not you? Is this some sort of pouting?"

"Pouting. What are you going to do if I was? Build a wall?"

"Now, this is what I have missed." Florentina clapped. "You two arguing. This is a sense of normalcy."

"We're not arguing," I said to my cousin as I stared daggers at Stapleton. "This is a discussion. Mr. Henderson and I are discussing our differences and varying tactics to determine guilt."

"Yes, the baroness enjoys sharp discussions when she feels slighted."

"You know, you are more alike than different," Miss Bellows said. She stood and adjusted her apron. "I think we all need to stick together. You and Miss Sewell will go to dinner. And I should go help the poor Frenchy in the kitchen. Mr. Henderson, can you escort me?"

If Miss Bellows served the men dinner, she would be in the sphere of the murderer. I stuck out my arm to Stapleton. "We stay together through the meal. We search together later."

He took my palm and placed it securely about his bicep. "You're right about the compromise part. We should go to dinner and meet all the suspects."

"You two? This is compromise?" Florentina ground her teeth a little, but she wasn't free of this.

"I need you to remember every verse of 'The Rebel's Rhyme,'" I reminded her.

"But Mama changed it when she was angry."

"Cousin, you are our only hope to figure out if it means anything."

"The moment you asked me, Abbie, it's flown out of my head."

"Mr. Peters," Miss Bellows said, "had eight in his rhyme, and Mr. Henderson has two. Who has the numbers in between?"

"Any of the men downstairs," Stapleton said and unlocked the door. "Please, think hard, Miss Sewell. What you remember of the rhyme may tell us what to expect."

"You're grinning, cousin."

"My mother had some funny lines for dealing with shopkeepers who tried to cheat."

"Let's not mention the rhyme to the other dinner guests." Stapleton stared down at me. "It may be our only advantage."

I bristled and almost withdrew my hand from his arm.

"Lady Worthing, please." Stapleton resorted to his most formal, most dignified tone. "Don't make yourself vulnerable. It's unnecessary."

Out on the landing, he took the brass key from Miss Bellows and locked the bedchamber, then handed the key to me.

"Later tonight, sir, we go examine Mr. Brooks. I won't faint this time."

With a shake of his head, not a sign that he had rejected my idea but more a show of frustration, he sighed. "Come along, ladies. Let's play this game and get something to eat. It's going to be a long night."

I took his arm again, slipping my hand along his wrinkled sleeve. Stapleton started moving, propelling me forward.

My cousin and maid followed.

I was anxious to see Lord Duncan. The strain of two deaths in and near his home must be terrible. That is, if he was innocent. I dreaded the very real possibility that my mentor had transformed into a criminal mastermind responsible for murder.

Chapter 14

The Dining Room, Nine Berkeley Square

Coming down the stairs, I looked over the banister and saw the marble sparkling below. If one hadn't witnessed the aftermath of Mr. Peters's fall, one would think that nothing unusual had happened here.

"Did the poor cook have to . . . ?"

"No, Abigail. I took care of tidying things," Stapleton said. "I swabbed many decks in my time in the service. None quite like this. Mr. Mayer also helped."

"You called for me?" A blond man in his late twenties or early thirties came from the long corridor. "Been warming myself in the orangery. Quite an engineering feat in there." His face became very sad. He squinted. "I hope that doesn't mean more unpleasantness."

"None that we know of." Stapleton's boot thudded as it struck the marble. "Have you found any?"

"Oh, no, Henderson." Mayer paused at the banister and

seemed to look appreciatively at me and Florentina. "Ah, the new additions to our dinner. You'd said that they were lovely but hadn't mentioned exquisite. Had I known, I might not have objected."

"Why did you initially object to having us join the dinner?" I made my voice sweet. It might be easier for Mr. Mayer to be truthful if he found me charming.

"Well, ah . . . the talk sometimes can be a little coarse." He offered this response with dimples, and Florentina and Miss Bellows seemed to accept it.

"And given the nature of the dinner, what would two gentlewomen have done and be willing to admit regretting?"

He laughed a little. "I find women admit to nothing, Lady Worthing."

I kept my chin high and my lips closed as Stapleton formally introduced Florentina and Miss Bellows.

"But I have heard that you are inquisitive, Lady Worthing." Mayer added an extra bow. "That should offer something interesting to our table."

"When the world stops being interesting, I'll stop asking questions."

"Henderson, you weren't exaggerating. She is as witty as she is beautiful."

It might be my imagination, but Stapleton stayed well at my side, keeping somewhat of a distance between me and the young Mr. Mayer. Then I remembered that a polite man might've helped the valet *leap high*.

Giving up on trying to untangle my hand from Stapleton's, I offered a nod to Mr. Mayer. "Pleased to meet you, sir. I'm looking forward to dinner."

"Likewise." His gaze went from me to my cousin. "Very pleased to meet you both." Mayer kissed Florentina's hand. "Very pleased. How do you know Lord Duncan?"

"Math," Stapleton said. "She's a mathematician. I can attest that she's quite good with numbers and ratios and sizing things into their proper perspective." Stapleton stepped aside and let Florentina pass. "Duncan is a fan of that, too, perspectives. Miss Sewell, Mr. Mayer is in banking."

Her cheeks had darkened, either from the rare compliment offered by my neighbor or the way the banker kept looking at her.

"It's finance, Miss Sewell," the young man said.

"Very pleased to meet you, Mr. Mayer." Her voice went a little pitchy when she asked, "You live in Berkeley Square?"

"Yes, ma'am. I'm the newest to the neighborhood. Been here only five years." His tone grew low. "Hope to make it to six."

Was that an indication that he'd received a stanza of the ominous rhyme? Before I could ask, Lord Duncan stepped out of the pink parlor. His frown had grown worse. It made his cheeks droop.

His attention drifted to the marble floor, then to us. "Ah, Lady Worthing. Glad you accepted my invitation."

"Under the circumstances, I had no other appointments. It takes a good man to change his decision."

Stapleton still had my arm clasped to his side. "And a wise woman to forgive an unintended slight."

"Well, look at us." Mr. Mayer ushered Florentina closer to be a part of the conversation. "So progressive in our manners and seeking a little levity under the circumstances."

Duncan half smiled. "Again, Lady Worthing, this is not how I intended to welcome you to my home."

He had said as much before. I wished I could believe him. Until I could clear him of suspicion, I couldn't.

Nonetheless, Stapleton's argument about not provoking anyone held merit. I decided to be charitable. "Thank you for taking us in from the storm. My maid, Miss Bellows, has volunteered to help your cook serve tonight. I know you're short-handed, more like short . . . shorthanded."

He blinked as if he'd only just started listening, or maybe he had ignored the "hand" part, as in the place where Benjamin Brooks was injured. "Yes, Lady Worthing, that will be a great help."

"Mr. Henderson, would you mind escorting Miss Bellows to the kitchen? I wouldn't want her to get lost. I'll take Lady Worthing and Miss Sewell into the dining room."

"Of course." It took a moment for Stapleton to release me. He eyed both Mayer and the magistrate before leading my maid down the corridor.

"Oh, Mr. Henderson, you will get to see the orangery," Mr. Mayer called. "It is amazing and so warm."

Stapleton looked back for a moment, then began chatting with Miss Bellows as he led her to the kitchen.

"Shall we, Lady Worthing?" Lord Duncan lifted his arm to me.

I was without gloves. My tan hand clasped his dark sleeve.

He didn't seem bothered or annoyed. The man simply looked terribly sad.

"I'll help you, Lord Duncan, escort these ladies." Mr. Mayer lifted his arm to Florentina.

She took it, and as if we were opening a ball, a procession was formed.

A short one. The dining room was directly opposite the pink parlor, on the other side of the grand hall.

Polished walnut paneling and a line of ancestral portraits greeted us as we entered the room. Smelly tallow candles had been lit in the sconces. The light was enough to highlight the men painted in armor and the lone woman captured in an elaborate violet gown.

A high glass chandelier hung over a polished mahogany table. The chandelier was similar to the one in the pink parlor but larger, with a dozen more lights.

The men who'd already taken seats were arguing.

"He's heading to Warsaw," Talson said. "Fresh from defeating the Prussians, the emperor of the French will try to take over the world."

"Napoleon is aggressive. Our embargo should be affecting him." This was Mr. Holston. Didn't someone say he was a military man?

He started pointing. "You can't possibly tell me Napoleon did not have a hand in Dessalines's assassination. He's still smarting over the loss to the Blacks."

The earl, a man with a pointy nose but a light voice, looked in our direction and bared his wolflike teeth. "The rebels must be contained before they think they are due everything."

My heart lunged.

It had been a while since becoming Lady Worthing that I had walked into such direct hostilities. It was hidden from my view, like the blood mopped from the marble floor.

Lord Duncan coughed. "Gentlemen, please. Contain your talk of war and stand. My other guests have arrived."

Mr. Talson leapt up, then balanced himself on his cane. "Good of you ladies to join us."

Holston, sporting a reddish-gray beard, rose at the end of the table.

The last to rise, the haughty earl, barely moved. He was closest to Holston, with Talson sitting in the middle. That left one seat open on that side for me to sit, putting me near the gossip and Lord Duncan, who I was sure would sit at the end of the table.

Three vacant seats on the other side of the table would go to Mr. Mayer and my cousin, with the final one left for Stapleton.

This configuration of three seats on each side, with the magistrate and the army man at the ends, left room along the spacious table.

I went to the seat I'd mentally chosen.

Florentina looked relieved not to have to sit between Talson and the magistrate, our leading suspect.

"Lady Worthing, Miss Sewell," Duncan said, "these are my guests whom I'd invited for the evening—they are colleagues, neighbors, and old friends. These men live right here around the square."

"Where's the physician?" the refined Mr. Holston said. "We should get his opinion on Napoleon. He's just been out of duty since January. Henderson might have more relevant information that will prove me right."

"Holston," Duncan said, "Mr. Henderson will be here shortly. Due to the unpredictability of the night, he's escorting Lady Worthing's personal maid to the kitchen."

Mr. Mayer chuckled. "Is she going to get lost going down the corridor? Or will the hum of the pipes entice her, along with the exotic plants? I'd never seen a pineapple plant."

"Miss Bellows has volunteered her services for the night." I said this, then immediately regretted how I sounded as if I was trying to assert my resources to impress these men.

"I suppose that means we are in your debt, Lady Worthing." While shaking his head, the Earl of Constock raised his brow. "We are grateful." The laugh he added was as if he rubbed salt into a wound.

Florentina chatted again with Mr. Mayer.

Ignoring the banter between Talson, the Earl, and Holston, I took the opportunity to enjoy the large blue and gold tapestry running the length of the room and all the portraits. Most were of old men. The one closest was of a young woman. A slim brunette with large green eyes. She seemed to stare at me, maybe at Duncan, too.

Mr. Talson leaned over and patted my chair. "Lady Worthing, you are in Brooks's spot. It's fitting since you are the last woman he made faint."

Chuckles erupted.

Another first since becoming Lady Worthing, I was the butt of a joke. Forcing a smile, I said as sweetly as I could, "Well, unless someone thinks it's a bad omen to take the seat of man barely a day dead, I will make the best use of it."

That earned me a few nods and laughter. I assumed that was consent. Pity I wasn't content.

"But no one here seems particularly upset at his passing, so this is the best use," I added.

That silenced them.

Before my ascension, I'd been my father's outspoken daughter.

Stapleton whipped into the room. He seemed winded, like he'd run from the kitchen. The man slowed down and took the open chair.

"Now that you are here, Mr. Henderson, I will proceed with a formal introduction of everyone sitting at my table."

Duncan sipped what looked like water from a goblet. "To my right is Lady Worthing. Her husband is James Monroe, Baron Worthing." He pointed to Talson. "To her right is Frederick Talson. He's been a fixture of Berkeley Square."

"Some call me 'the father of the square.'"

"Yes," Constock said. "You are in everyone's affairs."

"You should be glad my daughter knows none of yours."

The earl didn't deny this. Instead, he said, "She's a forgiving woman and understands the value of discretion."

As Lord Duncan continued, formally introducing John Clayton, the Earl of Constock, and retired colonel William Holston, I whispered to Mr. Talson, "I suppose the Countess of Constock is one of those connections you spoke of."

"Guilty," he sighed. "I could've done a lot worse. And my adorable grandson, Viscount Jadonal, is a consolation."

Lord Duncan's introductions concluded with Derrick Mayer,

Miss Florentina Sewell, and lastly former commander Stapleton Henderson.

Holston stood and reached for the wine bottle at the center of the table. He was a large man with heavy, thick fingers, and I could see that in his prime he was probably very intimidating.

"Where is the food? Is your maid competent, Lady Worthing?"

"Now, Constock," Talson said, "you must show you have manners. An earl should have them, don't you think, Lady Worthing?"

Feeling all eyes on me, I reached for my water glass and tried not to wonder about things like poison or laudanum. "It's not for me to say what a man of dignity is to have or not have. I suppose that is his countess's duty."

Talson laughed.

Constock shot daggers at me with his eyes. I hoped he wasn't the killer.

"Touchy subject," the old gossip whispered. "The Constocks are having difficulties."

"You gossiping old man! Stop talking about me. I know that you will lead my wife astray."

"I mentioned none of your foolishness or my daughter's concerns. But feel free to inform the baroness and the rest of the table."

Constock's fingers fisted around the stem of his goblet.

Poor Florentina looked a little confused or terrified.

Mr. Mayer said, "We should all calm down and be patient. Things will work out."

Duncan, sitting far from everyone at the other end of the table, looked very glum.

"Our host is out of sorts," Mayer said. "While we wait on Mr. Villers, perhaps I can talk of my capital raise. I have room for new investments."

"I can vouch for him," Constock said. "You must be able to take a risk, but he's tripled my money."

"Yes," Mayer said. "You could've made even more if you'd been patient. I had to liquidate your position early."

Holston reared back in his chair. "So you did make money? I'd heard rumors—"

"Just rumors," Mayer interrupted. His brow shimmered with perspiration. "And rumors are bad for business. Constock, now that you've seen your returns, you can help spread the word."

"I'll do more than that. I want to invest again."

Mayer waved his hand. "No. My lord. I need a client who can be patient. That is not you."

"Turning him down." Holston nodded and seemed to look at Mayer with new respect. "Well, then, perhaps we should talk later. I could become your largest investor."

"And he's not talking girth," Mr. Talson joked. "Holston is very wealthy. He has property and holdings everywhere."

"Even in the Caribbean?" My question popped out before I could stop my tongue.

"I had some, Lady Worthing," Holston said. "But my portfolio has been completely divested. Like Duncan, I'm an abolitionist now."

"You mean, you got out before another revolution happens and you lose everything, like the French. Their Grand-blancs lost it all, if not their lives." Lord Constock hiccuped. "Don't sound so noble, sir."

"Yes, I did," Holston said. "Economics and principles can go hand in hand."

The earl guffawed and helped himself to more wine. "Well, I have enough of a return that I can make investments in my property, like Duncan. One visit to the newly enclosed orangery proves you care nothing about the window tax."

"Sir, I . . ." Duncan's lips lifted, as if he was ready to brag, but he merely shrugged.

"Oh, he's modest," Mr. Mayer said. "The changes to the grounds, the gardens . . . Even the bees are happy. I think it's the new Lady Duncan's interests."

"Bees?" Constock looked panicked. "How terrible. I don't understand why anyone would keep the vile creatures like their dogs."

"Her family is very big into bees." Frowning, Duncan slouched in his chair. "Her son is particularly interested in carrying on the tradition."

Talson's eyes sparkled. "How old is this boy?"

"He's eight, and her daughter is four. I'm a stepfather." His tone sounded nervous, but it was unclear if this was from speaking of his wife or of his new status as a parent.

"But bees? Those nasty creatures . . . Having them on your property is a consequence of matrimony." Constock drained his goblet. "I cannot wait until she redecorates the interiors. This house must move forward on the inside, not just the outside."

The earl's tone was decidedly bitter. Why wasn't he happy for his friend? Duncan had a family.

"You're frowning, Lady Worthing. Don't mind Constock," Mr. Talson said. "At times, he's disagreeable. Often complaining about a cold or insects."

"You know too much about everyone, Talson." The earl clasped the wine bottle and poured more into his goblet. "When will we learn not to tell you anything?" He stood, then turned, prepared to abandon the dinner. "Seems I've told you all too much over the years."

"Oh, sit, Constock," Duncan said. "You know it is our way to poke fun at each other. But the truth is, we know each other's secrets, our victories, and our horrid defeats." He pointed to Talson. "Apologize. We are all distressed tonight."

"Of course. Sorry, Constock. And to balance out my comments, you're a wonderful baritone."

Another round of boasting, investment talk, and drinking consumed the table.

If dinner didn't come soon, I'd have to look to Florentina for the fight percentages.

I caught my neighbor's gaze. "Is Miss Bellows settled?"

Stapleton nodded. "Thank you again, Lady Worthing. It's very generous to allow her to be of help tonight."

"This is a night of generosity." I lifted my water goblet. "To Lord Duncan. Thank you for hosting this gathering and welcoming my party."

"Yes, thank you, Lord Duncan." Florentina's voice sounded very sad. In her tone, I could picture all the Sewells, all our friends and family gathered about the fireplace in her parents' house, drinking cider, passing roasted chestnuts.

We shall endure, cousin. I wanted to say that, but to draw attention to her or myself didn't seem wise.

Right before the earl looked ready to leave, the chef, an ancient-looking man dressed in white, with silver hair, had entered. He wheeled a cart with what looked like pheasant and roasted potatoes. Miss Bellows carried a platter that had beefsteak and brown sauce on it.

The room, which had formerly hosted anger, now smelled of heavenly garlic.

Talson leaned closer to me. "Hopefully, that scent will keep Brooks's ghost away. You do believe in ghosts, Lady Worthing?"

I believed in many things.

My upbringing had taught me not to ask about things that went bump in the night or about dinner arguments conducted in candlelight.

It had to be the Scottish mindset in me that needed to figure out what was occurring.

I refused to let the tensions at the table and the food distract me from finding Benjamin Brooks's murderer.

Chapter 15

The Dining Room, Nine Berkeley Square

Sitting in Lord Duncan's dining room, I enjoyed the lovely dark meat of the pheasant. The magistrate's other guests ate the same or slices of beefsteak and they all feasted on the breads and cheeses that came from the kitchen.

Mr. Villers was a master. Everything had the proper amount of salt and spices.

The wine never stopped flowing. Bottle after bottle came from the cellar. Pity the Earl of Constock finished many of them all by himself.

He tried to be sly, talking politics or about Napoleon, but with each discussion, he kept pouring and finishing his goblet.

The man wasn't exactly sloppy, but I suspected he'd begin to slur at any moment.

Mr. Holston's conversation gave me worries. The man kept taunting Stapleton, trying to get him to talk about Nelson's last battle. Trafalgar was a great win, a lasting moment to the hero of England, but it was also his last, as during the battle he was assassinated on the deck of the HMS *Victory*, four inches from where Commander Stapleton Henderson stood.

"Nelson's boat, aye?" Holston said.

"It was a ship of the line. One hundred and four guns."

"It was a lousy boat. I heard it took a beating at Trafalgar. What say you, Henderson?"

Stapleton cut into the hunk of beefsteak on his plate. "It was seaworthy. A sailor can't ask for much more."

My neighbor was a level-headed kind of communicator, very even in tone. I hoped that continued. From the way he held his knife, I had a feeling that things wouldn't end well for Mr. Holston if he kept needling Stapleton.

Conversations drifted as platters shifted about the table.

I found my attention drifting to the large portraits lining the rear wall and back to the sole one of the woman.

The brunette seemed so delicate in her features and lacy pink dress.

"That's the late Mrs. Flowers. Charles's first wife." Talson's whisper caught me off guard. I hadn't noticed that he'd begun to study me again. "Lovely woman."

"Yes, quite lovely. She seems timeless."

Duncan seemed to awaken from his trance. "Died in childbirth," he said. "Would've been my first daughter."

"I'm sorry, my lord."

He took a moment to answer, and then he said, "This time of year makes me think of them. I was working too much. Anna's time . . . the confinement came too soon. I returned from my office too late to say goodbye." His voice was raw. The loss seemed to swirl in his words. "That is my greatest regret."

"Is that why you do a Night of Regrets?" I asked.

Duncan started to nod, then stopped abruptly. "It is one of the reasons." He looked across the table and seemed to catch Mr. Holston's gaze. "Then there's the trial of the plantation owner from Martinique."

Groans sounded.

"Oh, please, Duncan," the earl said. "There's no such thing. Brooks did the research this year. He found out it was a lie."

Duncan started to laugh. "I did make it up."

"But you've droned on and on about Martinique for years. Every year I've attended," Mr. Mayer said. "Why do that?"

The magistrate offered him an odd gaze. Then he said, "Some men need to slow down, to take stock of what is important. That is my greatest failure. I invented something to make you each feel it was acceptable to admit when we've done something wrong."

Mr. Mayer pursed his lips, then started eating his cut of succulent pheasant breast.

"Funny," Constock said, "to think of you, of all people, as a liar, Duncan."

"Well, he's kept us entertained all these years," Talson said. "And we all know Brooks would've relished exposing this." He lifted his goblet. "To Benjamin Brooks."

The earl joined him in the toast. No one else.

Talson swiped at his brow. Why did he look uncomfortable?

Chef Villers entered with Miss Bellows in tow, bringing bowls of the melty Cheshire cheese. Miss Bellows also brought a special dish of freshly toasted buttered bread. They also had a fish dish.

Forget dolphinfish. Florentina looked enraptured by the molten cheese.

When a bowl was placed near her, she was the first to ladle some of the ivory goodness onto her plate. Then she took a big piece of the toasted bread.

Giddy, as if she'd been drinking like the earl, Florentina smothered her toast with cheese sauce and chatted about numbers with Holston and Mayer. They each seemed to appreciate her work with Mrs. Edwards on the naval computations.

Stapleton ate and sipped at his wine, almost as if he needed to sample it, make sure it wasn't laced with poison.

"Lord Duncan," Mr. Villers said, "are we ready for the dessert?"

"Yes. Please bring it." Our host waved an unenthusiastic hand at Miss Bellows and the chef.

The poor suffering magistrate. Dishonesty was a horrible thing, but to have the men here relishing his exposure made me wonder how they would act if the crimes were more serious, like murder.

As we waited to see what treat the Parisian chef had created, I watched my tablemates.

About everything from their weight to their politics, Mr. Talson teased everyone. He saved his best barbs for the earl.

Constock took them without complaint but with more gulps of ruby-red claret.

Sitting back, I was confused. I couldn't tell if there was any genuine affection among these men.

The displeasure I felt at not receiving an invitation to this dinner and the smidgeon of jealousy I harbored over Stapleton's inclusion faded. This wasn't a dinner I wanted to be at. Lord Duncan had done me a favor by not asking me to come.

Florentina giggled.

Mr. Mayer did, too.

I released the tension in my shoulders. She wasn't having a poor time. The food was excellent, and as much as I enjoyed our private moments of just us, I needed to be charitable.

This evening was for the men. Not everything had to be about pushing boundaries or being the model of acceptance that the world desperately needed to see.

"It is a shame about Dessalines, if the reports are to be trusted." Constock looked at me with his pointy nose upturned. "Not everything progressive ends well."

Yes. And now I wanted to leave the table, to be back in the guest room.

Ignoring the earl, I shifted my gaze to the portraits, the line of ancestors and especially the late Mrs. Flowers.

Lord Duncan glanced at me, then turned his attention to the painting of the woman, whom it was obvious he deeply loved. "The burdens and risks men or women take can be enormous. One must hope that whatever the risk, even for something as natural as childbirth, it be deemed worthy."

Holston scoffed, making a dreadful noise, like he had the sniffles. "Don't know how worthy Dessalines's struggles are or were. I'm hearing he was betrayed by one of his own men."

"Guess there truly is no honor among thieves." Constock grinned and guzzled more wine.

Holston dug in his pocket for a handkerchief. The edge of a piece of gilded paper shined against his dark jacket. It looked similar to Stapleton's invitation. "The Haytians weren't ready for power," the former military man said. "Most men aren't when it is suddenly given to them."

"It corrupts, I hear. Power, that is." Mayer ladled cheese sauce in a figure eight on his plate. "I'd like the opportunity to know."

Chuckles swept the table. I burned. Florentina's countenance sobered, too.

"I like you, Lady Worthing," Mr. Talson said as a cheese sauce bowl was passed to me. "You push. Many don't."

"Mr. Talson." I sat up straighter in my chair. "Someone must. Why not me?"

He raised his goblet and saluted me.

"Sir, you've been to this dinner every year. I suppose you've taken the opportunity to admit your regrets."

Constock laughed. "Not my father-in-law. He is most certain in his dealings."

"I have them," Talson said. "Outliving too many that I held dear. A wife with stomach cancer. A son a casualty of war." He glanced at the earl. "Not everyone can ignore service to the king."

"Just lucky, I guess." Constock filled his goblet and lifted it to Talson. "Long may you live to always be right. Or to be brave enough to admit when you are wrong."

Talson turned away and peered up at the dripping chandelier. "I take some comfort in meddling in my daughters' lives. But they are often too busy to admit they need the help."

"But if you're not contributing with something equally salacious is that fair?" I asked, perhaps slightly antagonizing the one time the man looked uncomfortable.

"Well, since Charles has been lying about his great regret, I don't feel I've done anything wrong. And I've tried to be helpful to others when I learn of their distresses."

Lord Duncan sighed. "Anna used to call you 'the father of the square.'"

For the briefest moment, Talson's countenance saddened. He didn't receive Duncan's words as a compliment. The old man dipped his chin. "She was a marvelous woman. We miss her zeal. Would she approve of you lying about Martinique?"

"She understood me." Showing no visible contrition for his deceit, Lord Duncan added, "The Night of Regrets was to honor her. But each of you needed some coaxing to be honest, so giving you an exaggeration seemed the best route."

Smirking, Mr. Mayer folded his arms. "Still can't believe you've been torturing us with the same story all these years."

Was Mr. Mayer admitting to just learning of this? Why did it seem as if he already knew?

Miss Bellows and Mr. Villers returned with what looked to be a white cake with a raspberry-colored sauce. With great fanfare, crossing knives like swords, the chef sliced and plated the dessert on elegant saucers that possessed a blue Wedgwood design.

Then Miss Bellows put them and the bowl of raspberry sauce on the table.

Hints of citrus and honey scented the air. It was relief from the fishy scent wafting from the burning tallow candles in the sconces. I guessed a light was merely light to men and the smell didn't bother them one whit. The pink parlor definitely had beeswax candles, the best for Mrs. Flowers.

Talson poked at his slice of cake. "I might not have many stories to contribute, but I find what others have come to regret fascinating."

"Talk. Talk. Talk." The earl pounded his hand on the table. The raspberry sauce, looking like blood, spilled down the sides of the white bowl. "You are the gossip of the neighborhood, not some revered father figure. Anyone who tells you a secret is in danger."

His head wobbling, as if he was trying to decide on a barb to shoot at his son-in-law, Talson took his napkin and carefully wiped his mouth. "Constock, I apologize. If it seems I've taken pleasure in your folly with near financial disasters, I meant no harm. And you and Mr. Mayer have proven me wrong."

The earl looked as if he would fall off his chair. He tightly gripped the table and straightened. "Well. I accept the apology. I know the countess was very distraught about my investments, and you antagonized her. I can't wait for you to tell her that you were wrong about Mr. Mayer."

"What?" the young man said. "Don't draw me into your battles."

"I was concerned. All my daughters' happiness is all I have."

"Perhaps," Constock said. "Perhaps we should say something about Brooks and Peters. They've died, and we're talking about old arguments."

Duncan motioned with his hand as Miss Bellows spooned raspberry sauce onto his cake. "Go ahead."

"Well. I hated Peters for leaving my employ. And I groused at him for it, but he was an excellent valet and a damn fine soldier," Holston said. "He came from Martinique and fought against his captors for his freedom."

Mr. Mayer looked up from his dessert and grabbed the cheese sauce again. "Talented man. I think once he was able to retire, he was going to open a warehouse for gentlemen. Cravats, I think. But hadn't he worked for all of you?"

"Not me," said the earl, "but I would've hired him next."

"Peters was good." Mayer fingered the impressive bulky thing about his neck. After all the activities that he'd participated in, his cravat was still pristine.

"Poor fellow. I think his dream was going to be delayed. Seems he couldn't count his money." The old man smirked to himself like he knew a secret, but before anyone could say anything, he pointed at Duncan. "Charles, say something kind about Benjamin. And it's no secret that you hated him as much as you admired him. Eulogize our poor comrade."

Lord Duncan's fist tightened, then relaxed. He picked up his crystal goblet by the stem. "Benjamin Brooks and I, we competed in trials, for acclaim, even for the appointment to be magistrate."

Holston laughed. "You're being modest. You even courted the same woman. But you won on that count, Charles. Anna Violet Flowers was a worthy prize."

A slight smile crossed the magistrate's face. It lasted for a few seconds, then disappeared.

"That's my friend Charles Flowers, the Lord Duncan." Talson chuckled, egging him on, and waggled his thick eyebrows. "How he hated you being appointed to the position of London's magistrate."

"I'm fortunate, Talson."

"One could say London's fortunate," Holston said. "The man would grift from the grave."

"Sir, please," Duncan said, but he didn't seem to have the energy to protest. As it was with stone-faced Stapleton, his mind was somewhere else.

"Be honest," Holston implored. "That's truly what this dinner was about. You and Brooks competing every year on who could tell a more depressing tale of regretful woe."

"On that, I think Brooks won," Talson said as he ate the last of his cake. "He always managed to have a client he didn't do enough for, or he found it politically inconvenient to do his duty at all."

"The man was a bastard about politics." Holston put down his utensil. "I wondered how a man of little conviction could rise so far."

"That sounds as if you didn't like Mr. Brooks." Stapleton looked down the table while taking a second helping of beefsteak. It was the bit left on the platter.

The earl started to laugh. "I assumed because he had powerful friends like Duncan or your father, he just knew how to maneuver."

The icy glare Stapleton returned was more unnerving than the wind howling at the windows. "Powerful friends do come in handy."

The snide look left Constock's face. He turned and greedily dipped into the raspberry sauce.

I thought I preferred Stapleton's distant countenance to this one, where it seemed he could do damage with the knife in his hand.

Wanting to change the subject, I asked, "Was Mr. Brooks depressed? A man alone, even with power, is still human. This time of year can be difficult."

"Lady Worthing, you think he did that to himself?" Lord Constock sounded angered. "Brooks was tough. Little bothered him. He wasn't weak."

From what Stapleton had said, I doubted the wound was self-inflicted, but I needed to see who'd be most bothered by the suggestion. "A slit wrist can be evidence of someone suffering in silence," I remarked.

Duncan shook his head. "I doubt Brooks would do this. I

suspect someone he wronged, or convicted, of doing this. Or perhaps someone he was about to charge."

"That's an odd take," Mayer said. "Why not a thief? Crime happens even at Christmas."

"Whoever did it," Stapleton said, "knew exactly where to cut him to ensure he'd bleed out quickly."

Talson sat back and blotted his mouth with a sparkling handkerchief. "Would someone here have that knowledge?"

"I would," said Stapleton. "I'm a trained physician. But he was dead before we arrived. But you would, too, Mr. Talson."

The old man held up his cane. "I love that you think I could injure a man my junior by more than a decade, but I didn't kill Brooks. And sounds like if I hadn't been enjoying Duncan's orangery, I still couldn't have helped him."

Mayer rubbed at his face. "I was in a hurry on my way here, and I saw someone coming through the middle of the park. That might've been Brooks or his attacker." He covered his mouth for a moment. "If that was him, was he already in trouble? Could I have—"

"Relax, Mr. Mayer," Stapleton said, interrupting. "With the way the snow has been falling, I doubt you could see anything clearly. And if you had stumbled upon Brooks, there'd have been little time to save him."

The young man closed his eyes for a moment. "I would have liked to have tried."

"Mr. Mayer," Florentina said, "you might've encountered the murderer and been made another victim. There's is no need to put that burden upon yourself."

He smiled at my cousin. Her eyes brightened, and she skittishly turned away and picked at the blue-veined Stilton, which honestly should be ignored.

Holston began shaking his head. "Neither of you would want to save Brooks. You wouldn't do it, either, Duncan."

"Please, sir," Talson said. "You are going to give Lady Worthing the wrong impression."

"Wrong impression?" Holston released the longest laugh. "Brooks relished tormenting everyone. And unlike Duncan, he relished every victory, even the ones he cheated to achieve."

"Mr. Holston," I said, "it sounds as if you'd been cheated by him or targeted."

"No. But Mayer had. Duncan. Constock. Probably even sly old Talson."

"Wait." The young man's cheeks reddened. "Don't drag me into this."

"Had you been targeted, Mr. Mayer?" Florentina asked him with a look of great concern on her countenance.

"No. Of course not. But he hurt business associates of mine. Their business was ruined just by the innuendo of wrongdoing. I hate to speak ill of the dead, but we all know he loved winning at all costs."

This pronouncement silenced everyone. For the next two minutes, nothing but plate and fork movements and the guzzling of wine serenaded the table.

Constock, who'd finished his latest goblet of wine, began to hum. Then, without prompting, he said, "Benjamin Brooks had to have been attacked. He was looking forward to being off with his latest mistress."

"You dolt." Mr. Mayer started to laugh. "His new bird was your countess. Were you too drunk to notice how many times she went to his house?"

The earl leapt up from his chair. "No. That's not true. He was my friend. He'd never."

Then his sotted red eyes caught hold of something. He staggered around the table and leaned forward next to Mrs. Flowers's portrait. "Well." The man stared at her portrait, then swung around and faced Duncan. "Maybe he did have it in him to be a blackguard."

Duncan stood. "Why don't you go up and sleep off this stupor before you disgrace yourself more?"

Constock glared at everyone, then barreled out of the dining room.

Talson shook his head. "I apologize."

"For what?" Holston said. "For your behavior or your daughter's?"

"I need air." Talson pushed away from the table and stood. Limping a little more, he headed toward the hall but turned back and reentered the dining room. "We are better than friends. We are neighbors. We must pull together. Remember Pitt? When Pitt the Younger, our prime minister, our neighbor, died in January, we came together."

"That's what good neighbors do." Duncan looked over at the picture of the late Mrs. Flowers.

Holston rose and helped Talson sit back down. "When will the new Lady Duncan demand changes to the parlor and even the paintings?"

Duncan sighed. "She's decorating the family home in the country. I'm sure it will be only a matter of time."

"That's terrible," Mr. Mayer said, "but to be expected. Out with the old, in with the new."

Miss Bellows and Mr. Villers returned with a service of coffee. I was proud of her. My maid did not spill a drop.

"Lady Worthing," Talson said, "will the baron be returning for you by the New Year? The weather should improve by then."

All talk at the table ceased again. Eyes shifted to me.

My foot fluttered for a moment. Then I sat up straight. "I don't believe so. Weather somewhere will be against him. If London is caught in a blizzard, you can imagine how rough the seas about our shores have become."

Talson nodded, accepting my foolish rambling that weather, not apathy or a ridiculous request, prevented a husband from returning to his wife.

Talson surely saw I was tense. I felt him lean toward me, like a hawk seeking a squirrel. "Surely, you haven't pestered him to come to you. A marriage—"

"I find no need to pester. A man will be where he wants to be," I interrupted. I bit my lip hard, almost enough to draw blood.

"Well, it serves Lord Worthing right if the fool ends up getting himself killed." Holston chuckled. "Leaving a wealthy young widow to fend off the fortune hunters would be a shame."

"Lady Worthing is quite adept at fending off fools." Stapleton's tone was sharp, but then he offered a rare small smile. "I'm sure she will endure the ordeal quite well."

Which ordeal? Widowhood or being in the marriage mart again?

Then he added, "Theirs is a love match about which plays should be written."

"Suppose you are right, Commander Henderson." Holston nodded. "She's doesn't appear to be easily fooled."

"Or to suffer fools." Mr. Mayer's voice piped up, adding another stranger's opinion of my life for public consumption.

"Mr. Mayer, I haven't the patience of Job. I don't particularly care to suffer a thorn like St. Paul. I prefer the truth. I believe that is the reason for this night, is it not?" I said.

"It's actually regrets, Lady Worthing." Stapleton's tone was soft and easy, but I preferred the one that sounded ready to fight.

I was ready to fight. "One can regret only consequences, not the right to act. Isn't that what we all want? To make choices and live?"

"Is that what you are saying?" Talson asked. "You don't mind Lord Worthing being away?"

"One can never mind anyone following their heart's desire. Worthing loves exploring the world. I prefer London."

My gaze went to Florentina, who knew the truth, that I wasn't reason enough for James to return. She glanced away, taking to stirring the cold cheese sauce.

Stapleton granted me the kindness of not offering me one of his penetrating glances.

He and the magistrate exchanged whispers.

"After coffee," Duncan said, "I think it best we all retire and hope the weather has improved."

"It will be Christmas Eve," Florentina said. She sounded so sad.

I was hot and bothered. The talkative Mr. Talson told me more gossip about the neighborhood. None of which had to do with the men attending Duncan's Night of Regrets. I drank my coffee, annoyed that I was no closer to figuring out which of these men who hated Benjamin Brooks had decided to kill him in the middle of Berkeley Square, utilizing one of the most elaborate manners of murder.

Chapter 16

The Orangery, Nine Berkeley Square

Worries wrap his soul. John Clayton, the Earl of Constock, sits up in bed. He can't sleep. His wife, Lily, loves him. She wouldn't have an affair with Brooks.

Mr. Mayer has been a trusted friend and financial partner. Why would he lie?

John will find out directly from the young man. He says they should meet later, when everyone—especially Talson—is in bed.

This latest investment has bonded them. The nights he's walked the floors of his house, waiting for word that his money is safe, has become a habit. The fear of failing has taken a toll. Seeking wine to ease the pain keeps him hungry for more.

If Talson sees how dependent John is on hunting down his next drink, he'll surely tell Lily. What wife can respect a man that needs a bottle?

John holds on to the bedpost, waiting for his head to settle.

Yet he can't help but hate how the old man is always in his business.

Nonetheless, wouldn't Talson know if Brooks has begun an affair with his daughter?

The thirst for berries and the sting of oak tannins takes over. He pulls on his tailcoat and breeches. John hasn't stripped off his shirt and waistcoat. Even the stupid invitation with Brooks's trick is still in the pocket of his tailcoat.

What a horrible Night of Regrets. Then he jokes to himself about Brooks finally regretting something.

With a lit candle in hand, John leaves his bedchamber. The upper corridor is quiet. Everyone has gone to their chambers.

He waits, wanting to make sure that no one will see him go down to Duncan's wine cellar.

Easing to the stairs, he thinks about Peters. Poor bastard, his investment has gone wrong. Like John, he put all his money into another of Mr. Mayer's holdings. That one lost everything.

John starts to feel bad again but then realizes this could've been him losing all his money. That would make Lily leave him.

Anything but that. Benjamin Brooks was the type of man to go after a friend's wife. Look what he did to Duncan. Mrs. Flowers might've been charmed by him, but Brooks made her pay for not choosing him.

The laughs they shared in secret, including over a nude painting supposedly of Anna Violet, now sting. Brooks would have done the same to Lily whether she rejected him or not.

John stands at the bottom of the steps, letting the light of his flame beam ahead of him. Like a glimmer of hope, it casts sparkles on the freshly swabbed marble floor.

Hard to believe Peters is dead. Everyone knew how the valet hated working during the holidays. Peters's wages were probably two or three times the going rate, but his services were well worth it. With his finances healed, John can afford a new, vibrant lifestyle.

Since the valet couldn't retire and still had to work for someone, John could have hired Peters away from Duncan.

The valet was a stalwart fixture in Berkeley Square.

His assistance helped Holston be a man of fashion. For years, Mr. Peters kept the former military man in the talk of society. Without him, everyone notices Holston's girth. With fickle London, a lack of looks means a loss of influence.

Holston's on the rise again. John knows he must've invested in another of Mr. Mayer's ventures. Maybe John can take half of the return and invest again. The more money he has, the more he can be assured of Lily's affections.

Looking into the dining room, he finds it bare. No glass or wine bottle sits on the table. He left his greatcoat upstairs. The cellar is probably very cold. He enters the hall again, purposing to be speedy in the place that holds the wine and two bodies.

Light flickers from the pink parlor.

John sneaks to the door and opens it. The room is empty.

He sighs, wondering if Duncan is lurking about. Maybe he can't sleep, either. Perhaps the two can have a drink together.

Maybe Duncan will tell him the advice that Peters surely gave the magistrate to enable him to become the talk of fashion. How else could stick-in-the-mud Duncan snare an heiress?

John enters the parlor and scans the open curtains, the sash window, which exposes all the falling snow. Will the new Lady Duncan rid the house of the pink parlor? If she does, then all the reminders of the truly regretful night will be gone.

Duncan's smart to sequester the woman and his new ready-made family away in the country. He hasn't let his new wife visit with any of the neighbors of Berkeley Square.

"That's the smartest thing you've ever done, Duncan. Nothing like keeping the vultures away," he says aloud to himself.

Shamed, John looks back at the writing desk by the window and imagines Anna Violet Flowers sitting there, doing her daily correspondence or, as Brooks said, pretending her contractions aren't painful to make him leave.

She was a good woman. Not a liar, like Brooks, like John.

Pity Anna became a pawn to be used in the war between Duncan and Brooks. John should've been a bigger man and said what was going on.

A smile rises to John's lips.

Duncan's new wife can't become the next Anna Violet and be used as a prize now that the barrister is dead.

John's Lily can't be tormented, either.

If John can convince Talson to forget the number of times his daughter has visited Brooks, all can be forgotten.

No one will know of any problems in the Constocks' marriage. There will be no reason for anyone to think John has had anything to do with Brooks's murder.

He starts to leave the parlor and again notices the swords. His father-in-law smiles every time he sees these. How can he when he was here when Anna Violet Flowers died?

John steps back into the hall. He'll leave the candles burning for Duncan. The man must be around here somewhere. Perhaps now that Brooks is dead, he should admit to everything that happened.

The marble . . . John glances at it again. He watched Mayer and Henderson clean it, but like with Brooks's body, he left without doing any work. He went and had drinks with Talson in the orangery.

What if Lily has become infatuated with Brooks? The barrister did help some close friend of hers out of a legal problem. John found out too late to stop her asking a favor of the barrister. Once she was indebted to Brooks, it was only a matter of time before he collected on what was owed.

The two, Lily and Brooks, haven't had an affair yet, but it is only a matter of time. John and Talson walked in on the two when they were very close to a compromise two weeks ago.

The benefit of the barrister being dead means no scandal and no more temptation for Lily. But how will she take Brooks's murder?

Will she think John did it?

Will she fear her husband?

In an odd way, will she be more attracted to a man who wields ruthless power to protect her reputation?

Power is like cologne water for his wife. She loves the smell of it, like she does the scent of roses.

John likes power, too. Though he hasn't had it in a long time.

As he moves down the corridor toward the cold cellar, he wonders if Duncan finally killed Brooks. The barrister loved regretfully talking about his affair with his *Violet* at these dinners to torture Duncan.

Talson says Brooks lied a great deal about her, but that admission came only after she was dead.

John hears a noise. His heart beats faster.

Holding his candle in front of him, he walks a little slower. A part of him begins to consider that there might be someone else in the house who wanted Brooks dead.

Sobering up more quickly than he likes, John realizes that the room in the cellar with the wine might be locked.

Mr. Villers would have the key. Is he in the kitchen, or has the chef gone to bed like everyone else?

A thirst for port or claret or sweet brandy ravages his soul. He knows he should stop or have more self- control.

He stops and considers returning to his bedchamber. Sleep may drive the taste from his mouth. The polish on the marble reflects the light of his candle.

Wasn't Peters here the night Anna Violet died? Maybe ole Duncan's getting rid of everyone connected to her death.

He swallows. What if Duncan knows the truth?

If John dies, and Holston and Talson are gone, there'll be nothing to remind Duncan. Nothing more to regret.

Lucky thing for Mayer is that he wasn't living in Berkeley Square before Anna Violet's death.

Nonetheless, Duncan is at fault, too. Everyone knows he'd rather his wife die than bring an heir into the world that was another man's babe.

Benjamin Brooks was a whoremonger. The worst kind of fiend, one that preyed on the wives of his associates.

John's hands tremble. A chill comes over him. He needs a drink badly.

Heading this time to the kitchen, he hopes to find a key.

Mid-step, John hears a noise. Then a door close.

Maybe someone is in the orangery, drinking again.

Pointing his candle, he heads down the long corridor.

The door to the orangery is open.

A breeze of hot air from the steam pipes rushes to his face.

Looking through the glass of the door, he sees two wine bottles on a table, but one glass.

Someone had his idea for a late-night drink but left.

"It would be rude to take someone else's treat." He repeats this in a louder voice.

No one responds.

Is there a secret meeting?

The only women in the house are the young Blackamoors and the older maid. The math girl and the baroness are pretty. In Martinique the free women of color are sought after for companionship. If they are enslaved, they're chosen to entertain.

He rubs his face of the foul memories and tries to forget his family still owns habitations in the West Indies. Many men, like Holston, still smart over their losses in old Saint-Domingue. Perhaps with the fearsome Dessalines gone, there can be reparations. Won't Lily love John more if their finances double or triple? Perhaps he can convince Mayer to let him into another investment. This time he'll keep his wife from fretting and spreading rumors about risky practices.

Having waited a few more minutes, John goes into the orangery and closes the door behind him.

It's quite warm in here.

He hears a buzz he hadn't heard when he was in here earlier. The technology that some hothouses use to bring in warmth must get noisy at night. Funny Duncan didn't mention it.

Perhaps he hasn't had the chance.

Ambling to the table, he admires the view. The glass wall shows that the snow is piled high. It's still falling.

But there seems to be a path on the other side of the glass. The fool who left the two bottles must have gone outside.

After setting down the candle, John taps one of the bottles. If a man freezes to death, he won't need wine.

He waits as long as he can. The path is almost covered in snow.

Pop. After uncorking the wine, he pours himself a glass. The bottle is sticky.

"What's that?" He wipes his hand on his sleeve and smells rich honey.

Licking at his fingers, he realizes it is something more than honey.

The buzzing in his ears is louder. "Damn pipes."

He toasts them and drinks from the glass. The wine is good, but there is more of that taste.

He is dizzy but notices that the bottles aren't on a table but a bee box. The new Lady Duncan's bees!

Heart pounding, he's got to get out here. A beesting can kill him. One killed his father. That's why John is the Earl of Constock.

The buzzing is all around him. He sees the yellow things flying about him.

If he's calm, he can make it out of the orangery unscathed.

The door to the corridor closes behind him. A bee lands on his coat.

Another joins it.

He can't turn fast and run.

John wants to yell for help, but that might upset the bees. He's deathly afraid of *bees*.

Summoning his courage, he decides to leave the orangery, but he has to be as calm as possible. Glancing at the bottles on the bee box, he decides he'll take one with him. After this, wine will calm him. He'll enjoy it in the safety of his room.

John tries to pick it up a bottle, but it's slick and slips from his hand. It hits the floor.

Smash.

Shards fly everywhere. His shoes and stockings are splattered. If Peters were alive, he'd be mortified having to clean wine—

Not wine, more honey.

The buzzing sounds closer.

Chest raging, heart beating like a military drummer heading to battle, he stands completely still, even as bees land on his sticky boots.

But then he starts to move.

A tap on the orangery glass startles him when he turns.

He sees a shadowed figure. John can't risk picking up the candle to see who it is.

Through the window, over the sound of ice pelting the orangery, John hears, "'Hiding, six little Grand-blancs flee a buzzing hive. A bee stings one. Then there were five.'"

A man at the outer door of the orangery has sung this horrible rhyme.

That was the stanza in his invitation. That was the joke Brooks intended to play on Duncan. Brooks had told them all he was the mastermind of it. Or was he?

"Not funny," John whispers. "Open the door. The cold air might make the bees settle."

The man, who should help, pulls on something shiny.

John has missed the silver wire leading through the glass to the door of the bee box.

With another tug, the box opens fully. The hive inside falls out and crashes to the floor.

Freed, angry bees buzz all around.

One winged creature lands on John's sticky fingers.

Panicking, he runs to get to the door. It's locked.

A stinger slams into his palm. Others into his leg, his back. Heart thrashing, he tries to scream, but his throat constricts.

"Lily, I love—"

Everything stops.

Lungs burning, John falls against the locked door, then slides to the floor.

Chapter 17

Sitting on the chaise, waiting for Stapleton to come so we could go to the cold cellar, I tried to rub my temples and rid them of my slight headache.

Florentina yawned as she lay in bed. She'd taken off her carriage gown and slipped into a robe from her portmanteau. "Abbie, get some sleep."

"Yes, ma'am," Miss Bellows said. "I'll sleep on the chaise."

"No. You've worked too hard tonight. I need you to rest. Sleep in the bed," I told her. "It's the least we can all do, knowing you oversaw the food and kept us from nasty tricks."

"You mean poison, Abbie. You might as well just say it."

I wiped at the crusts of sleep forming about my eyes. "The valet may have been poisoned. Whoever did it hasn't been identified. They may strike again. And since you haven't remembered all the lines of 'The Rebel's Rhyme,' we don't know what to expect."

"In the morning, Abbie, I promise. I can't think, and dinner hasn't made anything clearer. Why would Duncan make up a fake regret?"

That didn't make sense when life typically offered plenty. "Take a nap, both of you. Then, Flo, as soon as you can, remember the rhyme. We need all the lines of the rhyme to hopefully be ahead of the killer."

"I will try." She sat up from the pillows. "Have you had a vision? Anything that could help us?"

Miss Bellows's snores sounded. The poor woman, wrapped up in Flo's robe, had fallen asleep as soon as she lay down.

"I know she will have a good rest." I glanced at my cousin's frowning face. "Nothing. I've seen nothing. I know nothing. I think I hate this even more than having a dream I don't understand."

She snuggled into the covers. "You need to sleep. Hopefully, Mr. Henderson is too exhausted to play—"

A light rap on the wall almost made a giggle burst from my lips. I stretched and tapped a response.

The next moment, a similar knock came from the door.

I rose from the chaise and eased the lock open and let him inside. The flame of the small candle in his hand illuminated his tired countenance.

"We've waited two hours. It's not quite midnight, but I haven't heard any movement, not in half an hour. I think it's safe to proceed, unless you've changed your mind, Abigail."

"Her changing her mind about folly?" Florentina shook her head. "That would be too much of the wise thing to do."

"Flo, we need answers. And we need the full 'Rebel's Rhyme' before someone else is killed."

"Both of you, be safe and tell the dead Mr. Brooks I said hello."

I took the key to the room from the table and held the cold

brass in my hand. I dealt with keys all the time. This one felt different.

Nerves. Shaking off this feeling, I joined Stapleton in the corridor.

He tugged at his withered cravat, freeing it, and putting the linen into his tailcoat pocket. "It's late, Abigail. Perhaps we should abandon this. Brooks is not going anywhere, not until the coroner can dig through the snow."

"Why are you so resistant to searching the body?"

"I spent over an hour with him in the cold. He has nothing more to tell."

"I could go by myself."

The way he gaped at me, like that was the stupidest thing in the world to say, made me step back. "Sorry. That was nonsensical, since you are here."

"Abigail, you babble when you are tired. Perhaps you can go back inside your room. You can get some sleep. And we can search the barrister tomorrow."

"Let's go. You've put up with my ramblings before. This is no different."

He frowned a little deeper. "Yes, no different."

I was not sure that I could last another minute wondering if Brooks had a stanza from "The Rebel's Rhyme." "If he has a foolscap with a stanza from the rhyme, particularly one that alludes to his fate, like Mr. Peters's, then we will need to reexamine everything in his possession."

"You're thinking that Mr. Peters was murdered, Abigail?"

"After the bickering I heard tonight, I wonder if someone Mr. Peters refused to work for or whose employ he left held animosity toward him."

"Enough to kill him? He was a free man. He could choose his employer as much as they could want to hire him. I think you're wrong."

I took his arm. "Only one way to find out."

He patted my hand and started toward the stairs.

The length of his sigh sounded as if he were in pain. Then I remembered the day he'd had, from nearly getting frostbite outside, to mopping the hall, to being made the stand-in coroner. I stopped moving.

"What now, Abigail?"

"If you think that we will learn nothing by searching Mr. Brooks, then I will believe you."

He blinked at me, I thought.

His expression softened. I thought I had completely stunned him. "You trust me that much, Abigail? Or is this some sort of jest?"

When his fingers threaded with mine, he drew closer and studied my eyes, as if the answer were written upon my irises. "You *do* trust me."

Stapleton started moving, taking me with him. I was not sure what he'd seen in my face, but it seemed to be enough to give him confidence to journey with me to the basement. I prepared my mind, my heart, not to faint when I came face-to-face with Benjamin Brooks, the murdered barrister of Berkeley Square.

We started down the steps to the lower level, and I motioned to Stapleton. Light glowed about the doorframe of the pink parlor. Someone was in there.

With a finger to his lips, he slowed our pace. Almost on tiptoes, we reached the last step and then walked across the marble of the hall.

"Weren't all the sconces snuffed after dinner?" I whispered.

Stapleton nodded. He pressed an ear to the parlor door.

A noise buzzed.

A bee floated by, and I almost jumped out of my skin. I moved a little farther into the corridor that led to the cellar and the kitchen.

He doused his candle.

In the dark, he wrapped his arm about me and held me in place. "Are you all right?"

I nodded and pointed to the creature crawling up the pink parlor's door. "What on earth? Isn't this the wrong season?"

"Duncan keeps bees. He's asked my advice on ways of protecting them during the cold. It's odd that one is inside the house, though."

"You're a man of many talents."

"I like flowers, Abigail." He released me from his embrace. The familiar scent of bergamot was missing. I smelled the fishy tallow of the dining room candles. "That means understanding everything that inhabits nature and is a part of the chain of life that keeps things beautiful."

"I didn't realize you and Duncan had become so well acquainted."

"That's your doing, Abigail. He inhabits your sphere. Now I do, as well."

That could sound like a threat or a warning from anyone other than Stapleton Henderson. His odd twist of words meant he'd not abandon me. That was the best kind of friend. "Tell me what he said about the first Mrs. Charles Flowers."

"A great deal. He loved Anna Violet with his whole heart, but . . ."

"But what, Stapleton?"

"I will not break his confidence. But I will say he blames himself and his neighbors for her death."

"What do the residents of Berkeley Square have to do with a miscarriage?"

He looked away, not answering.

"Stapleton?"

"He greatly misjudged her. He feels very responsible for her death."

"Childbirth is a danger. Things do go wrong."

"He has his reasons, Abigail. And I think he's right."

"And you agree? That Lord Duncan is guilty of causing his wife to die? Do you know what you are saying?"

Something screeched. The sound echoed down the long corridor, as if it had originated at the far end.

His head whipped around, and he craned his ear toward the sound. "Abigail, why don't you ask him yourself? He's in the pink parlor. He goes there quite often to feel her presence and make amends."

"I'm not leaving you. We're in this together."

I couldn't see him well. In the dark, I could make out only his outline, but I felt him smile, smile like he had upstairs when he saw my trust in him in my eyes.

"Someone else may have plans to see Mr. Brooks, which may mean delaying the cellar visit."

"No. Stapleton—"

"We can't be seen together at night. I will have no one besmudge your character. Go into the pink parlor. I'll stay here. Perhaps after you ask Duncan your questions, the three of us can visit the cellar."

"Is it wise to delay seeing Mr. Brooks?"

"He's not going anywhere. Ask your questions of the living."

Stapleton opened the door to the pink parlor. I went inside, trusting Stapleton, and with him trusting me to find out if Duncan's admission was true, that he was responsible for Anna Violet's death.

Chapter 18

The Pink Parlor, Nine Berkeley Square

Bright beeswax candles lit the pink parlor. The honey smell hit my nose as soon as I entered. The flickering flames in the sconces shined on the crossed swords above the fireplace.

I cleared my throat to announce myself as well as to interrupt his reverie.

Lord Duncan didn't turn. Wearing a brocade dressing gown of burgundy and reds, he stood with his back to me right at the window. His hand lay gently on the top of the writing desk.

He could be a statue, frozen in place, looking out at the night and the falling snow.

Like earlier this afternoon, the room was immaculate. He'd brought no tea or even a glass of wine with him.

"Lady Worthing, I presume. Except for Mr. Henderson, men don't step lightly. I wouldn't hear him at all." He peered at me, then turned away. "Why are you out of your room? There could be a lunatic or a calculating killer lurking."

I came a little closer. "I couldn't sleep."

"When Anna had difficulties sleeping, she'd come down here and write. Those last few months she was here constantly."

"It's a very cheery room. If I were in Westminster, I'd be in my parlor, reading or watching my terrier, Teacup, play."

"Oh, yes. I hear the little rascal has become domesticated."

"Yes, my lord. But he still acts as if he is the lord of my manor." Duncan chuckled but still faced forward.

"Mr. Henderson showed me the invitation to the Night of Regrets. Very fancy. I loved the gold."

"That would be the late and great Habesha Peters. The man was so detailed. I had to do nothing. He came up with everything."

At the back of the floral sofa, I placed my hands, not to steady myself but rather to help me be patient and listen. I knew Lord Duncan had a story to tell.

"Please, Lady Worthing, don't be disgruntled about not being invited. It was designed for men, the men of Berkeley Square."

"I'm not disgruntled at all. Well, not anymore." I took another step, daring to further invade his privacy. "Mr. Peters . . . Was everything his design or that of a particular stationer in town?"

"The genius is . . . was . . . purely Peters. Brilliant man with large hands who could make the most imaginative cravats and write with a light, airy touch."

"The valet was a man of many talents. I know I'd be lost without Mrs. Smith and Miss Bellows, all my intimate staff."

He half turned and glared at me. "This will be the last Night of Regrets. How could I do them without Peters? Yes, he complained mightily about being here, but that was his way. He did everything, from planning the meal to creating and delivering the invitations. This year he had some sort of surprise, an added twist."

"You didn't look at the invitations?"

"Why? I trusted him explicitly. He never disappointed." Duncan rotated back to the sash window. From the corner of his mouth, I saw a small smile and wondered if he could somehow see the valet. "We'd sit in here after everyone left and have brandies. I'd open the window. The cold air would come inside. We'd share fine hand-rolled cigars and discus how honest we thought all were. Many years no one was."

"Sorry for your loss. It sounds as if you will miss him."

"Peters worked for me, before that for Holston, and even for Brooks. He told me about his life in Martinique and in the Americas. I will miss the man, but he was going to retire."

"When I recovered, I thought I heard that he wasn't going to be able to. Something about his finances."

Duncan groaned. "Mr. Mayer, the newest neighbor, has enticed a few with lavish investments. Constock just got his money back, plus twenty percent. It looked for a moment that he'd lost all of it. I hope that wasn't Peters's situation. Constock and Talson have resources. Mr. Peters didn't."

He sighed. "I suppose it doesn't matter. There's a cousin and his family. I'll contact them as soon as we are able." His head dipped. "Lady Duncan will be making many changes. I wanted Peters to help or give advice."

"Will this room change?"

The magistrate glared at me. Then his countenance eased. "She will be able to do whatever she wishes. She must know I am devoted to her and her ideas."

His words sounded as stiff as his shoulders looked. How did one ask one's mentor to share why he felt he must compromise to such an extent over something that meant so much?

One didn't.

One just empathized and talked nonsense. "Has the weather improved?"

"A little. Lady Worthing, please return to your room for your safety."

Wanting to take a look at the view, which had him transfixed, I moved closer, even touched the writing desk for balance as I stretched.

Duncan looked down and almost seemed aghast that I'd dared to touch and leave fingerprints on the polished surface.

I took a cloth from my pocket and swiped at the desk. "There. Good as new."

"Lady Worthing, I'm very particular about this parlor."

"Are you sure you're going to be able to give Lady Duncan permission to refurbish it to her comfort?"

He touched the glazing holding the window's leaded panes. "I'm going to have to be. It's such a sight on a sunny spring morning. When the park is in bloom, there is no better view."

Sighing, he slipped his hands to his sides. "Daffodils surround the bench in the springtime. The wind has uncovered it a little. I can see the top of the wrought iron."

"You're staring at the bench where your friend died?"

"Was Brooks a friend? He targeted my wife to humble me." His tone became heated, angry. "Is that what someone you've taken to your bosom does?"

"No, I don't think so. But maybe that is where men and women differ." I peered around his shoulder and focused on the candles in the window highlighting the falling snow, the ice dangling from the plane trees like jewels. "The storm keeps raging."

"Talson has gathered icicles to put in his cocoa. The last thing the old gossip needs is more hot liquid to expand his puffed-up chest."

"So, your oldest neighbor is not a favorite, either."

"He's a friend. But he loves gossip so much that it misguides him." Duncan turned to me. "It's difficult to see the truth.

Then, sometimes, it's too late to change anything. Regrets. Everyone has them unless they are a demented fool."

"Sir, may I be frank?"

"When are you not, Lady Worthing?"

"You have a night for men to talk of regrets. You made up one for a trial of a man from Martinique. Why do that when it's obvious you regret the circumstances of your wife's death?"

After biting both lips, then pressing them closed for a long minute, he said, "Peters felt if I directed everything at Anna Violet, then no one would talk about her, about what happened."

It was obvious that the magistrate had learned something awful that involved his first wife and this room. This part of the house seemed to stand still in time.

But being timid and not questioning him would lead to nothing. So I asked, "You loved Mrs. Flowers deeply? I take it your first marriage was not a matter of convenience."

He looked alarmed, but I said the obvious to set him at ease. "You must know Lord Worthing and I wed for convenience."

Duncan bit at the corner of his lip. "Worthing is a family friend of the Carringtons. One could hope that there was more."

"There can always be more, sir, but how things begin is important."

He closed his eyes, then focused on the window. "Ours was a love match. I loved her the moment I saw her. It was at a country dance. She wasn't that good at a reel. I wasn't that great at anything. But we were enthusiastic about failing together."

Bringing his hands together, he clasped his neck. "We were very happy. Then she was with child. Then she grew depressed. I'd often find her here, drawing or writing her letters. Her penmanship rivaled Mr. Peters."

He chuckled a little. It was forced.

Humor wasn't going to help him. Perhaps honesty and a woman's perspective would. "Confinement can be difficult."

"It wasn't carrying our babe that made her weary. It was the rumors circulating the neighborhood."

"Rumors, Lord Duncan?"

"Yes. Two."

My mind began to turn, and I wondered about the horrid people I'd met tonight. Then I decided that he needed to talk, and I wanted to listen. "What were they?"

"Are you sure you want to know?"

"I am asking, sir. And I know that this was years ago. People change."

His head dipped. His hand reached forward to touch the glass. "That Anna Violet Flowers had an affair with Benjamin Brooks. That wasn't true. Brooks loved making people think this was true. Didn't care if it hurt her reputation. Just that it made me look foolish. The rising barrister with problems at home."

"And, of course, such a rumor never hurt a man."

"No. Not exactly. I believe that was why he was passed over to become magistrate. I looked at it as Anna's revenge."

"The second rumor?"

He drew his hands behind his back. "That . . ." His voice broke. "One of my last nights as a bachelor, I was very drunk with Holston, Constock, Talson, and Brooks. And when asked if my future wife committed adultery, what I would do if it produced a child . . ."

My stomach knotted. "You can look at me and tell me the worst."

Very slowly, with the speed of a dropping snowflake, he turned. Tears ran down the length of his stone face. "That I'd cast her and the child out. That I'd even pray she miscarried."

I didn't want to move or react, but my hand had another idea. It flew hard and fast to my mouth.

"These men told Anna. It made her distraught that I could possess such thoughts. She was right that wine can't make one have evil in one's heart. I begged forgiveness. I promised her that I'd never think such terrible things again. I even told her that if something happened and that was our fate, I'd win her back and love the babe as my own, for it was part of her."

"A desperate man will say anything to be forgiven."

He swallowed and wiped his face with a sleeve. "That was the problem. She never believed me. And I did everything to show her that I loved the ground she walked on."

That wasn't the end of the tale. "What happened, Lord Duncan?"

"Brooks began to tease that they had had an affair. He'd send her notes and flowers. Everyone in Berkeley Square saw."

"And they thought it was true. And when she became pregnant—"

"They thought it could be Brooks's," he said, interrupting me. "The teasing from everyone was silly. But it put Anna in a depression. She wrote him, asking him to stop. Even asking Brooks to tell everyone these rumors of seduction were false."

"He didn't stop, did he?"

"No. The night she died, he was here, telling her about a portrait he had painted of her to commemorate their love."

Hands balling, shaking, Duncan released all the air in his lungs. "Mr. Peters tossed him out of the house, but Anna was already having contractions. Nothing could stop them. Nothing could save her or my stillborn daughter. I didn't even get a chance to say goodbye."

My heart broke for him, for the woman who had lived within these pink walls. "I'm so sorry, Lord Duncan."

"You know what's worst of all? The neighbors insinuating that this mishap was God's design. And one saying how important it is to know the bloodlines of one's heir."

Now my other hand flew to my mouth.

"I let gossip and lies destroy her. I never thought that rumors could hurt. They weren't true. I knew I was true to her, and she stayed true to me. But the falsehoods, the lies wore on her. I'm sure the strain caused her and our babe's demise. How does one forgive oneself for not understanding the person one is supposed to care for and protect the most?"

The pain in his voice, his whole heart breaking anew, ripped through me. "You didn't know, Lord Duncan. And you didn't spread the rumors. That was Mr. Brooks. He was central to this deceit, and it sounds as if he had no regrets over what his lie caused."

It took a moment, but the magistrate answered yes.

The second question, I tried to ease into, but there was no soft way to ask. "You wished you'd killed him, don't you?"

Candles flickered.

The wind howled and rattled the glass.

Then a low yes was said. "Though duels are illegal, I should've taken down those swords and done the deed. If I'd defended her honor, maybe Anna would be alive. My daughter, too. If I had been the executioner, then it would feel as if I'd done something for Anna. I'm glad someone did what I couldn't."

It was a confession. Not one for a court of law, but a simple declaration of fact. Charles Flowers, Lord Duncan, magistrate of London, had celebrated his rival's death.

"And you had a man you despised in your house every year around the time of your wife's, your family's death. Why?"

"Lady Worthing, I wanted him to confess. I wanted him to remember how he had tortured her ruining her good name. I wanted him to feel some shame. I wanted the friends who laughed with him to feel it, too. In the end, fate has intervened. The man died too quickly to feel anything."

"Well, he's gone. I suppose you are free. You can begin to forgive yourself."

"No, Lady Worthing, I'll never be free. I can't forget what I allowed to destroy my wife."

Shrinking, taking a step back, I let Lord Duncan have the

whole window. The controlled rage in his voice made me concerned for his safety.

How could I not be when he envied a murderer?

Looking through the window, I noted again how the bench looked sort of majestic in the light falling snow.

And close.

I could see it in plain sight.

Then the worst realization hit. The magistrate wasn't merely jealous of the killer. He had seen Benjamin Brooks's murderer and would do nothing to bring the guilty person to justice.

Chapter 19

The Hall, Nine Berkeley Square

"Lady Worthing?" Talson poked his head into the parlor but remained in the hall. "And there you are, Charles."

As if he wished to ignore the disturbance, Lord Duncan half turned. "Where else would I be?"

"Right. I don't mean to disturb an intimate conversation between the two—"

"Talson, if you insinuate something untoward about this one, especially in this room, I'm not sure I can control myself."

The old gossip wiped at his mouth, maybe wished to cut out his tongue. "Sorry, Charles, Lady Worthing. My words are all twisted. Something has happened. Charles, it's imperative you come. We found Constock."

The magistrate marched toward the frowning man. "Was he missing?"

"Well." He put his dripping cane over his arm. "My son-in-law . . ." Talson stared ahead, then at the floor. "I've bad news. I don't want to upset Lady Worthing. Perhaps she can leave."

It must be terrible. His voice sounded raspy . . . grief-filled.

I drew myself up and kept my posture straighter. "Just say what it is. I'm fully recovered from the afternoon's shock. It's well into the night."

Duncan nodded. "Out with it. I'm done with secrets."

Talson stayed at the door. "I tried to wash the honey off my cane. I don't want it to drip in the parlor."

"Talson." Duncan's tone sounded softer but was still direct, the tone he possessed during investigations. "I need you to say what's occurred."

"How am I to tell my daughter? My grandson?"

"Talson, what is it?" Duncan came to the threshold. "Say the worst."

"It seems the earl's hatred of insects, bees in particular, was well founded. He's been stung in the orangery. Numerous times. He's dead."

The magistrate rushed into the hall.

Talson stepped into my path when I tried to follow. "Ma'am, you don't wish to see this. It's pretty bad."

Rolling my eyes, I pushed past him and caught sight of Duncan charging down the corridor.

As fast I could, I caught up to him, and we both entered the orangery.

Hot steam had condensed on the cold glass windows.

Mr. Mayer and Stapleton were already inside, surrounded by broken glass and two crates, which bees circled. Others crawled in and out of the one with the open lid.

"Constock. He's not moving, Mr. Henderson." That was Mr. Mayer's voice. "Can we try something? Anything?"

"No pulse." Stapleton was on his knees next to the bloated purple face of the Earl of Constock.

Duncan stood beside a table and chairs that could be on a patio. "I don't understand what has happened. A pane of glass on the back side of the orangery had shattered. The bee boxes are on the ground." He tied his falling robe belt. "Who discovered him?"

"I did," Mr. Mayer said. "We were going to meet to talk about his holdings, but I fell asleep. When I awoke, I tried to find him to ask if we could talk about a more aggressive strategy tomorrow."

The young man stood and swiped honey from his hands. He had stings on his fingers. "The bees were swarming. Poor Lady Constock. She'll be devastated."

From the corridor, Talson poked his head inside. "She will be devastated. But I'll help her all I can. My grandson. He's eight. He's the Earl of Constock now. Lily. She'll still be a countess, albeit a dowager countess for a long time."

He caught Mayer's eye. "Thank goodness you've paid out her investments. Their family fortunes have been returned."

"I'm glad of that, but right now I must mourn my friend."

Mayer's shoes were off; he hobbled to the corridor door in his stocking feet.

Why would he go looking for someone with no shoes on?

The young man almost bumped into Talson as he barged out of the orangery and into the main house.

Holston came racing down the corridor. Wearing a greatcoat he stepped into the orangery. There was water dripping from the bottoms of his boots.

"Been outside, sir?" I said to him. "I thought it wasn't safe to do that."

"My house is the closest. Right there to the right. But I couldn't make it," he replied. "The snow is too thick. I didn't make it far. I returned to see chaos in the orangery. I broke the glass, trying to help. Poor Constock. There was no helping him."

Holston seemed unnerved. "Bees," he kept saying. "What are bees doing here? It's winter."

"People have honey all year round," Talson said.

"It's my fault," Duncan said. "Lady Duncan's bees are important. I built the heating system to warm the orangery like a hothouse for roses. She wanted to preserve these hives. Those bees are from her father's estate. I've already failed her."

"The cold air is putting the ones that are alive back to sleep," Stapleton said. "A lot of the bees are dead, not from the cold but from their stings. Honeybees don't survive their stings. They rip themselves to shreds when they strike and fly off."

Well, Stapleton did know about bees. Not that I doubted him; it was just interesting to see a rugged man concerned about such topics. My view of him would continue to expand.

And in a year full of chaos, he still found ways to surprise me.

"Cheer up, Duncan," Holston said. "Looks like a number of the winged beasts are still alive. There's hives intact in the box, but shouldn't you have more concern for our dead friend?"

"*Your* friend," Duncan said.

Something had changed. It was the harshening of the magistrate's tone.

Mouth open, Holston backed up, shivering. "I'm going inside. I need to get warm before I get sick. Not that I'm keeping score, but I know what will happen if I do succumb."

"What will happen, sir?" As I asked, Holston and Talson exchanged grim looks. "Mr. Holston?" I said. "What will occur?"

"It's an old saying from Saint-Domingue or Martinique that Brooks said. 'Five, huddle and keep score. One gets very cold. Then there were four.'"

When Talson turned his face to Constock, the military man took the opportunity to retreat.

I didn't have to glance at Stapleton. He had caught what sounded like a "Rebel's Rhyme" reference.

A fresh wind blew into the orangery. More snow came inside, too.

"Everyone, return to your bedchambers," Duncan said. "Forget about the bees. Another death has happened. Everything must be preserved for the coroner."

Stapleton stood and blew on his reddening hands. This was the third time today he'd dealt with death and cold. "Should we take the body downstairs with the others?"

"No." Duncan moved to the steam pipes and doused the flame heating them. "It will become freezing in here. That will preserve evidence. The coroner needs to see Constock as he is."

He held open the door to the house. "Out of here, everyone. Back to your rooms until morning."

I had no reason to protest. Holston had given us the biggest clue to this mystery. Stapleton wasn't the only one of the men to know about "The Rebel's Rhyme," and somehow, Brooks, not Duncan, was behind it.

Turning back to the house, I saw something shiny near Stapleton's hand. I went to get it.

"Lady Worthing, what are you doing?"

Duncan sounded frustrated, but I wouldn't be deterred. "I think I found something important."

When I tugged the thin silver wire, I felt pain. It had bitten into my finger. Resorting to pulling on it with my nails, I dislodged it and held it high. "This was tied to the door of one of the bee boxes. Is it used in the operation of the door? Could it have caused the door to open and release bees, to Constock's detriment?"

"No." Duncan's voice became like gravel—uneven, gritty. "I built the boxes myself. No silver . . . but you're bleeding."

Stapleton popped up and wrapped my whole hand in a handkerchief. "Heavily bleeding? Why must you poke and pull everything?"

"It's nothing." I took off the cloth and showed him the wire. "My guess is that this may have something to do with opening the box."

"And you're bleeding," Talson said. "Just like Brooks."

The look he and Stapleton exchanged was telling.

Or perhaps it was affirming.

"Just like Brooks," I repeated as Lord Duncan took the sticky wire. My voice didn't sound triumphant. It sounded light, wildly light, like my head.

The next thing I knew, I was again in Stapleton's arms, being jostling about as he ran from the orangery.

"I found the connection." I rested my heavy head against his shoulder.

"You found trouble. I might as well call you Lady Trouble."

We slid across the marble like the carriage had on the ice.

"It's Worthing, sir. But I thought you'd grown comfortable calling me Abigail."

"I've grown too comfortable in a lot of things. I should never have indulged you by coming down here with you. And now you are hurt."

Wham. Stomp. Stomp. His boots hit each tread. The noise echoed, vibrated down my spine. The cloth about my finger was scarlet. The shade of red on the white linen mirrored what I fell into when I discovered Brooks and his discarded items about the bench.

"Sorry, Stapleton."

He reached the landing and lugged me to my room. "The key is in your pocket?"

It was hard to think.

Then he started banging on the door.

"I didn't want to awaken Miss Sewell and Miss Bellows unless necessary," I said.

He pounded on the door. "It's necessary."

"Yes?" That was my cousin's sleepy voice.

"Ma'am, open up. This time Lady Worthing is actually hurt."

The lock slid; hinges whined.

Stapleton crossed the threshold and set me on the chaise.

He began working on my index finger, squeezing and pinching. "Keep your eyes open, Abigail, my Lady Trouble."

"I will. But you must stop frowning. The urgency to see Brooks's body and find evidence to link him to the other murders here has lessened."

"Abbie." Florentina's voice shook. "You'll not be going anywhere if you don't listen to Mr. Henderson."

Why weren't they happy?

The thin wire was sharp enough to slice through flesh. It had to link Brooks's and Constock's murders.

"Hold the handkerchief taut on her finger, Miss Sewell. I need to find something for sutures."

Miss Bellows shrieked as she sprang out of bed. Mobcap falling to the side, she said, "I have silk thread. I always carry my kit to support Lady Worthing."

"Get it, Miss Bellows. I will return with wine. I'll need it to clean the wound. Keep squeezing, Miss Sewell."

"Call me Florentina," she gasped. "But it may not be faster to say."

Stapleton stopped at the door, nodded to her, then ran.

"All will be well, Abbie." My cousin prayed and crushed a fresh handkerchief about my stinging index finger.

I wanted to comfort her, but I was tired and sat still.

The truth and I had much in common. We both seemed to be too much trouble.

Nonetheless, I wondered when it would be understood by all that my discovery meant murder. And the person or persons responsible had no reason to stop their killing spree.

Chapter 20

December 24, 1806
Abigail's Guest Bedchamber, Nine Berkeley Square

My fevered dreams, instead of seeming like plays at the theater, ordered the mystery in my head. The searing feeling in my index finger awakened me to the light coming through the curtains.

Though hearing Florentina's snores and seeing Stapleton asleep on the floor next to the chaise might be becoming more of a commonplace experience, it took a moment for me to realize I wasn't in my parlor in my townhome on Greater Queen Street.

Shifting to sit up a little, I winced. Pain shot through my hand. Then it all returned, how I'd spent the early morning nearly bleeding out because I had retrieved the thin shiny wire. One that I no longer possessed.

Stapleton shifted. He looked ready to fight. "Abigail?"

"I'm still alive, if that's what you are asking."

His lips pressed together, and he settled down. His head lay near my propped-up hand, and his back was against the chaise.

"I'm sorry."

"For what, madam? Risking your life again? Forcing me to dump laudanum down your gullet so I could stitch up a wound? Making your poor cousin the responsible party to give consent for a barely lucid client?"

He folded his arms. His eyes were shut. "Just pick one."

Peering up to the ceiling, at the dentil molding crowning the room, I hunted for what to say. Nothing particular came to my mind. "Sorry. Sorry. Sorry. Triple sorry."

He blasted air from between his frowning lips. "You're welcome. At least you live to the fullest, Abigail. I suppose it should be counted as a good thing that you put your zeal into fighting for the truth."

"And that my neighbor is a skilled physician."

He opened his eyes again. "Lord Worthing is a lucky man."

"Is he? I don't think he notices. Or cares."

"The man's a fool. Always thought James Monroe was a coward, but now I know him to be a fool, too."

Before I could ask or offer my agreement, Florentina bounced up. "I remember."

She slid from the bed and went to the table.

The pencil that she kept for emergency mathematics was out of her portmanteau. Next to my famous lists, she began marking the foolscap that I'd taken from the pink parlor.

"Stapleton gave me the stanza to the rhyme that Mr. Holston recited. I think I know that version," she announced.

I sat up all the way and became very dizzy. Then I sank like a rock. "Flo?"

She scribbled, her hand moving furiously across the paper. "The Rebel's Rhyme."

"Don't distract her, Abigail. Let Florentina finish."

I didn't know what to be more astonishing, that we'd soon have the full rebel's poem or that my nearly bleeding out had brought my cousin and neighbor to some sort of peace.

It was painful to move my hand, but I refused to accept any more laudanum. I found it particularly hard to make sense of all that had happened under its influence.

"Mr. Peters had consumed a great deal of this medicine. How could he walk from his room or Lord Duncan's all the way to the stairs?"

"He was a bigger man, much bigger than you," Stapleton said. He lay again on the floor next to my chaise. "And Talson and Holston talked about his gout. If he'd been treating himself with laudanum, I imagine he could've had a high tolerance."

His death didn't feel like Brooks's or the Earl of Constock's. Yet his death fit the stanza from the rhyme that he had on his body. "Did you get a chance to search the earl's body? Did he have—"

Before I could finish, Stapleton had reached into his coat pocket and whipped out a folded piece of gilded parchment, a match to his.

I reached for it, but bending my hand made everything hurt.

"Don't read it yet, Abbie." Florentina must've seen me stir. "I'm almost done."

I should tell her to take her time, but with three men dead, I didn't know how much time we had.

" 'The Rebel's Rhyme' might point us to the person responsible. Or foreshadow who'll be the next one targeted," I mused.

Mr. Holston had said, " 'Five little Grand-blancs keep score. One gets cold. Then there were four.' " With Mr. Talson, Mr. Mayer, Mr. Holston, Lord Duncan, and Stapleton still alive, there were five possibilities.

"Done," she said and set down her pencil.

As she passed the paper to me, I saw she wore the biggest frown. "What's wrong, Flo?"

"If I'd remembered this earlier, the Earl of Constock might still be alive."

"You can't take that burden upon yourself, Flo. His murder was elaborate. The killer surely thought about how to do it for a long time. You couldn't possibly think a poem—"

"Read it, Abbie," she interrupted. "Then see if you feel the same."

Florentina was a direct soul. She was plain in her speech, mostly matter of fact in her opinions. This had to be bad.

"Read it, Abbie. Then condemn me for pouting about not being in Cheapside and thinking that everything was ridiculous."

Holding the paper up to the light creeping inside from the window, I read aloud "The Rebel's Rhyme."

Braggin', eight little Grand-blancs think they own heaven.
One leaps high. Then there were seven.
Stunned, seven little Grand-blancs mourn in sharp cliques.
One slits his wrist. Now there were six.
Hiding, six little Grand-blancs flee a buzzing hive. A bee stings
one. Then there were five.
Scared, five little Grand-blancs huddle and keep score. One
gets cold. Then there were four.
Running, four little Grand-blancs take weapons to flee. One
twirls a sword. Then there were three.
Forsaken, three little Grand-blancs gather rope and fight anew.
One hangs himself, and then there were two.
Trapped, two little Grand-blancs sitting in the sun. One got
very warm, and then there was one.
Guilty, one little grand blanc left all alone. Closed his eyes forever. And there were none.

Stapleton had arisen. He and I exchanged papers, "The Rebel's Rhyme" as remembered by my cousin and Constock's invitation.

Unfolding the gilded parchment, I found the curled foolscap. I unfurled it. . . . The stanza from the rhyme matched exactly.

"'Hiding, six little Grand-blancs flee a buzzing hive. A bee stings one. Then there were five.' That was the earl's fate."

Stapleton folded the pink stationery upon which Florentina had written. "This means that Mr. Peters's death was no accident. He was pushed."

"He put together the invitations. I believe he included the curled stanzas to the rhyme," I replied. "Who would know about it and then give Mr. Peters all that laudanum? He had to be carried to the stairs. There is no way he could have made it there himself."

Florentina gaped at me. "The man did tell us how much he worked during the Night of Regrets, how much walking about he did, but he died after Mr. Brooks, not before."

"The stanza about slitting a wrist, which is the barrister's demise, comes after the leaping to one's death." Stapleton sat and stretched back out on the floor. "This doesn't make sense."

I felt sorry about assigning him again to an uncomfortable place to sleep.

"What do you think, Abigail?" he asked.

"The next time the three of us solve mysteries, I will be more considerate and provide more pillows."

"Mistress loves her pillows." Miss Bellows turned and snuggled deeper into the bedclothes. "And blankets. Lady Worthing loves thick blankets."

My maid settled to sleep again, leaving Flo, Stapleton, and me to puzzle out these clues.

"There are different versions of 'The Rebel's Rhyme,'" Florentina said. "I wouldn't be surprised if the massas, or those grands blancs, came up with their own version to talk about the people they enslaved."

"Cruelty begets cruelty." I looked at my snoring maid and remembered her sentiment, her questioning why hate was taught in rhymes. "Brooks. Holston said he'd heard it from Brooks."

Slowly, I moved to the edge of the chaise and stood.

Stapleton drew near me, as if to lend support if I wobbled. "And?"

I waved him off, then waited for the world to slow down. "And help me down the stairs in an hour. We need to refresh ourselves and then join the others for breakfast. It's Christmas Eve. Should be a lovely breakfast."

Steam left his nose as he released a big sigh. "I won't even ask if you are strong enough to do this. Abigail, goddess of war, is ready for battle."

"No goddess, but I am ready to battle. I feel like we are being led by the nose. Pieces of this mystery are being doled out for our consumption, complete with a script that announces how men will die."

"But not *when*," Florentina said as she put her treasured pencil back into her portmanteau. "Stapleton you are at risk. The killer is changing the order of the victims."

"We all are at risk," he said. "Mr. Peters wasn't a Grandblanc."

"But he lived in this neighborhood, and he had plans to join the merchant class."

"That would be a *petit blanc*, so to speak, if this were a French colony. But this is England."

Stapleton's logic made my temples ache, but I had to agree. "Mr. Peters's death doesn't make sense. But we need to understand how Brooks would be talking of 'The Rebel's Rhyme.'"

Stretching, my neighbor rose and moved to the door. "Fine. Ladies, be ready in an hour. I, for one, don't like all this uncertainty."

"The only certainty is that we are all at risk and the killer is among us." I rubbed at my temples. "We need to be careful."

Emotionless, Stapleton wiped a small smile from his face. "One hour, ladies."

After pointing to the lock, he left.

Florentina stepped to the door and slid the brass mechanism in place. "Abbie, it's Christmas Eve, and we are in danger."

"I think we are missing the obvious, but I am sure the truth will find us."

I turned and looked out the window. Our view was of the front of the house. I hadn't noticed before, but the storm seemed to have relented a little, though not enough to free us.

The race was to discover the culprit or the next dead body.

The Rebel's Rhyme

Braggin', eight little Grand-blancs think they own heaven.
One leaps high. Then there were seven.
–Mr. Habesha Peters

Stunned, seven little Grand-blancs mourn in sharp cliques.
One slits his wrist. Now there were six. –Mr. Benjamin Brooks
(Possible)

Hiding, six little Grand-blancs flee a buzzing hive. A bee stings
one. Then there were five. –John Clayton, the Earl of Constock

Scared, five little Grand-blancs huddle and keep score. One
gets cold. Then there were four.
–Mr. William Holston

Running, four little Grand-blancs take weapons to flee. One twirls a sword. Then there were three.
–Unknown

Forsaken, three little Grand-blancs gather rope and fight anew. One hangs himself, and then there were two. –Unknown

Trapped, two little Grand-blancs sitting in the sun. One got very warm, and then there was one. –Mr. Stapleton Henderson

Guilty, one little grand blanc left all alone. Closed his eyes forever. –Unknown

And there were none.

Chapter 21

The Dining Room, Nine Berkeley Square

Miss Bellows entered the large dining room of Lord Duncan's Berkeley Square home, carrying a tray of jellies and scones on a bed of evergreen fir. Delicate and beautiful, the red and green festive dessert made me release a gasp. It seemed a bit much for breakfast, but I doubted the chef had planned his menu around murders and a house full of suspects.

She placed one plate in front of the magistrate. Another in front of Mr. Talson. I waved her over to Mr. Holston when she had one last plate on her platter. I could wait, especially for something that looked so red.

Was it cherry or tomato based?

"Something wrong, Lady Worthing?" Lord Duncan finally lifted his head. It had been down for most of the meal. "Are you well? You bled quite a bit."

"Quite fine, sir." I tested my linen-wrapped finger as I wrapped my hand about a knife and scooped butter for a scone. "I'm sorry to have given everyone a scare."

Mr. Mayer, who'd helped himself to a third cup of coffee, banged his porcelain cup into his saucer. "Are we going to pretend that last night didn't happen? The Earl of Constock is dead."

Mr. Talson sat back in his chair. "Well, you seem a mite more upset over this death than the two prior ones. I suppose since neither the barrister nor the valet was an investor, your concern wanes."

"Peters had invested, but unfortunately, that didn't do well. I was unable to recoup anything."

Duncan glared at him. "That was the man's life savings. It was what he depended upon for his future."

"I'm sorry. That's how these investments go sometimes."

"Don't be so down on Mayer," Talson said. "Constock made twenty percent on his. Mayer paid him out earlier this week."

The young man grabbed his coffee cup and slurped it like it was ale. "Happy to have made sure his widow is in a strong financial position."

"It breaks my heart to see my daughter, any of my daughters, in pain." Talson's voice, while somber, had a tone that I assessed as boastful. He didn't mind that his son-in-law was murdered.

The chef and Miss Bellows returned with more scones and jellies, even a plate for me.

Mr. Villers shivered. "The corridor is freezing. Snow is filling the orangery."

"Don't go in there," Duncan said. "A crime has taken place."

"Are you sure, Charles?" Talson pulled a dessert in front of him. "Jellies molded like a crown? Why weren't these served at the Night of Regrets?"

"They took longer to set," Villers said. He bowed at the door and left with his silver tray.

"I suppose even men want crowns or crown-shaped desserts." Miss Bellows chuckled and followed the chef.

Talson leaned over. "The maid has me there, Charles. I like a crown, even a wiggly one."

Mr. Holston entered the dining room. He again had on his greatcoat. Sitting on his chair at the end of the table, he blew on his hands. "Is it cold in here?"

The room was warm. Though the snow and ice pelted the window, the coal in the fireplace raged.

"Are you not feeling well?" Stapleton added cream to his coffee. He wasn't eating much.

Holston put a napkin on his lap and picked up his fork. "I just feel cold. I don't want to be sick."

"You're fine," Talson said before asking me to pass the platter of bacon.

I did and thought of my boy. I hoped Teacup was well and enjoying his Christmas Eve.

"Of course, you'd dismiss me." Holston dropped his fork. It made a bell-like sound on his porcelain plate. "You are as bad as Brooks. Only interested in when your next bit of gossip will come. Brooks said you gossip like a woman. No offense meant to the ladies."

The way he slurred the word *ladies*, like it was offensive, stung like my finger. I wondered what he'd say if my cousin and I, a mathematician and a peer, weren't present.

Talson grunted. "I hardly mention you ever, Holston. You are too boring."

"You're a broken, lonely man, Talson," Holston retorted. "You take pleasure in lurking. You find secrets and hold them over other's heads. I'm surprised you're not the first one to be killed over regrets."

For once Talson had no reply.

"Gentlemen." Duncan pushed his plate aside. "Please. We are all stuck here today and perhaps tomorrow. It's Christmas Eve. Let's make the best of it."

"Easy for you to say," Mayer said. "You always pretend to be above every matter. Maybe for once, say how you feel. You know Brooks always complained about you. Constock too. How exactly were the three of you friends?"

"I suppose we weren't."

Duncan's tone, hard like marble, silenced everyone for five minutes. Then the arguing began again.

Holston pointed to Talson. "Did you even care for Constock? He was your son-in-law."

"What will there be to miss?" Talson eyed the sculpted jelly on his plate from two sides. "He was always drunk or fearful. Not much to contribute to society."

Mayer's face became scarlet like the jellies. "Stop talking about Constock like that. The earl was a good man."

"Tell us how he was easier to manipulate when he was sotted." Talson shook the ruby thing on his plate. "The earl was your biggest client because you could take advantage of him."

Miss Bellows returned to the room with more scones and wiggly jellies.

This time she set a plate in front Stapleton and Florentina and another near Mr. Mayer. "If there is nothing else, I will go help Villers prepare dinner."

She'd walked here by herself. Miss Bellows might be getting too comfortable, but if the killer sat at the table, he wasn't roaming, trolling the corridors, looking for his next victim.

I relaxed and didn't say anything. I hoped it wasn't something I'd come to regret.

Listening to the men argue, hurling insults over the table, I studied the bright red jelly and tried not to think of blood.

"So, Mr. Brooks wasn't well liked by any of you." My voice stopped their fusses. "No wonder you all can go about these days not thinking of a kind word to say of him."

"No one has even mentioned informing a loved one. And it's the holidays." My cousin's voice strengthened. "How can you all be neighbors and have so little care for one another?"

"Repeat the question, dear lady," Talson said and stabbed at his dessert. "Hard to hear over the bubbling hypocrisy. It's a Berkeley Square attitude."

"And don't fret over the Countess of Constock." Holston sniffled and smirked. "She'll be more distraught over Brooks's death."

"Stop," Talson said.

"She won't care. Her sentiments had moved on." Holston chuckled. "She'll truly enjoy being a dowager countess, being courted as a rich widow."

"Stop, Holston. Do not defame the countess."

"You mean like you've defamed others?" The dry voice was Duncan's. "Or have the past few years been imagined?"

Talson clasped his hands. "I've done a lot wrong. Many things I'm not proud of, but my daughter's a good woman."

"But many good women got caught up with the barrister." Holston's words made Duncan and Talson wince.

"Sounds like the barrister was popular. Perhaps some jealous husband killed him." Mr. Mayer poked at his jelly. "Jealousy can be a big motivator."

"Then that would mean the earl killed Brooks." Stapleton tapped his jelly with his spoon. No one had yet tried it.

He scooped a spoonful and put it in his mouth, then spit it into his napkin. "What is this, Duncan?"

"What!" The magistrate leapt to his feet, as if Stapleton were choking. "Are you all right? Is it poison?"

My friend wiped at his tongue with his napkin. "I don't eat cows' or pigs' blood. Please let this not be a new part of the ritual of the neighborhood. I live in Westminster."

Mayer dipped his spoon into his jelly. He wiped the spoon

on a napkin, which turned bright red. "I will also have to say no to consuming a bloody jelly."

Swoop. In unison, everyone pushed their desserts to the center of the massive table. It was if we were tethered puppets. Of course, we were all being pulled by strings, being led by whomever was behind this mystery.

I gaped at Stapleton, trying to detect any sign of illness. Then I turned to Duncan. "Does the chef have a name for this dish?"

"I don't know. He and Mr. Peters came up with the menu."

Holston sneered. "Perhaps he should come to us and explain. I'll go get him."

"Wait a moment. We don't want to overreact." Duncan turned back to Stapleton. "Are you well?"

My neighbor cut into his jelly with a knife. He appeared to be dissecting it, slicing the crown shape lengthwise.

"What is it you note, Mr. Henderson?" I asked. "Please say it is merely a red dye."

"Like from the bug, the cochineal? No, Lady Worthing, this is not from a bug." Stapleton wiped his blade on his napkin. "Merely verifying that the substance goes all the way through the jelly." He sniffed the napkin, then held it up. The linen had been stained exactly like the handkerchief on my wound. "Unfortunately, it is blood."

"Something died. That's for sure." Mr. Talson laughed. Then he looked uncomfortable. "You don't think it's Brooks's blood, do you?"

"I don't know," Stapleton replied.

For once, just once, I wished he was the kind of man to make a joke, but his familiar grimace told his truth. The jellies were colored with blood, and he couldn't tell if the origins were human or animal.

Wide-eyed, Duncan stood. "Mayer, Holston. Go get the chef. We need to question him."

The young man pushed to his feet first. "Should we take a weapon?"

The cockiness of yesterday was gone. The younger man looked nervous but straightened his shoulders when my cousin gazed at him.

Holston's bravado was also shaken. "What if these bloody things are meant to frighten us? What if he's in league with whoever killed Brooks and Constock?"

Duncan pointed to the door. "Take care and go get the chef."

The two men left the table and passed the fear-frozen Miss Bellows, who'd returned with a tea service.

Stapleton's gaze held mine. "Lady Worthing, I'm fine. The chef will tell us everything shortly."

Duncan grunted and sank into his chair. "He's been with me for years, almost as long as Peters."

"And he'd do anything for you," I said, "like you'd do for him. Just like with Habesha Peters."

Before Duncan answered, Mr. Talson leaned over me, as if to get at him. "Seems to me someone has taken things a bit too far, Charles."

The magistrate sat back. "Of what are you accusing me?"

"Brooks was murdered." Stapleton's tone was low but again resounding. "That is a clear fact. So was Constock."

Talson glared at Duncan. "That means someone here is guilty. Perhaps someone waited a little too late to exact revenge."

The look the two men exchanged chilled the marrow in my bones. I was no longer sure that Duncan merely knew who killed Mr. Brooks. He might have arranged for it to be done.

"You're not about to faint again, Lady Worthing? We can't forget how easily this one faints." Talson laughed. "The dessert getting to you?"

"I'm fine. I'm more concerned about the two men confronting the dangerous chef. Someone wants us to think he's behind all of this."

Duncan huffed. "Villers must know something, Lady Worthing. He made a dessert with blood."

The circumstances looked bad, but this mystery was all about how things appeared and how that differed from the truth.

The question in my head was, was the mastermind of the murders one man or two?

Chapter 22

The Dining Room, Nine Berkeley Square

Sitting in the dining room, I watched Lord Duncan interrogate his poor chef, Mr. Villers. The thin man, whose English tongue wasn't strong, looked beleaguered.

He ran a hand through his balding white hair. "I am not a murderer."

The magistrate had asked the same question in differing tones, even with various accents, only to get a bewildered stare in return. "Why did you wish to kill the Earl of Constock?" he asked again.

Why he did not simply ask the man in French about the horrid ingredient in the jelly was beyond my comprehension.

Bursting through the door and sliding across the polished floorboards, Miss Bellows ran into the dining room, carrying something that looked like a broken bull's horn. "Excuse me, sirs, ladies," she said, still trying to catch her breath. "Mr. Villers might be able to answer better if he can hear the question."

Half the table groaned.

Mr. Mayer and Mr. Holston looked sheepish or maybe ashamed. They had to feel awful about basically dragging the hard-of-hearing old man into the dining room like a lamb to slaughter. They weren't Duncan's legendary runners who administered justice.

I glared at them and then at Stapleton, whose solemn demeanor broke. For a moment, a grin crossed his countenance. I thought he'd actually laugh out loud. "Excuse me," he said.

He and Miss Bellows left the room.

"I suppose it was silly, manhandling Villers as if he was a wanted criminal, gentlemen." My voice was loud. "Shameful."

The chef nodded. "Manhandled."

"That's why you never answer my French," Duncan said. "All this time I thought I insulted you with my pronunciation."

"It does hurt, my lord. Your Scottish brogue can be thick. But who am I to tell an important man what to say?" The poor man cupped the horn to his ear and waved gnarled fingers. "Qu'est-ce que c'est? Ask your questions again."

Wearied, Duncan dipped his head for a moment. "I asked about the blood, Mr. Villers. How did blood get into the dessert?"

"Blood?" The chef scowled like he'd been insulted; then he went into a lengthy diatribe about beetroot and a burgundy or maybe a Bordeaux.

Then he worked himself up and delivered a full preacher's sermon on the intricacies of working with calf's-foot jelly.

Having nodded off, Talson shook himself. "Does that mean you refuse to confess to murder and putting blood in the jellies?"

"I have killed no one."

The man seemed fragile. Even though the silver wire was incredibly sharp, and a little effort would be needed to make an incision, it would take some strength to hold a victim in place or even tighten the wire if Brooks fought back.

This old man was no murderer, but was he willing to tamper with his art, the jelly dishes? He couldn't have attacked Brooks in Berkeley Square, and he had no reason to set a trap in the orangery.

Villers might be able to subdue beefsteak, but I doubted he'd be able to injure a man Duncan's age. I surmised the chef was fifteen or twenty years older than the magistrate. He might even be more aged than Talson.

"I give up," Duncan said. "It is obvious that you are guilty of some conspiracy, or I'd not have a bloody jelly on my plate."

When Duncan sat in his chair, as if he'd spent all his energy yelling at a man who was hard of hearing, I decided to try.

After slipping from my chair, I stood in front of the chef. "Mr. Villers, how did you decide the menu for Lord Duncan's Night of Regrets?"

Blue eyes sparkled. "I work very hard, madame. Months in advance, I come up with . . . How you say *liste des ingrédients*?"

"Ingredients, a list of ingredients?"

"*Oui*, madame. Yes. And then I work with Mr. Peters to acquire them. One year he traveled to Liverpool for turtles. My terrapin soup is best sourced from Saint-Domingue."

His brow rose as he glanced at me. "I mean Hayti."

"Good. Tell me about the colorant for the jellies. It's not beetroot or cochineal?"

"*Non*. The colorant is special beetroot," Villers said. "Mr. Peters ordered the beetroot for me. It's deeply colored. He demanded it for my lord. Stating it was his wish. Everyone knows that Mr. Peters speak for Lord Duncan."

The magistrate shifted in his chair. "I did not request blood."

"You keep saying *blood*." Mr. Villers straightened his sagging posture. "*Non. Non*, no blood. In sausages or stew, delicious." He kissed his fingers. "But in the dessert? Never. Why do you charge me with this insult? I did as Mr. Peters said you wished."

The chef moved to the table and held up one of my intact jellies. It slid and danced on my plate. "This is a masterpiece. Not blood."

Eyes shifted around the table, but most gazes landed on Mr. Mayer.

"This is blood, Mr. Villers." I handed him a fork.

He took it and dipped it into the jelly, getting a nice chunk, and stuffed it into his mouth. Mr. Villers's face turned as red as the dessert. "This is not beetroot. I do not understand. I tasted the colorant. It was beetroot."

"Being short staffed, Mr. Villers . . ." I paused when Talson glared at me. I think he enjoyed the taunting the poor chef had received.

I strengthened my tone, for I refused to let this innocent old man be made into the villain. "It's clear to me he was used. The man is another pawn in the Night of Regrets."

"Then who did this, Lady Worthing?" Mr. Mayer still looked sick to his stomach.

"I suspect that if you search Mr. Peters's quarters, you'll find the original colorant. At some point he switched them. The man was very busy yesterday. I suspect this was one of his tasks."

Taking the dessert from Villers, I asked, "Did Mr. Peters do more than gather the items on the list of ingredients? Did he help with the preparations?"

"*Oui*. He always helps." The chef put a hand over his heart. "The man could make a good stock."

Right on time, Stapleton and Miss Bellows returned to the dining room. In his hands was a flask holding a ruby-red mixture.

"What is this, Mr. Henderson?"

"Lord Duncan," Stapleton said, "we've just come from the attic, the servants' quarters. Mr. Peters's room specifically. Here is the substance that was supposed to color your jellies. This is the beetroot."

My guess that he and my maid had gone to search the valet's things was right.

When he set the flask on the table, Stapleton took a white piece of paper from his pocket. "And this is an invoice for goat's blood. I suspect that is what has made the jellies red."

A collective sigh went around the table. Nothing human, or from Mr. Brooks, was used.

Then Stapleton added, "I found another invoice for laudanum. Mr. Peters used quite a bit."

My stomach started to roll again. Peters was in great pain. Yet was that enough to resort to a high level of villainy for a man who wanted to provide a shock to participants in the Night of Regrets?

"Any other questions?" Duncan's gaze swept across the table and stopped at me. There was a slight smile in his eyes. He approved of our combined tactics.

That meant something.

It would mean even more if he was completely innocent of murder.

I shook my head, keeping the many questions I had to myself. Until I solved the original crime, determined who killed Mr. Brooks, everyone was vulnerable.

The other obvious question was, were there any other tricks that Mr. Peters had planned to bring additional terror to the men of Berkeley Square?

While everyone appeared shocked that Mr. Peters would pull a nasty trick, one man remained quiet. I watched Duncan send Mr. Villers back to the kitchen with Miss Bellows.

Then I watched everyone settle in around the table and eat non-bloody things, pushing the jellies farther away.

Except Mr. Mayer.

He hadn't touched the dessert at all. His remained on the plate in front of him. Did he know?

"Mr. Mayer," I said, "did Mr. Peters tell you of his plans?"

The young man turned his bright blue eyes toward me. "Why would he say anything to me? I didn't know him that well."

"But wasn't he one of your marks?" Holston said. "Didn't you brag about taking his three thousand pounds?"

Duncan leaned forward. "He'd worked a lifetime for that. When did you start going after servants?"

Mayer filled his coffee cup. "He was grateful I let him in on an investment."

Holston finished stuffing a scone into his mouth. While wiping crumbs from his mouth, he said, "It's good you don't discriminate, but Constock told me you sold Peters on there being no risk."

"The earl was confused." Mayer nervously added so much cream to his coffee, it overflowed. "There is always risk."

"You know Brooks was a blackguard in all respects, but he's indicted men who've indulged in fraud." Holston smiled at Mayer. "Saying there's no risk to a number of investors could get people talking."

"But who's going to believe him?" Mayer ducked his head. "I mean, Peters couldn't be credible. He put blood in our dessert."

"Peters worked for a magistrate and a barrister of the king's court." Stapleton wove his hands together as he added a missing piece, a motive for Mr. Mayer. "I think plenty would believe his statement about fraud."

The young man sat up straighter. He fingers lazily fluffed his cravat. "I would have helped him recover his funds. That's why

I promised low risk. If the earl were here, he'd attest to my good name."

"Are we all done tearing each other apart?" Talson wore a solemn frown. "Let's be honest. Peters was annoying. Brooks was hated. And poor Constock was a drunk. He probably stumbled into the hive boxes. His death was an accident."

"An accident?" Duncan glared at him. "Lady Worthing found a razor-sharp wire on the door to the hive. I looked again. The box was wired to open."

"And?" Talson shook his head. "As much as I find the baroness charming, she found sharp wire. It could've been part of your steam pipes or from the packing containers."

"Duncan put it together. Wouldn't he know?" Holston grabbed the bottle of red wine from the center of the table. He sniffed it. "Just claret," he said and poured a glass. "We don't know what happened."

"It's good to ask questions," I remarked.

"Lady Worthing, our interrogation almost convicted a hard-of-hearing cook. I think we should let the investigating be conducted by professionals." Holston sipped from his glass. "Oh, this is better than tea. And it will warm me up."

"I'm the magistrate," Duncan said. "Who else should look into these matters?"

"Oh, Charles." Talson chuckled. "Maybe the coroner would be less volatile. He'd rely on logical men, not pretty little ladies."

Duncan stood. "I can do my job. I'm the magistrate. I solve crimes and ensure the guilty are punished."

"Maybe you shouldn't be, friend." Holston's tone was sobering and clear. "You've done it for a while. Your rival is gone, and you have a new wife in the country. Perhaps you, too, should think of retiring."

Duncan's face hardened. "What would I be without all of you?"

"Happier," Mayer said. "The Night of Regrets, I suspect, has had a bigger meaning than merely a cleansing of souls."

"Gentlemen, let's not pick on Charles. Not with women present." Talson's furrowed brow eased. "This man still has many years of service to offer London. We couldn't be in better hands."

The grinning old man turned to Duncan. "But nothing like a long stay in the country to reinvigorate you. When you come back, this unpleasantness will be over. Spring will be lovely in the square for your and Lady Duncan's return."

"If Lady Worthing hadn't stumbled upon Brooks," Mayer said, "his body would've greeted you upon return."

Mayer, Holston, and Talson laughed.

It seemed rather ghastly, but it was obvious there was no care for the barrister by anyone. Duncan had told me the horrible things Brooks had done to harass Anna Violet. Yet no one else had a good word to share about the barrister. I wondered what type of life this man had lived that the people who invited him into their home truly didn't care that he'd died.

"Was the Earl of Constock also hated by all of you?" I asked.

Silence.

"Constock was a man most like us," Holston said. "Full of flaws."

"A supporter. No one believed in his friends more." Mayer grabbed the claret and poured his glass and then ran about the table, filling others' glasses. Huffing, he retook his seat and said, "The earl deserves to be memorialized."

As everyone took up their drink and celebrated Mayer's toast, it was crystal clear that Constock was liked by everyone except his father-in-law.

Then why had he died in accordance with the circumstances dictated by "The Rebel's Rhyme," just like Brooks?

"You seem confused, Lady Worthing." Talson leaned over to me. "What questions are in that fascinating mind of yours?"

"How duplicitous you all can be and smile."

My words cut away at his smirking expression, turned his dry lips to more of a dot. "Lady Worthing, that hurts."

I shouldn't have spoken my mind, but I had. I couldn't become shy now, no matter how much Florentina looked as if she wanted to kick me under the table. "Mr. Talson, I guess that is why men can be in politics and women cannot."

"Speaking of politics." Mayer's jovial tone interrupted the staring contest I now had with the gossip. "Remember the litigants to the big trial Brooks bungled over the summer?"

"What? Malfeasance?" Duncan shook his head. "Brooks never lost cases over such issues."

"The thievery gang he bragged about having his solicitor investigate . . ." Mr. Mayer took a dramatic pause, then said, "Didn't they threaten him?"

"Why would litigants threaten Mr. Brooks over losing a trial?" Stapleton, who had never touched the claret he'd been poured, chose to tap his water glass. "What was at stake?"

"Oh, Mayer, stop it." Mr. Holston shook his head. "I'm as jaded as the next man, but I refuse to believe one of my neighbors is a murderer. But we don't have to make up enemies to keep Duncan and Lady Worthing from deciding one of us is guilty."

"The litigants are true." Mayer's protest, without offering any names, sounded very hollow.

"Except we're not all neighbors. The physician and the women don't live here." Talson guzzled his wine. "The women and the physician could have brought the danger."

Holston huffed, then pointed a finger at him. "Sir, don't be ridiculous. They found Brooks. And as Mr. Mayer said, if they hadn't, the poor fool could've been out there until spring."

Looking up at the late Mrs. Flowers, Talson said, "Why

now? We've been at each other's throats for years. Not one has died, not until now."

This was ridiculous. I felt like standing up and putting a hand on my hip and arguing, but Mr. Mayer leapt up and put his finger in Talson's face. "Is this your best theory? Either a woman or the physician did it?"

"No," the gossip replied. "Could be both women and the physician."

Stapleton glared at the old man. "Do be careful with your words, sir."

Holston shifted in his chair. "Talson's just matching wits with Lady Worthing. Duncan has told us about her busy-bodied assistance in solving crimes."

"I've talked of the baroness's cleverness," Duncan said. "Her assistance has been warranted."

Well, that was an unexpected compliment.

Duncan stood. "I think we can adjourn until dinner. Do, everyone, stay alive."

"Is that all right with you, Madame Logic?" Talson had turned his venom on me. I realized he was the type who liked to tease but never took it well when others challenged him. "Perhaps you can simply tell us all now who you think is guilty."

Then I saw Mayer laughing. Holston too.

I kept my lips firmly pressed together, but my silence seemed to give Talson more energy.

"Lady Worthing, the floor. Dazzle us with your opinions."

There was no need to say anything. I had no wish to convince any man in this room of my intelligence.

When my cousin started making eyes at me, I gave in to the gnawing urge to respond. "Sir, I do have opinions, but unless I am sure, it's better not to accuse someone of a dastardly deed or deeds."

Holston raised his gaze to me. "As Constock would say, give

a woman an opportunity to say something important, and she will disappoint."

"He'd also add," Mayer said, "that certain types of women always disappoint." The young man looked at Florentina. "That's what Constock would say. Not my opinion."

"But you voiced it, sir." My cousin turned from him, like she had cast him off like a bad penny. "We should withdraw, Lady Worthing."

"Well, one of them talked." Talson clapped his hands. His tone was gleeful. "I suppose that is the best we can hope for with women."

"I'm not surprised by this poor attitude. Since many of you look at being a woman as if it were a curse."

"Being a woman," Talson said, "I suppose, must feel like one at times." Chuckling, he leaned against the spindles of his chairback. "These are just jokes. I do love how you rally."

"Gentlemen, please." Duncan's brow furrowed. "This is not helping. We're all stuck here for at least another day, if not two. We need to get along."

"Do we, Lord Duncan? It's obvious that your neighbors have no regard for cleverness or their own safety." I went over to my cousin. All the men, even Talson, who took his time, dragged themselves from their chairs and stood.

"Is that a confession, Lady Worthing? Did you kill Brooks?"

"Stop it, Talson," Duncan said. "You've had enough fun at Lady Worthing's expense. Please forgive them. I have bragged about your cleverness. And I hate thinking that what has happened has stumped us all."

Not sure what was worse, letting everyone believe that this mystery had me beat or that their boorish manners had.

Florentina caught my gaze. Her palm rolled forward, as if she was telling me to get on with it.

Hoping the odds were on our side, I agreed. "I thank you for trying to help me understand the neighbors of Berkeley Square.

Before I go ponder these circumstances, can each of you please share which stanza of 'The Rebel's Rhyme' you received with your invitation?"

Talson lost his chuckles. "Oh, you know about that. Then you know it was Brooks's idea? He was going to pull a prank on Duncan. Guess the joke is on us."

"Yes. And Brooks worked with Mr. Peters to put the foolscap with a stanza from the rhyme into each invitation." I glanced at Lord Duncan. "Your valet handled the invitations. This time would be no different. The script is done perfectly. It's Mr. Peters's hand."

Gaping, the old man reached into his coat pocket and pulled out the familiar bit of curled foolscap and lifted his haggard hand to me.

I didn't take it. "Please read it, sir. That way everyone can enjoy it."

He angled his spectacles higher up on his nose. "'Running, four little Grand-blancs take weapons to flee. One twirls a sword. Then there were three.'"

After making a note of that, I pointed to the young financier. "You are next, sir."

Mayer pulled from his money purse the curled piece of paper. "'Forsaken, three little Grand-blancs gather rope and fight anew. One hangs himself, and then there were two,'" he read aloud.

"Mr. Henderson, your turn."

Stapleton gaped at me but complied. "'Trapped, two little Grand-blancs sitting in the sun. One got very warm, and then there was one.'"

Not to be left out, Mr. Holston followed and tugged his invitation out of his greatcoat. "'Stunned, seven little Grand-blancs mourn in sharp cliques. One slits his wrist. Now there were six.'"

That was wrong.

The rhyme's stanza that Holston had should be the one he had alluded to last night. *Scared, five little Grand-blancs huddle and keep score. One gets cold. Then there were four.*

He had read the one that should be with Brooks.

I kept my face blank. I made sure not to express my confusion. "Thank you. Please stay well until dinner."

"Wait," Talson said. "We've let this one have her say. But let us men gather and do a formal Night of Regrets. I owe that to Peters and Constock. Maybe Brooks."

"Yes," Holston said. "That would be a worthy send-off for the three."

Everyone left the room but Stapleton, Florentina, Lord Duncan, and me.

"Very clever, Lady Worthing," the magistrate said, "to have figured that out. I didn't have Peters put that in the invitations."

Stapleton pushed his chair under the table. "It's obvious that Mr. Peters put the stanzas from the rhyme in there. From the bloody jellies to the rebel lyric, your valet had a plan of his own."

The magistrate folded his arms. "None of this makes sense."

He started toward the door, and I called to him. "Lord Duncan, please stay safe until dinner. Take no chances. There's a killer in our midst. I'm sure he's not done."

Duncan nodded and went into the hall.

Stapleton stepped to me. "He's not the only one who needs to be careful. We're now fully exposed. Our advantage is gone."

"On the contrary. We now understand the order. And it is clear that Duncan knew nothing of 'The Rebel's Rhyme,' but the other men did. It's also clear that Lord Constock had the only stanza of the rhyme specific to his fear of bees as how he died. He couldn't be behind any of this. We can't . . . I can't suspect him of being our murderer, not anymore."

"I will see you ladies to your room."

We followed my neighbor up the stairs. From the top landing, I saw Duncan go into the pink parlor. I could hear the others in the bedchambers along the upper level.

"Are you going to imbibe with them tonight, after dinner?" I gave Stapleton my key.

He twiddled the light brass between his fingers. "I'm not sure I have a choice. I think it will be best if I participate."

"But you will be vulnerable." I shook my head. "I don't like that."

Indigo eyes twinkling, he said, "I'm a retired navy man. I can handle myself."

That would surely be true in most circumstances, but it couldn't be safe to have wine with one killer, let alone two.

Lady Worthing's List

Murdered:	Mr. Peters
Murdered:	Mr. Brooks
Murdered:	Lord Constock
Suspects:	Lord Duncan
	Mr. Holston
	Mr. Talson
	Mr. Mayer

The Rebel's Rhyme

~~Braggin', eight little Grand-blancs think they own heaven. One leaps high. Then there were seven. –Mr. Habesha Peters~~

Stunned, seven little Grand-blancs mourn in sharp cliques. One slits his wrist. Now there were six. –Not Mr. Benjamin Brooks but Mr. William Holston

~~Hiding, six little Grand-blancs flee a buzzing hive. A bee stings one. Then there were five. –John Clayton, the Earl of Constock~~

Scared, five little Grand-blancs huddle and keep score. One gets cold. Then there were four. –Unsure

Running, four little Grand-blancs take weapons to flee. One twirls a sword. Then there were three. –Mr. Frederick Talson

Forsaken, three little Grand-blancs gather rope and fight anew. One hangs himself, and then there were two. –Mr. Derrick Mayer

Trapped, two little Grand-blancs sitting in the sun. One got very warm, and then there was one. –Mr. Stapleton Henderson

Guilty, one little grand blanc left all alone. Closed his eyes forever. –Unsure

And there were none.

Chapter 23

Stapleton's Guest Bedchamber, Nine Berkeley Square

After he checked the room, under the bed and in the closet, Stapleton exited our chamber.

Before the door could close, Florentina started yawning and looked at me. "Obviously, you want to tell him something. I know you're fretting about him enjoying the male-only gathering."

My cousin was right. I hated admitting how well she knew me. "I'll be back in a moment."

"I trust you, Abigail. Everyone does. That might be your flaw."

With a shrug, I dashed into the corridor. "Mr. Henderson, wait."

His brass key dangled between his fingers. He glanced back at me. "Everything all right? Did I miss something?"

He charged toward me, my door.

When he reached me, I put my hands up to his chest. "No. I didn't mean to alarm you."

Stapleton didn't move, even as my non-bandaged fingertips glided down his wrinkled silky waistcoat. "Yes, Abigail."

Why did he sound as if he'd been running? I must've frightened him with my tone. "Nothing's wrong, sir. I just had something to say to you."

He squinted at me. The tension in his brow eased as he stepped back. "Can we delay this? I didn't sleep well last night. I'd like to be well rested before tonight's performance. I fear my life may depend upon it."

A gasp left me.

Now it was his turn to draw closer and wave at me like I was a sinking vessel needing to know where to dock. "It's a jest, madam. Nothing more."

"But tonight is dangerous."

Noise sounded below. I thought it was Holston's heavy footfalls.

"Abigail, I can handle anything." He yawned like Flo, but louder. "It's best we discuss this later."

"You mean you truly don't want the opportunity to say you disapprove of what I've done?"

He frowned, moved again toward his door. When he reached it, he worked the lock. "Won't change anything."

"Stapleton, wait."

He had opened the door to his chamber and began to step inside.

"I wanted to say—"

"Say what, Abigail?" The volume of his voice had risen. Covering his mouth, he looked around me, probably checking to see if we were being observed. "If you want my opinion on something now, come inside. I'm inviting you in."

Big and bad and bold downstairs, how could I act scared or with a head for propriety while badgering a widower, a very single man, outside of his bedchamber?

I couldn't. Could I?

"This cannot wait." It could mean his life. With a nod, I went inside his bedchamber.

Whipping off his coat, Stapleton shut the door. He leaned against the smooth paneling of the door while he dropped his waistcoat to the floor. "Abigail, what is it you want?"

The blue room was neat. Not a pillow out of place. The curtains draping the nearby bed and the window were open. The fireplace had been used, but the coals had died out. The room looked inviting, peaceful.

It was untouched because Stapleton had slept on my floor.

"Abigail, I asked a question. What is it that you wish to say?"

His eyes had darkened to mirror black. They shined in the dim light that the snowy gray day let inside.

"Abigail?"

"I know it wasn't wise to allude to 'The Rebel's Rhyme.'"

"Wise?" He folded his arms. The tension in his forearms was great, like he'd considered grabbing me and shaking sense into me. "Couldn't help yourself? You had to let the killer or killers know you were on to them?"

"Yes. It seemed—"

"Someone could've tampered with the invitations, but sharing what you know, now you could make the killer desperate. You've given this killer targeting men a reason to target a woman. You."

"An unhinged person can choose anyone to die. Look at you. You're not a Berkeley Square neighbor. I doubt you know anyone here beyond Lord Duncan. You're on a killer's list. That's concerning."

"You don't have to be intimate friends to be killed. Sometimes, you die for sins of the past."

My heart remembered my housekeeper's warning about military men, especially those who'd served in combat. How many times had these indigo eyes sentenced someone . . . the enemy to death?

"In the scales of justice, Abigail, that might make things balance out."

"Stapleton, I will invite you to my Yuletide table every year. I will try to promise no hunting or tracking of wrongdoers during December."

His jaw slacked. I think he might've laughed.

Then we were silent, together.

"I'm sorry that your association with me and my inquisitive nature has made you unsafe, Stapleton. I fear tonight someone will take advantage."

"Abigail, I can handle myself." His arms dropped toward my hands, then were pinned to his sides. "No one can help being drawn to places and danger. You and I are alike in that way."

"And death is no stranger to us."

"We are no longer strangers, Abigail."

The heat of his stare made me feel warm. "Then you're committed to living to help me solve this mystery. I intend to solve it."

"No plans to die at Christmas. And, of course, you'll solve it. You're a rare creature, one that lives without regret. I envy and admire such strength."

He started to bow and lead me away, but I didn't want to go, not yet. "Most don't . . ." My tongue tied. I swallowed and tried again. "Have I been insulted or deeply complimented?"

"Take it as a compliment from a man privileged to be your neighbor. Being drawn to the same places and times with you is an honor."

"Stapleton, you're mocking me."

"Yes. It's better than trying to dissuade you from doing something that can have bad repercussions."

I looked away. Then turned back without regret or apology. "Why do I have to hide my intelligence to make others comfortable? What type of privilege is that?"

"If it means being safe or keeping yourself safe, hide. These people mean nothing to you."

"It isn't right, Stapleton. Those men are the magistrate, financiers. They hold the wealth of the ton. They make the laws. Except for Lord Duncan, they stand in the way of abolition. And don't ask me about the meetings I read about in the papers that they use to influence our Parliament in how the ministers deal with Black nations. If I can change one mind, I must seize the opportunity."

With a deep sigh, he said, "It's not good . . . their horrible attitudes or how they stifle progress to suit their bank accounts . . . But neither is it right for you to be targeted by men who'll never see your worth. They will not value your opinion, no matter how clever or poised or beautiful you are."

Silence enveloped us.

We should leave his room.

Or I should go into mine and abandon the friend giving me such compliments, making me feel seen and pretty.

No man had, not in a long time, told me that I was smart and beautiful.

My white half boots, polished and shining, stayed in place.

His head lowered. Was the sight of our soles, dark and light, more interesting?

"I'm sorry, Abigail. But you saw the reaction the men had when you talked about 'The Rebel's Rhyme.' They are complicit in whatever was planned to happen."

Complicit now, and years ago, these men bonded or became broken around the death of Anna Violet Flowers. Was justice for her crying from the grave or the pink parlor?

Stapleton touched my chin. It was for a second. His thumb grazed my skin for a second. "You are thinking too much. Come back to me. We're talking about disclosing our advantage, 'The Rebel's Rhyme.'"

"Duncan genuinely did not know anything about it. We needed to eliminate the possibility that he's actually the man behind all three deaths. Before this moment, Mr. Villers could've acted on the magistrate's orders for the invitations."

Stapleton's arm lowered to his side. "As long as you've known Duncan, you still doubt his innocence?"

"People are different under duress." I pulled my hands together and bumped my hurting finger. "He seems like he's gone on with his life after tragedy," I said through the pain.

My index finger was incredibly sore. "But I know the death of his first wife haunts him. If he can put the blame on one of his neighbors, that might be enough to make a husband seek revenge."

Flustered, with his cheeks reddening, Stapleton closed his eyes. He seemed to be struggling. "I'm tired, Abigail. I don't want to do or say the wrong thing."

"You don't think I'm not furious at myself. I gave away an advantage, merely to stop those men's laughter. I hope my actions don't prove fatal. I don't want you harmed."

"Well, you are now a target. That is what upsets me."

"The minute I walked into this house, I was a target. On the streets, when someone sees me go someplace they think is above my station, I'm a target."

He reached out and put a palm to my face. "What is it like in your world, where you can't be at ease for a moment and merely trust others?"

"It's not that simple, Stapleton."

"Do you ever have a day where you're not struggling to prove yourself?"

With my hurt hand, I clasped his thumb. My touch was tentative, and with the bandage, it was a torture to apply any pressure. "Even now I wonder if your kindness is some sort of test."

With care, he sought his freedom and moved away. "That's very sad, Abigail. Maybe someday you'll learn to trust your instincts."

I glared at him. "What does that mean for someone like me?"

"An independent woman with a good head on her shoulders, influential friends, and family? I think it means a great deal."

"My instincts?" My laughter came. I felt otherworldly; then I felt alone. The feeling mirrored how the emotions I possessed when I awoke in the middle of the night from having a vision and didn't understand the troubles I saw.

Except right now, I was miserable and hurting in ways I hadn't shared, not even with Florentina.

"Abigail, I'm tired. We will survive this. Your instincts are good. Now go."

"My instincts? They are terrible. My helpful, horrid instincts saved my family from ruin but gave me a husband who wants me to be a harlot. What exactly in me is there to trust?"

Oh, Lord.

My heart stopped.

I couldn't breathe. I'd just spilled my secrets.

Turning, fleeing, wanting to run, I spun deeper into Stapleton's bedchamber.

Wrong way.

Not the path to escape.

I pivoted, ready to sidestep him, but he caught my hurt hand.

Gingerly, tentatively, Stapleton brought me to him. Face-to-face, a breath away, I felt the heat of him. Then I smelled coffee and soap.

"You have great instincts, Abigail. Wonderful instincts. But you're human. You can't control others. Their failing is not yours." He clasped both of my limp hands. "And I was wrong to doubt you. If you felt the need to solicit information about the lyric, then it was rightly done."

The embarrassment of blurting out my horrible truths started to melt. I was snow at the dawning of a new warm day.

Wetness.

Relief or frustration formed within me. Droplets fell from my eyes. "What do we do next?"

He let go of my hands, glanced at me for a moment, then took his thumbs and wiped my cheeks. "I used my best hand-kerchief on your wound. My fingers will have to do."

I should pull away.

This feel of roughness and years of living in the world on my skin—I shouldn't allow such liberties.

Yet, this was a liberty, an indulgence to a woman tangled in her emotions. I needed support from someone who understood betrayal and broken hopes.

"A-bi-gail." His voice lowered and became more serious. "We need to . . . I need . . ."

"To visit Mr. Brooks below, in the cold cellar, after you're done with the men's meeting. We need to see if his invitation has the curled piece of foolscap. I believe an error has occurred or Mr. Holston has read us a fake one."

After a light tap of his thumb to my nose, he retreated. "You're wanting to see if an error has occurred? You think precise Mr. Peters gave two men the same stanza from the rhyme?"

"We need to be sure. To take the next step of making a claim, of solving this mystery, we have to be sure." I stood straighter, stopping my body, my soul from further leaning into Stapleton's tenderness. "And giving two men the same threat doesn't make sense."

"You believe Brooks was meant to have the stanza of the poem about the slit wrist."

"It makes sense. That's how he died. The earl died from bees, as his stanza suggests. Peters from a leap. But if Brooks has another stanza of the rebel's poem, then he wasn't supposed to die as a part of the Night of Regrets. Someone other than the man who killed the Earl of Constock killed Benjamin Brooks."

"Then we have two killers." Stapleton walked to his window and pulled back the curtain. When he let it go, the sheer panel offered filtered gray light. "The snow is lessening. If the weather improves, we can get out of here tomorrow. Christmas Day."

"What about the mystery? Stapleton, we need to solve the mystery."

He tugged on his blousing shirt. "We have to stay alive to figure out anything."

He craned his neck to the ceiling. I wondered if he enjoyed the dentil molding circling this room, just as it did in my bedchamber. I hated admitting that I stared and counted those plaster indentions as others slept.

Sighing like a teapot, Stapleton came back to me. "Tonight, when all are back in their locked bedchambers, we'll go pay our respects to Mr. Brooks. Don't go without me, Abigail."

"I won't as long as you promise not to allow these men to compromise you. I know them to be horrible to women, horrible enough to harm Mrs. Flowers, even when pregnant. They'll have no mercy on you."

"Miscarriages happen. But strain can induce troubles at the most dangerous time a woman experiences."

"That's why a babe must be wanted, truly made from love. I know their obligation that heirs be birthed, but I still wish for love." Oh, Lord. How did we start talking about me again? "Sorry. But thank you for suggesting I talk with Lord Duncan. He loved his wife. He wanted their family."

A heavier sigh, almost a groan, came from his lips, but the fire in his irises burned. "Babbling again."

He offered a little bit of a dimple, then again became sullen. "I will be fine, but I need you to defeat your worst instincts and wait for me. Wait for me, Abigail."

For the smallest moment, I forgot we had spoken about going to see Brooks in the basement.

"Seriously, Abigail, don't have me searching for you or fretting over your well-being any more than I already do."

Unexpected moments between us felt scandalous, and like

the most normal thing in the world. My, how things had changed between us.

"But you *have* to drink with the men?"

"Of course. I doubt someone who drinks only tea or lemonade would be accepted. I'm sure Holston has a gut made of iron. He's the only one I believe to be a challenge."

Probably sensing my unease, he said, "I'm going to be safe. Now go. I need to sleep."

After returning me to his threshold, he opened his door and looked out in the corridor.

Looking left and right, he took a step outside his door. "All clear."

Stapleton took my arm and towed me gently but quickly into the corridor, before rapping on my bedchamber door. "Lady Worthing, wear a coat tonight. The cellar is extremely cold."

The sound of the lock sliding preceded Florentina opening the door. Her sleepy dark eyes looked relieved.

Stapleton released me to my cousin. "Dinner will be sent up here, but please stay alert. And if you hear anyone trying to harm me next door, you can come check on me. Bring a weapon."

Chuckling, he nodded, and then he returned to his room.

"Did you tell him what you needed to, Abbie?"

"Yes. After his time with the men, he and I will tour the cellar."

Panic was etched along her face. "To see the dead man that made you faint?"

"After Mr. Henderson has finished socializing with the gentlemen of Berkeley Square, we will go together. I won't go without him."

"That's something." She shook her head and then went back to bed.

Once I had locked the door, I sat at the desk and looked again at "The Rebel's Rhyme." It looked so odd on Mrs. Flowers's pink stationery. Then I did my own calculation, like my cousin had, trying to assess the possible number of killers. Fewer than two would be ideal, but somehow, I thought my murder math was wrong.

Lady Worthing's List

Accidental Death:	Anna Violet Flowers
Murdered:	Mr. Peters
Murdered:	Mr. Brooks
Murdered:	Lord Constock
Suspects:	Lord Duncan
	Mr. Holston
	Mr. Talson
	Mr. Mayer

Chapter 24

Abigail's Guest Bedchamber, Nine Berkeley Square

Miss Bellows's snores sounded quite far from the music of the theater. Lying on the chaise in my guest room, I wished to be there, not here in Berkeley Square.

The robe Florentina allowed me to wear while my stays and carriage dress dried by the heat of the fireplace felt silky. It smelled like lilacs. Must be one of her hand lotions.

This sweet scent was wrong for this house and this mystery. Powdery violets should be the fragrance. For me, Anna Violet Flowers's death, though accidental, needed to be reconsidered. It was a pivotal moment for Berkeley Square. If not for her death, there would be no Night of Regrets.

"Dinner was delicious. And I loved the quiet." Florentina stretched her arms. The big lacy sleeves of her cream robe flapped. "Didn't you prefer this over the dining room?"

"Yes," I said, and she dimpled at my admission.

The dinner sent up was white, white soup and white Cheshire cheese sauce with crusty toasted bread. The toast was brown. It was delicious.

It was enough for the three of us.

That was hours ago.

Miss Bellows didn't help out with the men-only dinner. I refused to let her go. After dinner, she spent her time making me and my only outfit look presentable.

The woman was dedicated. Though she didn't mind helping Mr. Villers, she didn't protest my decision. She was ready to be merely my personal maid and not a server, not anymore.

Yet as I thought of Mr. Peters and his lost dream of retiring and opening a warehouse for cravats, I wondered about her. Did Miss Jane Bellows have desires beyond the current life she was living?

I'd ask her if she wasn't snoring.

Lying on the chaise, I wove my fingers into an old crocheted blanket and waited to hear either a knock at my door or movement next door.

Stapleton hadn't returned yet. It had to be close to eleven at night. I wanted to check the cold cellar and be back in my bedchamber before Christmas. Probably wasn't a good idea to sneak around, looking for clues on Christmas.

"Abbie," Florentina said as she gently helped Miss Bellows turn onto her side. "I hear your brainbox working."

"Over the snores?"

"Someone should find sleep." Florentina fluffed her pillow. "Have you figured out the mystery?"

"Which mystery?"

"Pick one." She sat on the side of the bed, pulling on new stockings. I wore a pair of them, too. I was glad she liked the soft woolen ones so much. It was a good early gift. Probably the smartest thing I'd done in what felt like forever. "Abbie, who killed Mr. Brooks, Mr. Peters, or Lord Constock?"

"Mr. Peters's death is more concerning." I freed my hand

and rubbed at the tight bandage on my finger. "Miss Bellows saw him fall. She didn't see anyone around him. The amount of laudanum Stapleton thinks the valet consumed makes it impossible for me to believe . . . he just stood at the rail, having come from . . ."

"Come from where, Abbie?"

"Exactly. Come from where? The servants' quarters aren't on this level. They're upstairs, in the attic. So how did he come down to this level, unassisted?"

She shrugged and smoothed the linen on her side of the bed. "Differing feats of strength? Different types of willpower?"

"So he was a strong Blackamoor man. He survived enslavement in Martinique, escaped slavery in the American colonies, fought in the great revolt against our king, so naturally, completely soaked in laudanum, he drew on that inner strength to navigate one set of steps and then suddenly lost his balance in the right position at the top of the stairs and fell over the railing and onto the marble below? That seems like an awful coincidence."

"Yes. I suppose. And you do ramble when you are tired."

She'd heard my conversation with Stapleton? "Oh."

Florentina glanced at me. There was warmth and understanding in her dark eyes. My dream of having to choose between friends must've truly been a nightmare, not a vision, for I think she'd come to understand that I needed them both to make my world work.

She climbed gingerly onto the mattress, not disturbing Miss Bellows.

The woman kept snoring. I assumed it was appreciative whistles.

"Abbie," Florentina said. "She has the right idea. Sleeping. And Mr. Peters should've done just that, unless sleeping was the last thing on his mind."

Her words were right. At least they felt that way.

"He had the foolscap with a stanza from the rhyme on him. He's not a grand blanc. He would know that coming from Martinique. Yet, he had the curl of foolscap."

"But not an invitation." Flo drew her knees to her chest. "He orchestrated the Night of Regrets. Maybe adding 'The Rebel's Rhyme' was meant to be a last joke on the people at Berkeley Square. He was to retire."

The loss of his money to Mr. Mayer's investments would change those plans. "Would he confide in someone or keep all his plans close to his smartly cut waistcoat?"

"It was cravats, Abbie." She yawned. "What if he told someone and they used the knowledge to set up these murders? Wouldn't Mr. Peters get the blame?" My cousin lay back. "He'd have to fear this. The same worries I had when we discovered the rebel lyric. The people from the islands would get the blame."

"Learning how Mr. Brooks died might have caused Mr. Peters to change his plans or perhaps hasten them."

My cousin fluffed her pillow again. "That is a good theory but a hard one to prove. Brooks's killer or even Constock's won't admit to anything."

She was right.

Who would admit to anything that would incriminate them?

Proof of what had happened to Brooks had to be on his person, unless his killer had already removed it. I went to the window. The top of the bench was more visible now. The snow hadn't become deeper. Some may have melted.

Time was running out. Once we were freed from here, the killer would escape. Lord Duncan might be blamed for the murders. I still didn't know if he was completely innocent of all the deaths.

"Abbie, come away from there. You've barely slept on that chaise. Here, please take the bed. I insist."

Since I planned to be investigating with Stapleton soon, I

didn't need to be comfortable. Stretching out on the firm mattress would mean nothing more than counting the dentils that formed the crown molding from a different position. "No, Flo. I am not sleepy. I need to listen for my neighbor. And you know how I get when I'm puzzling out things."

"Yes, I do. But are you sure, Abbie?"

With a nod, I tried to reassure her. "Sleep now. You know once we get to Cheapside, none will be had."

She smiled at me, all while shaking her head. "Suit yourself. Try not to get killed. And one injury is enough."

Florentina yawned, then settled into the bedclothes.

I sank again onto the chaise and waited.

By the time Stapleton and I finished searching the makeshift morgue in the cold cellar, my restless mind should be ready to sink into darkness—no dreams, no tossing and turning, no fearing my future.

"Try to sleep until Mr. Henderson comes for you." Flo's voice was a whisper. Her tone wasn't accusatory, more matter of fact when she added, "I see why you've changed your mind about him. He's honorable and protective."

And here.

My opinion of Stapleton was not exactly changing, but perhaps it was deepening. Behind the gruff exterior, there seemed to be a sensitive bee-loving soul. He seemed genuinely in agony over bringing us here.

But none of this was his fault. It was mine, as I'd waited until the last moment to leave Westminster.

It was also James's.

And even a little bit of Dessalines's, for not figuring out how to stay alive and keep people like me more fretful about what the world thought of freedom and power for all.

"Get some rest, Abbie. Mr. Henderson is wily. He will be all right. How much trouble can the clever man get into with Lord Duncan and a group of men in the pink parlor?"

It did sound ridiculous.

Nonetheless, bad things happened when one's guard was lowered.

Florentina could find sleep. I wouldn't be at ease until Stapleton returned safely and we were on our way to visit the bodies in the cold cellar. I needed to know definitively who the first victim of the Night of Regrets was.

Chapter 25

Stapleton's Guest Bedchamber, Nine Berkeley Square

Sixty-four. Sixty-four dentils adorned the crown molding at the top of the wall along the right side of this guest chamber. My new habit continued to occupy me as I lay on the chaise, waiting for Stapleton.

Waves of sounds—loud cheers, discernible banter—floated up from the lower level. I could tell the men had left the dining room and had settled in the pink parlor.

It was surprising that Duncan would allow them into Anna Violet's sanctuary. Perhaps he was giving them one last moment to confess to all the things that had made his wife suffer.

Another roar. This was shouting.

Someone was upset or sotted and having a good time. Part of me wondered how they could with three men dead and the memory of Mrs. Flowers surrounding them.

* * *

Noises close by made me open my eyes.

Something bumped the wall.

I went to the closet, where my carriage dress and coat hung. The cranberry dress was pressed and perfect again. Every brass button trembled as I slipped into the dress.

Though it was thick, I didn't know if it was warm enough for the cold cellar. I took the coat and hung it over my arm. It felt heavy. A brass key was in the pocket. Why would I have another? The first, the one for this room was on the floor near the chaise.

Something bumped the wall again. A low curse followed.

I finished dressing, then sat down to pull on my boots. When I picked up the key on the floor, I noticed the one in my pocket was heavier.

Feeling them, I noted the notches weren't the same. Having studied the dentils, I considered myself an expert in such things. The heavier one was thicker, too. It had to be an exterior-door key.

Another angry comment sounded from next door. Neither Florentina nor Miss Bellows moved. I'd figure out the key later. It was time to get to Stapleton.

Coat in hand, I left the bedchamber. One look to the left and the right showed me that all was still and calm. After fumbling with the keys, I found the right one and locked the bedchamber. I went the three steps to Stapleton's door. Then I knocked.

"Hello? Are you well?"

No one answered my whisper.

In a little louder voice, I said, "Stapleton? I'm here."

No answer.

The upper landing bore a dying sconce. It was enough light to expose the empty hall below. The absence of footmen and maids gave me confidence. Under the circumstances, I could explain going to Stapleton's room if caught. And the gentlemen . . . would mock me, as they had Anna Violet.

These men were bigger gossips than any I had ever known.

Looking over the railing, I thought of going to see Brooks all by myself.

As if he'd heard my thoughts, Stapleton opened his door.

I eased to it and pressed inside. The door shut behind me.

My heart beat fast.

Panic set in. This was his room.

My inner Mrs. Smith sounded loud bells in my head. My housekeeper would rail at this impropriety, my second one for the day.

Something, someone barged past me.

A life, a ghost, a murderer. I screamed into my palm.

Perhaps this wasn't the time to redeem myself for being a coward and fainting in the park of Berkeley Square. I readied to flee.

A man sank onto the mattress in front of me. "Go away."

"Stapleton?"

A moan answered.

Deeper into the room, I felt the heat of his fireplace. After stepping closer to his window, I fingered the curtains. Through the locked panes, I saw the snow had stopped, so I searched for stars. I needed them to prove me wrong or show me that my friend wasn't wounded or dying.

The added light showed glossy ebony boots.

"Stapleton? Are you . . ."

The body lying on top of the sheets didn't move.

Scared for him, for me, forlorn about not arriving in time, I went a little closer. "Stapleton? It's me, Abigail."

Holding on to the footboard, I made my way to the side of the bed. "Stapleton. Please tell me you are well."

No answer. Not even another moan.

The man was a light sleeper. I knew this because in Westminster he'd slept on my couch to protect me from a villain.

Last night he lay on my floor, close to me, checking makeshift bandages and stitches to make sure my finger had stopped bleeding.

My worst fears had happened. He wasn't all right.

Squinting, I saw what had to be his head. With my thumb, I felt his nose for a breath.

After dropping my coat, I hunted along his neck for some sign that blood still pumped within his veins.

My bandage and his cravat prevented a decisive confirmation.

I crawled onto the mattress and shook him by the shoulders. He smelled of medicine and brandy. Something had happened to him while he was downstairs with the men.

"Please. Please wake up."

I hung over him. With my good hand, I felt his chest for wounds. I finally felt a heartbeat.

His eyes opened, and Stapleton grabbed me, wrestled me to the mattress.

"What the . . . Abigail?"

"Yes." I struggled to catch my breath. "I take it you're not dead."

Pinning me in place, he grunted, then flopped over, falling by my side. "No. Alive. Alive and stupid." He spoke like his mouth was full of rocks. "I'm not myself. For your own protection, go."

I wasn't budging. Wasn't going to abandon him when I knew he wasn't right.

Then his arms slipped about me, and I wasn't right.

This wasn't right at all.

In the light of the moon, we lay on the mattress. His head curled onto my shoulder. Then he began to snore.

This was not our bargain.

And if I was going to be caught in a compromising situation, it would be in the cold cellar with dead Mr. Brooks.

*   *   *

Stapleton's hold was slack. I could wrench free.

That would be the proper course of action, rather than inhaling the scent of the soap he'd used to wash his face, a soap that smelled of crisp pine and violets.

Then I smelled his breath. It was brandy and medicine and darkness.

"Stapleton, I need you to tell me you are fine."

He coughed but kept snoring.

Well, at least he was breathing, sort of.

The beating in his chest, in mine . . . The sound deafened.

Minutes turned to infinity. I had barely shared a bed with James. I wasn't about to stay on a mattress with my snoring neighbor.

Stapleton shot straight up. "What?"

"At least I know you're not dead."

He looked down at me and towed me so that I was sitting alongside him. "I could wish for it. Sorry, Abigail." His tone sounded remorseful and sickly. "Look into my eyes. Tell me what you see."

I took a second, weighing my options, hip to hip with him on his mattress.

Like he'd done, I placed a thumb on his cheek and coaxed his face to mine. "Your eyes look bloodshot."

"Look again, Abigail."

I pulled myself to my knees and crouched beside him. Angling his face toward the window, I gently turned the chiseled jaw. His striking indigo pupils possessed gold halos. "There looks to be a ring are around your irises. It looks yellow . . . no, gold."

He flattened my palm against his flushed face and cursed. "Belladonna, Abigail. Someone tampered with my glass."

"What's that? Is it poison? Are you going to die?"

"We'll all die someday. But I have too much to live for, experiences I've never had." He coughed. "Can't believe I let a fool drug me."

"Which fool did this?"

"An old one, to be a menace. To make me sick enough to incapacitate me. Or to make me more talkative. Legend has it that belladonna is a serum for truth."

Under its influence, he'd tell me anything? "Is it truly a truth if one is forced to admit it?"

"A thing can be true *and* forced." Yawning, he rubbed his eyes. "Holston and Talson like to play jokes."

He groaned, fell back on the mattress, and tucked my palm, my arm about him like a blanket.

"Wake up, Stapleton. I don't think you should sleep. What if it's not Belladonna but something lethal?"

He mumbled something. Then his voice became clear. "The patient should be made to captain."

Then walking was what he needed to do. "Come on. Get up. Let's get you moving. That way I'll know you're fine."

I got him to sit up again, with his head falling on my shoulder, and then I tried to get him to stand.

He didn't budge but said, "You really care if I live or die?"

"Of course I do. Now, let's get up and walk."

"For you, Abigail, I live."

Not sure he meant to say that, but I understood. He'd try for our friendship. That would make me smile, the first opportunity we were all safe and I didn't fear being killed.

It took a little tugging, a little more cajoling, but Stapleton stood.

"I did it. I stood. Hmm. Could've been Mayer. Kept asking money questions. My father left me a lot of money, dirty money. I'm making it clean and protecting Mary."

Stapleton swayed, and I grabbed him and kept him upright. The distant look in his eyes faded. Indigo and gold shone brightly. "You do truly care for me? Not just my dogs. Talson said so. But I pretended not to believe him."

"The old man is looking for gossip."

"Is it gossip if it's true, Abigail?" He softly brushed the tip of my nose. "That you care for me as I care for you?"

With my arms about him, his torso pressed to my bosom and drumming heart, I surely gave every impression of a woman who did. "Let's walk a bit, Stapleton. I won't leave you until I know all is well."

"Then don't leave me, Abigail, Abbie girl. Stay for me."

Intoxicated sweetness was still sweet . . . right? I shook my head. "Let's walk, Stapleton."

With a nod, he started walking from the bed to the window and back.

His shirt was extra wrinkled, and an exposed sleeve near his waistcoat was torn.

"Have you been fighting?"

He paused, took a misstep, and offered me a befuddled look. "Maybe. Maybe, Abigail."

"Think, Stapleton. What have you done? What do we have to explain?"

He lowered his head to my shoulder. "I don't know. Too many drinks to remember."

That wasn't an answer. Was he being set up as the next victim?

> *Trapped, two little Grand-blancs sitting in the sun.*
> *One got very warm, and then there was one.*

That was his stanza from "The Rebel's Rhyme." There was no sun, but Stapleton's breath could ignite the house.

"We will beat this. Walk with me, Stapleton."

Back and forth we went—we did this action at least twenty times, walking from the window to the bed, then back to the window.

"I'm going to be fine. I just need to sleep."

Stapleton seemed better. Perhaps I could leave him for just a few minutes.

Then I thought better of it. "Let me take you next door. You will stay with Miss Sewell and Miss Bellows while I head to the cellar."

Yes, that was the new plan. I could lock them all inside while I investigated.

"I can do this quickly and be safe," I added. Ignoring him, I put on my coat. Stapleton followed me and adjusted my lapels.

"No. No. No. Brooks won't see you. He's dead," he murmured.

"Can you watch Florentina? Make sure she . . . everyone stays asleep—"

"Not Brooks, Abigail. He's dead."

He wasn't listening, or he was too inebriated to understand. I tried one more time by massaging his red, red cheeks. "I can get down there and look around and get back before anyone notices."

"I notice. I notice everything about you."

He took up his tailcoat and struggled to get it on. I helped him before he made more noise.

"Abigail, wait." He wobbled to his closet. The light from the window barely reached it. He was shrouded in darkness, mumbling about noticing things.

When he emerged, he had on his outer greatcoat, hat, and gloves. "Everything about you."

He seemed more alert when he came toward me and lifted an arm for me to clasp.

"We go together. There are men in this house who don't care for you." Stapleton counted on his fingers. "One. Two. Four. Three. A couple. There's no way I'm going to let you go anywhere near danger."

My neighbor, my friend, held his arm out again.

Us walking hand in hand. Wasn't that our mark, the symbol of quietly going together?

Though a wobbly man would slow me down, one freely wandering the corridors and perhaps falling over the railing wouldn't be what I wanted. I took his arm.

After closing his door, we started out just fine. Then we reached to the stairs. Boy, we looked high up.

"Lean on me," I said, "And let's go."

He grabbed me about my waist, and we started down the stairs.

A little tap, a tiny slap at his hands kept them from wandering. Convinced that his condition made him like this, I kept us going all the way to the bottom of the staircase.

When he spun me like we were dancing a reel across the marble that had claimed Mr. Peters, I began to question my choices.

And I also wondered what song the master pianist played in his head.

There had to be a tune.

He put a finger to his mouth and pointed to the light coming from the pink parlor.

Lord Duncan had returned. When would his mourning ease? He was newly married. And a stepfather to young children.

"To the basement. That's our objective, Abigail."

Down the corridor, we went. It was freezing. The door to the orangery was open.

Stapleton stopped, looked inside. "Well, Constock's still there. Wonder who has come this way?"

We started moving.

"Probably Talson. Duncan teased him too much. He left early, but he'll come back. Maybe it was Mayer. He was anxious about some legal papers." Stapleton's memory of the night had started to return. This was good.

"What about the financier, Mr. Mayer? Has he found widows to cheat?" I asked.

"Having lost his biggest client, Constock, he seemed to want to talk to the newly widowed countess. Talson had a big problem with that." Stapleton stopped. He scratched his chin. "Or maybe it was the paperwork she left with Brooks."

Brooks.

My hand fingered the key in my pocket. The big, bulky key. "And what was Holston doing this entire time? Sulking for being ignored?"

Right at the cellar door, Stapleton stopped again. "We argued. He said something about Nelson."

It wasn't my imagination, the evil grin crossing his face.

"Then he was quiet. Then he was gone," Stapleton added.

Gone? As in not accounted for?

My heart pattered, surely doing a faster, up-tempo version of the marble reel.

He grabbed the candle from the sconce. It made my pulse jitter more when I thought about "The Rebel's Rhyme."

"Shall we go, dearest Abigail?"

Nodding, praying, I followed him down the steps. The temperature in the cellar felt colder than ice.

Stapleton slapped at his cheeks. He looked down at me and pulled me closer. "So cold. The open orangery has made this an ice cave. We won't be able to stay long."

I had no intention of staying any longer than necessary.

With the candle in his hand, guiding us, I watched our shadows and hunted for anyone that moved.

By the time we reached the last step, I almost shouted with joy. No one had fallen or become injured or set a cloak on fire.

"Well, Stapleton, where is Brooks?"

Holding our light high, he swung his arm to the left. The brightness on his face showed his countenance shift from blank to lips pursed with concern. He took a step and waved the candle more.

"Stapleton, did you forget where you placed him? Is this

place deeper, like where you keep your wine bottles back in Westminster?"

"No," he said, then paused, delaying.

"Stapleton, you said we have to hurry. Then I'll get you upstairs and watch you sleep off whatever foul thing they gave you." I shook his arm.

"I know exactly where Benjamin Brooks is. He's over there, next to Mr. Peters and Mr. Holston."

He said these words so calmly and sounded so sober, I thought it was a jest. But that wasn't the kind of man Stapleton was. He'd not make jokes about life and death.

I grabbed the candle and aimed it to the left. The light landed on bare feet pointing up between two sheet-draped lumps.

The snide retired military man lay on the cold-cellar floor, between the bodies of Mr. Brooks and Mr. Peters.

Lady Worthing's List

Accidental Death: Anna Violet Flowers
Suspicious Death: Mr. Peters
Attacked: Mr. Holston
Murdered: Mr. Brooks
Murdered: Lord Constock
Suspects: Lord Duncan
Mr. Holston
Mr. Talson
Mr. Mayer

Chapter 26

The Cold Cellar, Nine Berkeley Square

Stapleton separated from me and moved closer to the bodies lying on the cold cellar floor. "This makes no sense. How did he get here?"

"Doesn't matter now. Is he alive, Stapleton?"

My neighbor sank to his knees. "I was sure he was behind everything, Abigail. Hold the candle over me and keep it steady."

Steady? How? My hand shook from the cold and shock. "This murder is in line with the stanza I thought the man had. 'Scared, five little Grand-blancs huddle and keep score. One gets cold. Then there were four.'"

"True, Abigail, if he were dead. There's a pulse."

Alive?

Blinking, like this was a bad dream, I tried to hold the light still.

"We have to get him warm and out of here. Then I'll try to

rouse him." Stapleton took off his coat and laid it on the man. "We've come in time."

I looked around, trying to spot a characteristic red pool. "At least he's not bleeding."

"No. But exposure can kill just as quickly. Snow doesn't have to be piled on him for him to freeze to death. That door to the orangery was left open to ensure a quicker death."

Stapleton blew on the man's hands, but he was cold, too. If my friend stayed down here too long, with whatever drug he'd ingested, who knew how it would affect his health.

After setting down the candle, I joined him. We worked together, rubbing Holston's arms and legs to get his blood circulating.

"I would have run if I'd come alone. That would have doomed this man, denied him any chance of living," I said.

Holston awoke, gasping. "You." He pointed a shivering hand at Stapleton. "You came back to finish me."

"I did nothing of the sort, you blithering fool."

The shivering man turned to me. "Lady Worthing, he did it. He hit me in the pink parlor. Then he jumped me from behind later, all because I called Nelson a coward, a fame-hungry fool."

Yep. That would get Commander Stapleton Henderson to attack.

My neighbor, my friend, clasped my hand. "Abigail, I didn't, but if he keeps saying terrible things about Admiral Nelson, I say we leave him here."

"Stapleton, let's get him out of here. We can settle this where it's warm."

Stapleton groaned, then helped the man sit up.

"I can't feel my feet." Holston couldn't stand. "It's cold, too cold."

He began to cough. "I came down to pay my respects. That's

the one thing Henderson reminded me about. But it was a trick to lure me here and leave me for dead."

"What was the argument about?" I asked. Leaning in a little closer, I noticed the sheet on Brooks looked like it had been disturbed. It was missing the perfect tucks that aligned the sheet covering Mr. Peters.

"Nothing." Stapleton's brusque response blended with Holston's cry of "The military."

After releasing a groan, Stapleton said, "Individuals always want to know about Nelson's last hours. It disgusts me to invade my admiral's last moments."

"As one of the three men who served and lived, I wanted to know." Holston began to cough. His lungs sounded ragged.

"We have to get you out of here." Stapleton pulled his coat tighter about the cold man. "You think you can walk? Your toes look bad."

"Valley Forge. Nearly froze everything working on the assault under General Wilhelm von Knyphausen." He coughed but for the first time drew his hands together. "Peters. That's when his gout first came."

Two soldiers who had served together. Of course. Mr. Holston had a long history with the valet.

"You came down here to say goodbye to him," I said.

"Yes. Henderson here reminded me of my duty as a man who wore the uniform." Holston tried to stand but failed. "Thought better of you, until you made good on your threat. Sailor!"

"For the last time, I did not attack you." Stapleton got behind him. "Get ready. Try to hold your weight."

They struggled, but Holston couldn't get up.

"Abigail, if you need to say your respects to anyone, do it now."

Stapleton's warning echoed throughout the space. "No one but the coroner will return to this place."

"No, Mr. Henderson. I've seen enough."

I was done here.

Whether Mr. Brooks had an invitation on him or not, it didn't matter. The person who attacked Holston had more than likely tampered with everything, setting all these events into motion. Then this person had ruthlessly used a soldier's regard for a fallen comrade as a way to cast guilt on someone else.

Stapleton wrapped his arms about the man's chest.

"Sir, you'll hurt yourself trying to aid Mr. Holston," I warned.

"A sailor must try. For king and country." Stapleton grunted. Strain was written on his face, but he hauled the hurt gentleman upright. Though he was successful, I doubted that he could manage to carry the man up the stairs, even if I helped.

"Holston," he said, "Lady Worthing's injured. It's just you and me. Two military officers. We need to take the hill. It's going to be difficult, but I'm going to need you to do as much as you can to stay upright."

"Wait." Holston took a big breath. "We argued. You made threats. You snuck up and hit me. How do I know you'll not toss me over the side like Peters?"

"If I had attacked you, you wouldn't have woken up." Stapleton's tone was matter of fact, and he put a hand to Holston's throat. "I'd have punched you right here. Your crushed windpipe would have been all the damage I required."

The fiery rage in his voice made me believe every single word.

"I'm going to move you about, Holston. We need to keep your blood moving." Stapleton pointed to the steps. "Abigail, go get Duncan. He's in the pink parlor. He's always there, especially at midnight."

"Midnight? It's Christmas." My first Yuletide as Lady Worthing away from Westminster, and I was in a cold cellar, freezing with Stapleton, Mr. Holston, and two dead bodies.

"Go now. Scream if you need me, but Holston is fevered. He's not out of danger."

I dashed up the stairs and ran to the pink parlor to herald the news of another attack.

Chapter 27

December 25, 1806
The Landing, Nine Berkeley Square

I followed Lord Duncan and Stapleton as they carried Mr. Holston up the steps to the landing. The three struggled. The former military man's weight challenged Lord Duncan and Stapleton. At times, the way they swayed, I thought all three of them would topple over the stair railing and take a leap like Mr. Peters.

Out of breath, chest heaving, Lord Duncan said, "Mr. Holston's room is down the corridor."

"No, we'll take him to my room," Stapleton said. "That way Lady Worthing, Miss Sewell, Miss Bellows, and I can take turns watching over him."

There wasn't much debate. The men started moving toward Stapleton's room.

Three feet from Stapleton's door, I waited for Stapleton to give me his key, but the door was wide open. Immediately, I clasped his shoulder. "Your door was closed. I closed it."

Groaning, Stapleton lowered his end of Holston, putting the semiconscious man on the carpet runner. He went inside the room.

Peeking in, I saw him do the check that he had done in my room, peering under the bed, punching into the closet.

"No one is here. Maybe it just rattled open. The window's open," he announced.

Though I didn't remember if the window had been open or closed, I was about to accept his wind theory. Then I turned and saw that the sliding lock mechanism on his door had been changed. Silver wire was attached to it.

"Don't touch, Abigail."

"What the devil is going on?" Duncan set Holston's legs down, placing him fully on the floor.

We traced the wire, which led out of the room.

Stapleton pulled it. The lock engaged and stuck in place. "Someone wants me locked inside this room."

Very carefully, he dislodged the razor-sharp wire and tossed it into his fireplace.

"'The Rebel's Rhyme,' I said. "'Trapped, two little Grand-blancs sitting in the sun. One got very warm, and then there was one.'"

Leaving Holston to fend for himself in the corridor, Lord Duncan joined Stapleton and me, and we began searching the room.

"This is too much," the magistrate said.

"You knew nothing of the rhyme?" I asked. "Or what Mr. Peters planned?"

"Nothing at all," Duncan said as he checked the closet. "I always let him handle the details of the Night of Regrets."

A gasp. "What is going on? Abbie?" Florentina's voice echoed.

I went out of the room, clapped my fully dressed cousin's mouth, and dragged her inside Stapleton's bedchamber. Fiorentina looked scared.

When I released her, she said, "You are safe too, Mr. Henderson. But what is that? Mr. Holston? Not another one!"

Gripping her by the shoulders, I gave her a little shake and then a hug. "Florentina, what have you heard since I left? Were you alert when someone came into this room?"

"Not much. Some noise. Then I got dressed. Wait, Lord Duncan's in here too? Abbie, what's going on?"

My cousin didn't hear anything and the killer was here. I blew out a breath. "Danger was right here, next to our room. I left you and Miss Bellows unprotected."

She took my bandaged hand and pulled it to her heart. "I'm fine, Abbie. Miss Bellows is, too. She's dressing. I think we have bigger worries for Mr. Henderson. The killer came for him."

Duncan closed the window. "It's cold in here. Let's get the fire going and bring Holston inside."

"A fire. 'Trapped, two little Grand-blancs sitting in the sun. One got very warm, and then there was one.' No, wait, Lord Duncan."

Stapleton looked at me, and as if he'd read my mind, he went to the fireplace. Sticking his hand inside, he soon pulled out a sooty blanket. "This was wedged up the chimney. It would've caused smoke to fill the room."

"But the blanket would've burned," Florentina said. She stooped close to a bucket of firewood.

"Lord Duncan, do you use coal or wood to heat your rooms?" I asked. "I saw coal in the pink parlor and in our room, but maybe this room is special. The pink parlor is the only room with beeswax candles."

"That's Anna's light. She loved those candles. But coal is used for all the rooms, I think. Mr. Villers would know. My housekeeper and butler are in the country with Lady Duncan."

Stapleton picked up a log. It wet his hands. "This would've smoked for sure. Like with the attack on Holston, I might not have died, but breathing in smoke or whatever these logs are soaked in could be deadly."

Gaping, I turned from him. The fear in my heart couldn't be shared. "Our visit to Mr. Brooks may have saved two lives."

With a hand on my arm, Stapleton sighed. "You have my thanks again, Lady Worthing. Since we do not know if there are more traps in here, let's move Holston to your room. I'm sure your room hasn't been targeted. Miss Sewell would have told us."

Florentina nodded as Stapleton and Duncan went into the corridor to the hurt military man.

"He did it!" Holston pointed at Stapleton.

"Who, man? Who?" Duncan grabbed the man's lapels. "Holston, tell us."

The freezing man's head fell back. Again, he lay there unconscious.

I sent Flo back to alert Miss Bellows. Our room needed to be made ready to save a man who could wrongfully implicate Stapleton in a near-fatal attack.

My bedchamber felt like an oven. Sitting at the edge of the chaise, I watched Stapleton stoke our safe fireplace.

Lord Duncan stood in the corner near our closet. "I can't believe any of this."

"What's not to believe, sir?" I pointed to the man burning with fever behind me. "Mr. Holston's been attacked, left for dead in the cellar. Mr. Henderson's room was tampered with."

Miss Bellows held the blanket, dirty with soot or ash or whatever was in the chimney. "There's no hope of saving this. Shameful, as it's thick. But someone in this house is trying to make Mr. Henderson's stanza from 'The Rebel's Rhyme' come true."

Trapped, two little Grand-blancs sitting in the sun. One got very warm, and then there was one.

"Who's left, Abbie?" Fiorentina paced. "I mean, Holston doesn't look well. I'm afraid to find Talson or Mr. Mayer. Oh, I hope it's not Mr. Villers. No one who can make a Cheshire cheese like that can be evil."

"He's a nice man. I know Mr. Villers isn't responsible," I replied.

"We should round up everyone," Duncan said.

"And do what? Give them a chance to change their stories? Then blame could easily be foisted on you, sir, or even on Mr. Henderson," I said.

"I cannot sit still." Duncan tore from the room.

When I started to go after him, Stapleton stopped me. "Let him go. You know where he is heading."

The pink parlor.

Florentina closed the door. She fiddled with the lock, but all I could think of was how someone had tried to sabotage Stapleton's lock.

Florentina hummed carols as she and my maid went to the kitchen. We'd decided to pretend that nothing had happened other than Holston being accidentally locked in the cold cellar.

The killer knew the truth, but we doubted he'd risk discovery, not with the snow beginning to recede.

The fire roared in my bedchamber, offering sparks and light. Stapleton tossed coals into the fireplace. He looked sleep deprived and angrier than I'd ever seen him.

I touched his shoulder. "Miss Bellows and I have brought every free blanket, even the linens."

"It might not be enough to get the fool warm."

"Stapleton, you're doing the best that you can. If Mr. Holston survives or if he doesn't, it has nothing to do with you, and everything to do with the person who tried to kill him."

"You heard him, Abigail. He thinks I attacked him. He thinks I left him in the cellar to die."

"But you didn't."

"I could've struck him." He put his hand to his temple, as if he could rub the answers out of his skull.

"You honestly don't remember what happened? Is that why you're trying so hard right now? You've gathered every bucket of expendable coal and tossed it into the flames. There's nothing more you can do."

He stood up straight. "I do have a temper, Abigail."

"No, you don't. You are levelheaded. You think, then act. If you'd planned to harm Mr. Holston, you would have done it. And I doubt there'd be a way to save him."

"But a man under the influence of belladonna could be tempted or made to do something. He disparaged you. He called you names, implied there was something untoward between us."

I put my hand on his neck. He stiffened, as if I were about to slap him.

Strengthening my hold, I let my palm sink into his tight muscles. "As long as we are friends, we will be friendly. We will act like we care about one another. I'm not afraid of these questions."

He reached over to embrace me but made it quick. Then he went back to stoking the flames.

In that motion, I witnessed something, a vision. I was on the deck of a ship. Cannons fired all around me. Then I saw Stapleton in full military regalia and a brilliant indigo jacket. His countenance burned with horror.

"Abigail. Abigail."

In his arms again, I shuddered.

"The cold, is it getting to you? Is your hand bleeding? Abigail, say something to me."

"Not your fault."

"It is. I let you tug on that silver wire. I saw it. I should've known it was razor sharp."

Putting my injured palm to his arm, I said it again, but clearer. "It's not your fault. You didn't see the shot fired at Nelson. Not your fault."

"There are the things we tell ourselves. Then there are things others say. Holston is one of Nelson's critics."

"Admiral Nelson is a hero to everyone with sense. You cannot be upset by what one man says or thinks."

"No. But he hints at the truth that haunts me. Four inches separated me from dying and Nelson from living. My fault. Distracted."

My godfather had let me see the notes on Stapleton Henderson's service. I'd seen his commendations, his ribbons and medals for valor. He was a brave, intelligent officer. Nonetheless, I'd read the officers' reports of the day Admiral Nelson died. Stapleton was central to the battle and one of the key men who was there when Nelson drew his last breath.

When Stapleton glanced at me this time, the truth, his truth, was etched in his haunted eyes.

"You knew who would be attending Lord Duncan's Night of Regrets. You were aware that Mr. Holston would be here. It wasn't 'The Rebel's Rhyme' or your father. It was Nelson and the guilt you bear."

Lids lowering, eyes roaming back to the fire, Stapleton nodded.

It had been a long time since I'd had a vision, particularly of something important. Fretting over James, politics, or even what my future held had blocked my gift.

My failings could harm a friend. That was unacceptable.

"Abigail, I don't know if I hit Holston, but I was angry enough to do so."

"If you did, and that is a big if, you wouldn't have dragged him into the cellar, openedl the door to the orangery to let him freeze to death. You would've just killed him."

He bit his lip for a moment. "Then, of course, I'd have told you and dared you to prove it. I think that was our original agreement when we first worked together to solve a murder."

"Working together." His face eased. Then Stapleton walked to the bed and felt Holston's sweating forehead. "His lungs are congested. His fever is high. He may not make it."

"Brooks, leave Anna Violet. Talson, tell him to do it." Holston had begun mumbling again. This was the third time he'd mentioned Duncan's wife.

"Stapleton, you mentioned Talson was upset about documents," I said.

He put both his thumbs to his forehead. "Lots of conversations about Brooks. Something about Constock's countess giving the barrister papers."

As he stared at the fireplace, I thought Stapleton had a vision.

"What is it? What do you remember?"

"In the pink parlor, Talson—He was unusually quiet, but then he perked up. I think he congratulated Mr. Mayer."

"That's odd. One, for the gossip to be quiet, and two, for him to congratulate a man whose business may go under because of the loss of his best client."

"It sounded like some other type of win. Maybe a legal one." Stapleton moved back to the fireplace. He pulled an iron out that he'd used to warm the sheets. "Could have used this before." He shoved it back inside the fireplace.

"Stop tormenting Flowers. Talson, tell Brooks to stop," Holston mumbled.

Lord Duncan came into the bedchamber. "Mr. Talson's ready to leave. He doesn't want to sit around and be killed."

The magistrate walked to the bed. He seemed anguished. This wasn't the face he had had with Brooks's or Constock's deaths.

"Mr. Henderson, will he recover?" Duncan asked.

"His fever is high. If it breaks . . . when it breaks, then we will know."

Duncan folded his arms about his robe. He still hadn't dressed. "He was the only one to show my wife kindness."

"We surely found him in the nick of time," I said.

"Oh, yes, Lady Worthing." Stapleton went back to stoking the fire for the hundredth time.

I went closer to Lord Duncan. "You started your Night of Regrets for a bunch of men you couldn't stand. Was it worth it?"

The magistrate turned away, looked at the blue walls. "Brooks is dead. Constock too. I'm sure they tormented Anna Violet. Maybe this does even out things."

Rubbing my hands together, I tried to ignore what sounded like a confession. "Sir, why don't you go get dressed? Refresh yourself, and then return."

Duncan's brow rose, and his countenance appeared pained. "I guess that sounds about right."

He patted Holston's arm. "Come on, you old trooper."

If the old soldier died, his confusion about Stapleton went, too. That was definitely a new thing for me to root for, death. No, I needed to figure things out to prevent my friend from being unnecessarily harassed. And to save the last man.

> *Guilty, one little grand blanc left all alone. Closed*
> *his eyes forever. And there were none.*

"I will leave you all," Duncan said at the threshold. "I will start my day." He sounded so sad and broken. "It's not the same without Peters."

As soon as Duncan left, I put on my coat again and gathered Florentina's, too.

"Lady Worthing," Stapleton said, "where are you going?"

"I think I need some air on this Christmas morning."

Stapleton narrowed his eyes. He shook his head and mouthed, "No."

The man knew me well. He surely suspected my getting air meant I had a plan to solve the mystery.

"Miss Bellows is with the chef. I will send them both to you. Then maybe you can rest." I walked to the door.

Stapleton beat me to it and held it open. "Please don't make any rash decisions. I can't come save you this time."

Staring at him, I told him the truth. "You saved Holston's life. I must save yours and Lord Duncan's. Nothing will be the same if the killers aren't caught."

"Killers, Abigail?"

"Yes. The power of getting away with hurting and killing must be stopped. Holston is innocent. He was attacked while honoring a friend. His would-be killer meant to frame you. Then your demise was initiated to make you take the blame for it all."

Swiping his sweating brow, he motioned for me to stay. "I'm alive. They failed."

"They'll kill your reputation. 'The mad commander who let Nelson die lost his way and killed several alleged leaders'— that's what they'll say. I don't think they wanted to trap you, but with Peters's death, they needed a new plan. Framing you is it. And the gossip and innuendo will stick."

"Abigail, no. It's too dangerous."

"This isn't just for you. Your sister, Mary, needs you strong to help her. And Duncan, the man who created the Night of Regrets, is racked with guilt. The wrong person being blamed or convicted will destroy him."

As I stepped into the corridor, I could see that Stapleton wished to waylay me but was holding himself back. "You heal Holston, Stapleton. That's what you do. I'm going to do what I do best."

By my insisting that I go, by my brooking no interference from him, I undermined his privilege of granting a woman consent. Men begrudgingly allowed a woman to own her power.

256200

264   *Vanessa Riley*

Though he was a different kind of person, protective and honorable and fearless, he knew letting me go was for the best.

It was time for Lady Worthing to act. I had had the key to the mystery all along.

Lady Worthing's List

Accidental Death: Anna Violet Flowers
Suspicious Death: Mr. Peters
Attacked: Mr. Holston
Attacked: Mr. Henderson
Murdered: Mr. Brooks
Murdered: Lord Constock
Suspects: Lord Duncan
~~Mr. Holston~~
Mr. Talson
Mr. Mayer

Chapter 28

The Orangery, Nine Berkeley Square

Buttoned up in our coats and pairs of Mr. Peters's boots, Florentina and I slipped out of the house through the orangery.

We tried to be discreet, but I had a feeling that someone saw.

It didn't matter.

If it took trudging across the snow and ice to find the missing clues to solve the murders, so be it.

Florentina yawned and beat her hands together. "You couldn't steal gloves, too, thicker ones?"

Our calf gloves were pretty but not suitable for being outside in the howling wind.

Brrr.

"Straight through the woods. If we hurry, we won't be outside for long." My tone sounded confident. But I wasn't. I was cold and was hoping that Benjamin Brooks had the answer to why so many had to die.

Snowflakes floated in the air. They weren't from freshly falling snow, but from the powder blowing off the trees. It was fitting. Powder. Violets. Anna Violet should lead the way.

The ground beneath us felt solid. No tracks would be left to attract more attention or to be seen from the window of the pink parlor.

"Did you hear something, Abbie?"

What was there to hear?

My ears were numb. The frilly bonnet did a poor job of protecting me. I supposed it wasn't designed to endure winter's frost outside of a carriage.

We'd been in the cold, making our way around Duncan's house for about twenty minutes. I didn't realize the orangery was at the back of the house. The magistrate had a very large property.

When we crossed the drive, I wanted to rejoice and decided we'd return through the front door. A quick look back showed me the big window of the pink parlor. Candles and emerald fir branches lined its sill.

Overhead, I located our bedchamber, and I prayed that Stapleton was at the fireplace, not looking out at us.

When Florentina and I approached the bench where I had found Mr. Brooks, I slowed. My hands felt cold and sticky. "The killing was brutal. It was intentional."

"Come on, Abbie. We have to keep going."

Florentina was right. Standing around in the cold meant getting sick or caught before we completed this mission.

"Forward," I said. "We must get to the houses on the other side of the square."

Halfway into the park, we trudged beneath tree boughs. The

gray light of the day danced on crystalline icicles. It would be beautiful if I didn't feel scared, if I didn't believe we were being followed.

The wind whipped up flakes. Snow crunched under our feet.

Each gasp of the wind made these borrowed boots feel like slippers.

"Abbie, did you hear something?"

My heart drumming. My teeth shivering. My good sense leaving.

"The plane trees, Flo. They are shifting in the wind. Ice is cracking. Don't pay attention to any of it. Mr. Brooks's house is straight ahead."

"Talson's is on the far corner," she said. "I don't know where Mr. Mayer's lives."

"Holston's is on this corner near Lord Duncan's. It's a shame we know where these men live. I doubt we'd ever be invited or that it would be wise to attend, since one of them is a killer. Could be more."

"Mr. Mayer talked about visiting Cheapside. He's intrigued with my mother's black cake."

My face was frozen. My smile was in place. "It's Christmas Day. Wilson Shaw has eaten it all if he made it to your parents' house. If Mr. Mayer is not in jail, he can come next year."

"Oh, you found your sense of humor." Florentina stumbled a little. A downed branch from the storm had been covered up, and it made the ground uneven.

"Let's move together." I locked arms with her. We moved as one.

Snap.

I looked over my shoulder and saw nothing.

The killer or killers had to know we were missing. If they thought that two women couldn't figure things out, we were probably safe. Yay for misogyny.

The trees, dressed in white, dripping with ice, looked like ghosts. The quiet, broken only by the sound of our footfalls, made me walk faster.

"Brooks's house number is Thirty-Seven." I pointed at the house visible in front of us through the trees. "It's directly across the square from Lord Duncan's."

The townhome was dark. It seemed completely evacuated. The entire row of town houses was dark except for one room at Mr. Talson's.

Did he keep a servant through the holidays? Or had he left, like he'd told Duncan he would?

"Suppose word has spread that the master of the house is dead?" Florentina asked. "Or did Mr. Brooks decently let his staff leave for the holidays?"

I shrugged. I honestly didn't know. "We've heard nothing good about this man. Of course, it could all be lies. I don't dismiss anything when it comes to male gossipers."

The steps in front of Brooks's had iced over. Grateful for the traction that Mr. Peters's boots offered, Florentina and I climbed all the way to the top.

After knocking hard with the brass knocker, I waited.

No footman ran out.

No doors opened.

Brooks's servants were gone.

"Well, that is that, Abbie. I know you are not going to—"

My pulling the heavy brass key from my pocket made her quiet. When it went easily into the lock and I opened the door, I thought she might faint.

"Hurry in, Flo."

"How did you . . . ? Oh, don't tell me you took it from the body."

"No, Florentina, I didn't. I found it under the bench where Brooks died. I must've grabbed it up before I fainted. It's been in my coat the whole time."

"Well, that's good," she said. "No need to find a rock and a side window."

Feet pounding the marble, we discovered the exact layout as Lord Duncan's house—same stairs, same wide grand hall with two rooms on either side. "Another Inigo Jones creation," I observed.

"I overheard Mr. Peters in the kitchen telling the chef about Brooks. He said Mr. Brooks was a tidy man who kept everything in his study. That was before the valet's mood changed." Florentina cupped a hand to her eyes. "What room would that be? We don't have time to search every one. And that wouldn't feel right. The man is dead. You have a stolen key."

"I *found* the key. And nothing is right about this square." Nothing was right about a rivalry that had cost Brooks his life and an innocent woman and child theirs. "As I said, this is another Inigo Jones creation. You think he'd take one of the grand bedrooms upstairs to make his study? I think it would have to be something to stir envy."

"Quite so, Abbie."

One glance into each other's countenance had us screaming together, "The pink parlor."

We crossed through the grand hall and dashed into the room that was the same as Anna Violet Flowers's parlor.

Once inside, I found a sconce and took its candle and lit it. A huge shelving unit partially blocked the entry. "Guess Mr. Brooks wanted more privacy."

We went deeper into the room toward the duplicate of the window where Duncan stood guard. To the side was a picture of Anna Violet Flowers in the nude.

Fiorentina gasped. Then she shook her head. "Guess we know why Mr. Brooks wanted privacy."

The wife that Lord Duncan adored, her picture the same

pose as in the portrait in his dining room, hung here, but not a strip of linen or velvet shrouded her.

"I think that is Mrs. Flowers's face, but some artist imagined the body. I believe this was part of the rivalry between Brooks and Lord Duncan," I said.

She shook her head. "It's very cruel to have this, unless Duncan's wife truly had an affair with the barrister."

That would be a horrible discovery, especially since I believed that was why Benjamin Brooks was killed.

"Well, it's not pink." Florentina went toward a desk.

My teeth chattered less as I noted the white dentil molding and the very white walls.

"Even if Brooks was perverted and was a horrible human being, he didn't deserve to be murdered. The killer or conspirators are trying to draw Mr. Henderson into this dark web. That shall not be borne out."

"You can't have that. Can you, Abbie? Then he wouldn't be in your web."

Shooting her stinging glances, I approached the desk she'd begun to search. It was disorderly. Nothing like the way Mr. Peters had described. "Has someone already searched this desk?"

She lifted her shoulders, then started looking at documents. "Do you know what we are looking for?"

"We'll know it when we find it." I pulled open a drawer, cluttered with pieces of foolscap and stationery. "This disarray would drive my neighbor crazy."

"Abbie, I heard you and Mr. Henderson."

Which moment had she heard and misunderstood this time?

My eyes lifted to her.

Her expression was genuine, filled with concern and even shame.

My cheeks burned as I turned back to the chaos on the desk. I waited for her to say I was wrong to want his friendship.

She didn't say anything for a long time. Florentina sifted through papers. "I trust you know what you are doing."

My emotions were clogging my throat. "No condemnation for putting myself into his sphere?"

"None. He's going to wait for you to decide what your life is going to be. I believe he will support you. I will, too, if you divorce James Monroe and are no longer Lady Worthing."

She dug a little more, then stopped. "I can't pretend as well as you. Abbie, you shouldn't have told him what your husband insisted upon."

"I don't do well holding in all these scandals. They make me have worries. They make me feel less me."

"Nothing is worth being less than. Not even a title or a precarious position in society."

Fighting my tears, I sorted through papers and ribbon-wrapped pieces of parchment. "Did I mention I love you, Florentina Sewell, the woman who has always seen me?"

"Not today. But it's Christmas. You can be generous."

Laughing, wiping a tear or two, I held up a ribbon-wrapped piece of parchment. "These are indictments, Flo. I saw the one with Lord Worthing's name on it. I was frightened for him. One never knows how the jurymen will decide one's innocence or guilt."

After a fast glance in my direction, Florentina flipped through the largest pile of papers sitting at the edge of the desk. "These have recent dates."

She put down a piece of paper and started to do calculations in the air. "These are talking about a lot of money. My wish for you, Abbie, is to be happy. I don't want you to be like this Lily T. Clayton, swearing to statements of her misfortune. Lord Worthing might not have been swindled by his financier like she was, but whatever his reason is to ask you to break your vows, it has to be equally awful."

With my bandaged palm, I cupped her hand and kissed it. "I . . . you and I, we will survive. We will thrive. But we must find what I believe to be here. The true reason for Brooks's murder."

We started searching the piles again. My cousin was doing calculations on something she had read. She picked up another page and did the same.

"Did you find ship coordinates?"

The light of my candle showed such a frown growing on her face. "Abbie, how wrong is it to take money from one client, pretending to make an investment, only to use the money to pay another client?"

"I don't know. That sounds like a Wilson Shaw question."

"Perhaps, but it reads like fraud." She pulled the paper to her chest. "These are signed by witnesses all saying that Mr. Derrick Mayer has cheated them."

She looked so sad. Mr. Mayer had paid attention to her, offered her compliments. He may not have become a favorite, but he spoke her second language, numbers.

Then it hit me. "Why would one of the Crown's barristers have so many statements? He was planning to indict Mr. Mayer."

"Well, that's one motive." She flipped to the last page of her pile. "And here's another complaint . . . saying her husband has been completely taken in by Mr. Mayer. Mrs. Lily T. Clayton, the Countess of Constock."

I put a hand to my mouth. "The countess was meeting with Brooks not for an affair but to provide testimony for an indictment."

"She desperately wanted Mr. Mayer exposed."

"Perhaps her husband, too. This shows her full name."

After taking the paper, I focused on the signature—*Lily Talson Clayton, the Countess of Constock.*

"And Mr. Brooks is so twisted. He pretended to Mr. Holston to be having an affair with her," I said.

She flipped through more pages. "Though Mr. Mayer repaid Constock, there are enough claims against him to still indict him."

After stuffing a few papers in my pocket, I kept looking. "I'm sure Lord Duncan would like to review them."

After going back to the first drawer I had opened, I dug through the foolscap and found a piece of paper that looked like the invitations. "Here's 'The Rebel's Rhyme,' and Brooks has assigned names to each stanza."

Stunned, seven little Grand-blancs mourn in sharp cliques. One slits his wrist. Now there were six.
—Put this in mine.

Hiding, six little Grand-blancs flee a buzzing hive. A bee stings one. Then there were five.
—Give this to John Clayton, the Earl of Constock.

Scared, five little Grand-blancs huddle and keep score. One gets cold. Then there were four.
—Give this to Mr. William Holston.

Running, four little Grand-blancs take weapons to flee. One twirls a sword. Then there were three.
—Give this to Mr. Frederick Talson.

Forsaken, three little Grand-blancs gather rope and fight anew. One hangs himself, and then there were two.
—Give this to Mr. Derrick Mayer.

*Trapped, two little Grand-blancs sitting in the sun.
One got very warm, and then there was one.
—Give this to Mr. Stapleton Henderson.*

*Guilty, one little grand blanc left all alone. Closed
his eyes forever.
—Give this to Charles Flowers, Lord Duncan.*

And there were none.

I handed the paper to her, and she gave me a witness statement from Mr. Peters.

Before I could comment on my thoughts, I saw pink stationery.

Not just any paper. It was Anna Violet Flowers's, with the fine weave and her name in gold ink.

After grabbing a handful of letters, I gave half to Florentina.

We read through them. Twenty letters in all of Anna's private thoughts, thoughts that she'd sent to a friend, a friend who wanted more, a friend who turned into an enemy when he refused to leave her alone.

This confirmed Lord Duncan's version of the events. I wanted to put these painful letters back, but Florentina took them. She gave me half and put the rest in her coat. "Truth, Abbie, we both have it. One or both of us will make sure it is known."

My mouth opened. I had started to utter my agreement when I heard a creaking floorboard.

At my house in Westminster, that was a telltale sign of a person's movement.

With a finger to my lips, I eased from the desk and snuffed the candle.

To distract whoever was coming, I released the lock on the window and let the wind open and rattle it.

Then we hid behind the shelf partially blocking the door.

Taking a long breath, I waited to see if we'd been followed by Benjamin Brooks's murderers.

Chapter 29

Thirty-Seven Berkeley Square

Hiding in a dead man's house, in his personal study, Florentina and I waited to see who'd followed us.

Well, I knew who.

The sound of the footfalls was too familiar. I'd have to thank Stapleton for making me so aware of how men moved about in the world.

A darkened figure shined an oil lantern inside the room.

I held my breath, Florentina, too, as bursts of light illuminated the white walls, even the signature dentil molding.

A little to the left and lower, the lantern would find us.

The person, the fiend—surprisingly, just one person—came fully inside the parlor.

I gulped.

That meant his henchman waited for us outside. If we successfully fled this villain, the other would harm us like he'd harmed Brooks.

As we huddled together, I felt Florentina's heart gonging against my shoulder. I wondered if she could sense mine. The rhythm of our hearts seemed to echo in the parlor as footfalls neared.

The long bookcase that had offered the disgusting Mr. Brooks privacy acted as a shield, keeping a murderer and his lantern from catching us.

Labored footsteps, labored breaths . . . He stopped.

I covered my mouth with my bandaged hand. My teeth had begun to chatter. The window I'd tossed open let in gusts of freezing air.

Silence.

Was he distracted?

Or did he see us and merely want to toy with us, as he had with each victim of the Night of Regrets?

The figure went to the desk. Florentina put a finger to my lips. The man stood where she had and rummaged through the pile she'd just searched.

He cursed.

I prepared to throw myself at him so my cousin might get away, but he shifted. His light cast shadows along the floor where he'd set down his cane.

Right when I thought he'd pivot and see us, the window slammed shut.

He rushed to it.

The moonlight exposed Mr. Talson and a swordlike weapon in his hand. He opened the window wide and looked out. "You thieves. You went out the window. You cowards."

As he hung out the window, yelling to someone to find us, I grabbed Florentina and motioned to her to run to the hall. We slipped out to a blessedly empty space.

Unfortunately, we didn't have Stapleton's silent footfalls, not in these borrowed boots.

Panicking, we started toward the front door, but that way would make us easy prey for Talson's accomplice.

Hand in hand, I steered Florentina down the corridor, hoping it was truly an exact match to the one in Lord Duncan's home.

It was, complete with an unbroken glass door looking into an open-air orangery. It hadn't been enclosed like the magistrate's.

No buzzing bees or monstrous steam pipes. It led to a garden and freedom.

"Ladies!"

Talson. He was right behind us.

The whip of his sword cut through the air. I pushed forward, leaping into the cold and light flakes.

Florentina and I ran. We ran for freedom.

Snow and ice crackled under our boots.

"No one will help you. You broke into my friend's house."

"Yes, so much a friend!" I pushed Florentina to go faster. "You're complicit in his death."

We kept going, taking the long way, rounding the pavement that formed Berkeley Square. "To Duncan's house," Florentine said. "Someone will see us and the madman swinging his sword."

For a fellow who'd walked with a limp, Talson moved fast. He might catch us.

"Let us rationalize, ladies. I won't harm you." His cackle and his lie were carried by the wind.

We were halfway to Duncan's now. Coming from the side, getting closer, we had to make a ninety-degree turn. From there it was a straight shot to his steps.

Then Florentina tumbled. She rolled in front of me.

"Get up, girl! He's coming. He'll kill us."

We were too far from the pink parlor's windows, or any of Duncan's windows, to be seen.

"Come on, Flo."

She grabbed her ankle. "I can't! I love you. But go, Abbie. Save—"

I dropped to her side and found the strength, the adoration for her in my soul, and lifted her onto her feet. I used my anger like Stapleton had when he first hoisted Holston. I made her lean into me. "Walk with me."

We started again. Our pace was so slow.

The crackle of boots on ice sounded behind us. Talson would soon overtake us.

"Abbie, please." Tears streaked her face. "One of us has to make it."

"Never. We die or live together. Don't give up."

As she leaned on me and kept moving, pain washed her countenance.

Then I saw two shadows—one behind, one coming toward us—running from the woods.

We were so close to Duncan's house, but not close enough.

The blade, shiny and long, whipped toward us. I pushed Flo out of the way to take the brunt of it.

But the blade missed me and whacked Talson's arm.

Lord Duncan wielded this sword. He'd taken one from over the fireplace in the pink parlor.

The old man fell back onto the snow-covered ground.

His weapon had fallen at my boot. Scrambling, I picked it up.

"You ladies all right?" Duncan didn't take his eyes from the man bleeding into the snow.

"Yes," I gasped.

"My ankle, my lord," Florentina said. "I think it's broken."

Talson moaned and tried to cover the deep cut in his arm. "Duncan, have you gone mad? I was scaring them. They'd broken into Brooks's house for some morose reason."

The magistrate sneered at Talson. "I should leave you outside to bleed to death. I'm sure that you'd have no problem letting these women suffer. You had no problem letting Anna suffer. You let her suffer until she died. One bit of truth from the gossip who knew all could've silenced the talk of an affair with Brooks. You could've done that."

Miss Bellows came outside, along with the chef. "Mr. Henderson," she said, "he asked us to watch for all of you. We saw Lord Duncan running. We knew we had to come."

"Help Miss Sewell." The magistrate's breath frosted, fogged the air like a dragon's breath. "Get her to Henderson."

The old chef and Miss Bellows went on either side of my cousin and helped her back to Duncan's house.

Talson yelled after them, "You should help me. I'm . . ." He groaned. "I'm in worse condition."

"Keep going, Miss Bellows," I called. "My cousin needs the best care. That is Commander Stapleton Henderson."

Like a good woman, Miss Bellows kept the chef and Florentina moving forward to safety.

Stone-faced, unflinching in his resolve, Duncan said, "No one will help you, Talson. Not even the man you're in league with."

"Then you know that Talson is working with Mr. Mayer," I said.

Duncan gaped at me. "Yes, and you have deduced that I saw the financier attack Brooks as I looked on from the pink parlor."

Now Talson's eyes widened. This was the first moment his snide lips puckered. Fear had finally taken hold. "You watched Brooks die and said nothing. Charles, I didn't think you had such evil in you."

"I am about justice. If administered by a neighbor, so be it."

"Lord Duncan, Mr. Brooks was about to indict Mr. Mayer for fraud. He swindled people out of their investments."

Lowering the Viking sword a little, Duncan half turned toward the square. "Brooks was finally going to indict someone over that?" Then his grimace returned. "But it wouldn't get

Mr. Peters his money back. I told him I'd help, but he said he was done."

"Mr. Peters's gout was terrible," I said, preparing to tell Duncan how the Night of Regrets went amok. "He had also lost his dreams. For a courageous man who survived enslavement and war, he couldn't think about living without the money he'd worked so hard to save. He couldn't retire."

"It frightened him," Talson said. "I tried to help him. I did help him."

"Of course you did. Both you men did."

Lord Duncan looked at me. "He was done. Peters was in such pain."

"You found him in severe distress. You helped him down from his quarters. Probably thought you could put him in a lower bedchamber and have one of the physicians attend him. You had two staying at Nine Berkeley Square, but you didn't know he'd taken enough laudanum to numb the pain of a fall."

"She's lying, Charles. You'd never . . . You helped Peters die."

"Oh, yes, he did." I nodded. "Peters put a stanza from the original Caribbean version of 'The Rebel's Rhyme' in his pocket. It wasn't one of the stanzas that you and Brooks decided upon. That was going to be your twist to the Night of Regrets. You gossiped and told Mayer and Holston, everyone but Lord Duncan and Mr. Henderson."

"That's not murder." Talson bled through his coat. "Help me."

"No one is going to help you. You killed Constock, attacked Holston, and attempted to kill Henderson with smoke. Why show you mercy?" Duncan said.

"You truly believe anyone will think an old man did all those things? You both are mad."

He'd have a point if the man wasn't a master manipulator. "You set traps for Lord Constock and Mr. Henderson with silver wire. The same sharp wire that was used to cut Brooks. None of that takes brawn. Just cunning. A willingness to use a man's weakness for wine and to wait in the snow to set a trap, but forgetting to dry your cane of melting ice. Or the savvy to induce weakness by drugging a younger man with belladonna. To make him irritable and willing to fight."

Talson tried to sit up. Scarlet drops collected in the snow. "Is this how you solve things, Charles? A woman rattling off lies?"

"I'm not done, and you shall listen." I looked at Lord Duncan. "I haven't said how Mr. Talson was helpful to Mr. Peters."

I held up the gossip's sword, letting the gleam of light stick to it, and pointed to the wire-wrapped handle. The same type of wire but thinner adorned the Viking swords of Anna Violet. "You took Mr. Peters to Brooks. You knew he'd been swindled, like your son-in-law Lord Constock. And like the Countess of Constock, your daughter Lily, Mr. Peters gave a statement. But Brooks pressed him for a favor. He wanted to pull a prank during the Night of Regrets. The barrister wrote out 'The Rebel's Rhyme' and told Mr. Peters which stanza to place in each invitation."

With his eyes shifting almost as much as he winced, the cornered man didn't deny a thing.

Waiting for him to confess, I kept going. "I'm sure the man who uses fine silver wires to repair swords enjoyed picking the stanza of how Brooks would be killed. Then you struck a bargain with Mr. Mayer. If he gave the earl and your daughter back their investment, you'd help him get away with silencing Brooks. A bonus would be that the valet from Martinique, who knew the 'The Rebel's Rhyme' and sent the invitations, would be the prime suspect."

"Mayer killed Brooks?" Lord Duncan puffed a cold cloud of white air. "I watched Brooks die, but I didn't see who did it."

"Must've been something, Charles, to watch your rival die."

Catching the magistrate's gaze, I said, "And Mayer agreed with framing your valet. I'm sure that weighed in Mr. Peters's head. The minute he knew how Brooks was killed, I believe the fear of his good name being sullied wore on his thinking as much as his pain."

Talson writhed. "Are you believing this, Charles? She's wrong. I had no reason to kill anyone."

"I'm sure you will grieve heavily when you tell your daughter that her spendthrift husband can no longer put their fortune at risk. With Constock dead, he can't reinvest with Mayer. And Mayer can't tell a soul, because you know he killed Brooks."

Duncan shook his head. "You killed your own son-in-law, and with bees."

"I'm not saying that I did, but Constock was weak. Weak for wine and a little buzzing creature."

"Talson, you're a monster," Duncan said. "Lady Worthing, your powers of deduction amaze me. You've put together this fiend's crimes. I should let him bleed to death like Brooks. In fact, you run inside."

"Woman, don't go. Charles has gone mad. You heard him. He watched Mayer kill his rival. It was his Night of Regrets. This is Duncan's doing. You have it all wrong. That's why he wants you to go. He wants his crimes to die with me."

"I'm quite sure of your guilt, Mr. Talson. I have the statements from your daughter and Mr. Peters, dozens of others. I even have 'The Rebel's Rhyme' in your or Brooks's hand."

"Must be Brooks." Talson writhed. "I never heard of such, but you broke into Brooks's house. You could be Charles's accomplice."

"I had a key." I held the brass thing up in my bandaged hand. "You can't break in if you have a key."

"Brooks is not going to complain," Lord Duncan said. "She found him. I think he'd be fine with you getting your comeuppance from a woman."

"Well, he loved women. Didn't he, Charles?"

"But not as much as you, Mr. Talson." I pulled pages of pink parchment from my coat and handed the letters to Lord Duncan.

Talson closed his eyes and cursed.

"It wasn't Benjamin Brooks harassing Anna Violet, at least not at first. It was Talson," I explained. "He befriended her, then used all the little things he knew about her from their friendship and his daughter to torment her. When she rejected him, he made a game of teasing her and giving all the details to Brooks."

"Brooks was outlandish, even making scandalous pictures of her," Talson muttered. "Then he told other neighbors intimate conversations I'd had about Anna and her beauty. Brooks took my esteem and made it tawdry. And I couldn't tell the truth without destroying my own reputation."

"So, you let Anna Violet Flowers be destroyed." I shook my finger at him. "All the letters she wrote to make the gossip stop, begging you to end the rumors of an affair, Brooks had them all. That was his leverage over you. 'The father of Berkeley Square' was a tired old leech who couldn't take rejection. And you laughed as a malicious man made her life miserable."

"Brooks made her a joke to everyone." Duncan stepped forward and stabbed Talson in the other arm. "Lady Worthing, go inside. I need to duel for my wife's honor."

"I admit to nothing, Charles." Talson tried to staunch his wounds but failed. "I'm glad that my daughter and my grandson, the new Earl of Constock, are protected."

"Yes, the grandson, who'd be about the age of my daughter had she and her mother lived. But girls don't matter to you, Talson."

"These are fantasies, Charles. You let this meddling woman who's done nothing but disrupt your household use you. Her fanciful talk is turning man against man. She and her ilk want what we have. I've been your friend for years. All these women want to belittle us. They want to make decisions, *our* decisions. They want to lord over us."

Duncan stepped close to the fiend. "Talson, if Lady Worthing were in control, her kind heart would be trying to get you aid."

"I'm not that kind or that foolish, Lord Duncan," I declared. "I merely want you to think of what you are doing and the kind of man that you are."

"He chose this path." Duncan took his sword and put it to Talson's throat. "This is one mystery you don't have to see through to the end."

"You can't trust her, Charles. She's twisting you up."

"Lord Duncan," I said, "you don't have to be like him."

"Just do it, Charles. Run me through. Let this all be over."

The magistrate stood up straight. "Let's both go inside. Let spring have him, like he wished for Brooks."

Not knowing what to say, I decided to stand with the magistrate and watch Mr. Talson make the snow scarlet and gain admission to hell.

Chapter 30

Derrick Mayer hears the commotion entering Lord Duncan's house. Hearing Miss Sewell's voice, he knows he's finally done something right. This feeling, warm and full in his soul, is one he hasn't experienced in a long time. Cheating people eats at the spirit.

He lays his head against the cold glass, and his breath frosts the pane. He'd started out hunting for the ladies with Talson, but once he passed the bench and saw the shadows hovering in the trees, he felt convicted.

It was one thing to go against the worm Brooks, but quite another to turn against innocent women. Even a scoundrel can draw lines in the snow . . . lines that should never be crossed.

"Duncan and Lady Worthing should've been back by now." Miss Sewell's voice echoes in the hall. "Talson, too, but in the magistrate's custody."

Could the sword-wielding old man have done them both in?

"Miss Sewell," the maid replies, "should we go back to help?"

"No, Miss Bellows." This is a man's voice, the chef's. "The magistrate will come in when he's finished outside."

Derrick should go into the hall and say something.

But how can he face her?

A moment earlier he'd contemplated doing Talson's bidding again. The murder of one became two, almost three. When Talson murdered his son-in-law, that should have been the point at which to confess. The wily old man would figure out a way to blame Derrick.

If only Brooks had had that key, then Derrick could've gotten the evidence Brooks had collected. That would have been worth trying to kill an old soldier grieving in the cellar.

Mr. Henderson shouts in the hall. The commotion sounds like he's going to aid Miss Sewell.

Hoping she's not badly injured, Derrick sighs. He laments again not getting that key, the witness statements, and finding whatever Brooks had on Talson. It had to be bad to try to set Mr. Henderson up to be convicted.

Hands sweaty and sticky, Derrick wipes them on his shirt and the tails of his cravat. Nothing stops the feeling that blood stains his palm. Probably more now, for he doesn't hear Lady Worthing's voice at all.

It's too late to help her.

He told Duncan when he confessed that he'd not leave the room. It's about time Derrick Mayer's word means something.

There was no reasoning with Talson. He meant to kill the ladies. The fool kept saying that breaking and entering is a crime punishable by death.

Derrick glances out at the snow, waiting for Duncan to come back and tell him all the many charges he holds against him and Talson.

The rhyme he's heard since his childhood in Martinique, since he met Mr. Peters and planned to participate in Brooks's . . . Talson's big scheme, he sings it like Mr. Peters always did.

> *Braggin', eight little Grand-blancs think they own heaven. One leaps high. Then there were seven.*
> *Stunned, seven little Grand-blancs mourn in sharp cliques. One slits his wrist. Now there were six.*
> *Hiding, six little Grand-blancs flee a buzzing hive. A bee stings one. Then there were five.*
> *Scared, five little Grand-blancs huddle and keep score. One gets cold. Then there were four.*
> *Running, four little Grand-blancs take weapons to flee. One twirls a sword. Then there were three.*
> *Forsaken, three little Grand-blancs gather rope and fight anew. One hangs himself, and then there were two.*
> *Trapped, two little Grand-blancs sitting in the sun. One got very warm, and then there was one.*
> *Guilty, one little grand blanc left all alone. Closed his eyes forever. And there were none.*

He stops singing and thinks of the men who've perished the way the rhyme dictates. Duncan was so angry and frightened for the ladies that he surely has made *Talson twirl a sword* and become no more.

Part of him is relieved that Talson will be dead.

He and Talson and fate have arranged this, except for Mr. Peters's death. The cravat that Derrick wears about his neck was a gift from the valet. It's made of the best linen. Peters gave it to him as a present the day Derrick let the man invest.

The poor valet . . . Derrick swindled him out of his retirement. The man was so frantic the day Brooks died.

Derek scratches his head, then pulls on his cravat. It's generously made, bulky and strong. He sings again the poem, but this time he adds the men's names.

> *Braggin', eight little Grand-blancs think they own heaven. Peters leaps high. Then there were seven.*

> *Stunned, seven little Grand-blancs mourn in sharp cliques. Brooks slits his wrist. Now there were six.*

> *Hiding, six little Grand-blancs flee a buzzing hive. A bee stings Constock. Then there were five.*

> *Scared, five little Grand-blancs huddle and keep score. Holston gets cold. Then there were four.*

> *Running, four little Grand-blancs take weapons to flee. Talson twirls a sword. Then there were three.*

> *Forsaken, three little Grand-blancs gather rope and fight anew. Derrick hangs himself, and then there were two.*

Ignoring the final two stanzas, hoping Henderson and Duncan escape, Derrick repeats the stanzas that came to pass, then sings extra loud the one about him. *Forsaken, three little Grand-blancs gather rope and fight anew. Derrick hangs himself, and then there were two.*

Hanging is a just punishment for someone who steals, and for a man who's killed one and tried to kill another. Beating up Holston and leaving him for dead in the cold cellar was terrible, but Holston knew Brooks was going for a fraud indictment.

After stepping back from the window, Derrick clasps Mrs. Flowers's sainted chair. He lifts it and moves the padded thing from the writing desk to the center of the room.

Right under the sparkling crystals of the chandelier, he looks up and eyes the hook that supports the light fixture. After loosening the long strips of cloth that form his cravat, he knots the ends and forms a loop. He decides to hang it on the center hook that supports the chandelier.

His fingers slip over the smooth fabric again, and he thinks of poor Mr. Peters. He didn't know what to do about no longer having money. He'd imagined retiring and being off his feet, resting that gout-filled leg. Derrick told him Duncan would take care of him, would even let him work till he died.

That was unacceptable to the valet. He said he was done serving others after this Night of Regrets. The man surely meant he was done.

Derrick will take his advice and be done, too.

" 'Forsaken, three little Grand-blancs gather rope and fight anew. Derrick hangs himself, and then there were two.' "

Singing the rebel stanza over and over, he climbs onto the chair and puts the loop in place. The knots are strong. The hook will hold his weight.

" 'Forsaken, three little Grand-blancs gather rope and fight anew. Derrick hangs himself, and then there were two.' "

Derrick slips his head through the fabric loop.

It is time to make his stanza from "The Rebel's Rhyme" true.

With a swift kick, the chair falls away.

He struggles, even fights, but he hasn't the strength to escape. He'll need a miracle to outlast this mistake.

The door opens.

Salvation comes from the physician. Vision darkening, he sees Mr. Henderson entering the parlor.

"Mayer, now that my patient is stable and Miss Sewell, too, I need to know where Lady—"

The physician glances at him, at his dangling legs, and sees that he is breathless, gasping.

Salvation leaves.

Mr. Henderson backs away and closes the door.

Chapter 31

The Lane of Berkeley Square

Standing outside with Lord Duncan, I watched him let Mr. Talson bleed. I refused to leave him. I'd never seen the magistrate in this dangerous state of mind. I feared for his safety.

I wouldn't leave him alone to make "The Rebel's Rhyme" for him come true.

Guilty, one little grand blanc left all alone. Closed his eyes forever. And there were none.

"Lord Duncan," I pleaded with him, "let the courts punish Mr. Talson. He will be publicly humiliated. That will hurt him more."

"But he made Anna suffer." His sword was again at Talson's chest. "Perhaps I should just end him. It's a matter of honor."

"Yes, Charles, honor." The man winced. His breath fell rapidly. Talson must know he couldn't continue to bleed and live. "She believed in redemption, remember."

With his sword still extended, Duncan backed up an inch.

"She thought the Yuletide season was supposed to be about second chances. I made the Night of Regrets for Anna. I made up the trial that went wrong in Martinique to give everyone a chance to admit their wrongs. But every year they told of new sins. And then they gloated about them. Talson most particularly."

"Lady Worthing! Lord Duncan!"

That was Stapleton. When I turned, Talson moved. He lunged forward. I wasn't sure if he tried to take Duncan's sword, but he ended up impaled by it.

The magistrate didn't move. In fact, he twisted the hilt in the man's gut before pushing Talson to the ground.

Stapleton ran to us. His gaze went toward the red blade of the sword, then to me. "Are you two all right?"

I nodded but couldn't move. My eyes stayed affixed to the menace who was dead and all the scarlet snow.

Taking the sword from the magistrate's hands, Stapleton said, "You saved Lady Worthing from the fiend who wished her harm. You are a hero, Lord Duncan."

Firm jaw slack, Lord Duncan said, "Lady Worthing, these men were the reason you've never had an invitation here. Lady Duncan's never dined with anyone here. You need to be able to trust your neighbors. It's good you can trust yours."

Finding myself nodding again, I fought the queasy feeling growing in my gut. "Mr. Henderson is a good man. I'm lucky."

The wind blew snowflakes around us. It could be considered pretty and wintry, this view of Berkeley Square. None of us stirred. I didn't want to, not until blanc snow covered the scarlet ice.

Stapleton took Talson's sword from me and clanged it against Duncan's. "It's Christmas Day. Let's go inside. Holston has recovered. He will make it."

Duncan started moving. "We'll need to take Mr. Mayer into custody until I can formally indict him."

"Mr. Mayer has taken 'The Rebel's Rhyme' form of punishment. He's in the pink parlor. He won't be leaving there until we decide to make him go."

It was an odd way to say where the criminal was, but the look these two exchanged indicated that Mr. Mayer was no more.

On the steps of Number Nine Berkeley Square, the view was white and grand as fresh snow covered every sin.

Epilogue

December 26, 1806

The day after Christmas, I sat back in Stapleton's carriage as it moved through the streets of London. I didn't think I had ever been quite so happy to leave a place, but we did wait for the coroner and Duncan's runners to come make their pronouncement and remove all the villains and victims from his property.

"Abigail," Stapleton said as he sat on the other side of the carriage, holding Florentina's foot in place. "I see the crinkle on your brow. Do not fret. The magistrate and Mr. Villers are on their way to the country. He'll be with his new family. He's not alone. And I believe for the first time in years, he's without guilt."

"Oh, Mr. Henderson, she won't stop fretting, not unless you promise to return with Teacup to my parents' house for dinner. She doesn't want you alone, either."

My cousin smiled at him.

That eased my spirit.

"Miss Sewell," he said, "I know you're anxious to frolic or

do math, but I need you to be off this ankle for a few more days. You twisted it badly. I want it to heal so you will not need a cane."

I had to look away. I was sick of canes. The memory of hearing Talson's cane on wood floors or marble gave me chills. "Yes, Flo. Say no to canes."

Miss Bellows shook her head. "Do you think Lord Duncan will keep a residence in Berkeley Square?"

Stapleton shook his head. "I've a feeling he will be putting it on the market. Who knows? He might end up as one of our neighbors, Abigail, right in Westminster."

"Not sure what that would mean to the neighborhood. But it might bring more mysteries."

Everyone groaned.

I sat back, quite content that we, the four of us, were alive and we'd helped Lord Duncan.

Leaning my head against the seat, I made my Yuletide request. "Wake me when we are in Cheapside and Aunt is ready to serve black cake."

Perhaps for the first time all week, I closed my eyes and rested in peace.

When I opened my eyes, I didn't see cake, but the blue doors of the Sewell residence. Footmen in silver and blue rushed out their door, followed by two of the best sights I could ever see, my godfather, Mr. Vaughn, and Wilson Shaw.

Sitting up, I noticed Miss Bellows was out of the carriage, getting them to carry portmanteaus and presents into the house. I think she ordered a bath for me, too.

"Ready, Florentina?" Stapleton waited for her to nod.

She slipped her arms about his neck, and he proceeded to carry her from the carriage.

"Wait one minute." Wilson stepped to Stapleton and blocked

his progress. "This one is mine. From the look of you, you've had enough of her."

"Is it fine with you, Miss Sewell, to give you over to Mr. Shaw?"

"Men are fighting over me, Abbie. I think I like this." She nodded to Stapleton. "You can put Mr. Shaw to work. I think you've done a little too much." She smiled at him with true Florentina warmth. "Stay and help my friend. Then we'll see you at the Sewells' dinner tonight."

"Yes, ma'am." Stapleton did as she requested and gently handed her off to a seemingly impatient solicitor.

Once she was secure in his arms, Wilson looked spry, like he'd bested Stapleton, and whirled Florentina around and around as he returned to the wonderful three-story stone house on the corner. "Little girl, you and your cousin had us worried. And I see the physician had to doctor your foot."

"Yes, I twisted my ankle badly while running with Abbie."

Wilson stopped and looked back. "A run, huh? Probably for your very lives."

May have been my imagination, but his hold about her tightened.

"I can only imagine what our dear Lady Worthing had you running from." Wilson frowned and passed Vaughn on the steps. "We didn't know what to think. I did my best to keep your parents entertained, for we couldn't go anywhere to look for you."

"We were stuck, as well. Horrible experience."

The two bounded upstairs, chattering the whole way, but the world could hear her shriek as he apologized for eating all her mother's black cake.

Vaughn laughed and came closer to the carriage. "It seems Mr. Shaw arrived early and became stranded here during the snowstorm."

Clasping Stapleton's offered hand, I stuck one stiff leg out and then another. My neighbor's arms went about me quickly, too quickly, as he helped me to the ground. "And I'm sure my aunt babied Mr. Shaw like the son she never had."

My godfather dipped his chin. "My sister-in-law means well, and I'm sure Shaw loved the attention."

Vaughn glanced at us, his full lips flattening. "I received a startling message before leaving my residence. The mayhem at Lord Duncan's is being called a Yuletide massacre. Thank you for keeping my niece and my goddaughter safe."

A comforting look passed between them before Stapleton said, "They both kept me safe, as well. It was a team effort to survive."

"Well, then, I congratulate you both." He was wearing a heavy ebony tailcoat and only one glove, so my godfather must've just arrived. He started up the steps to the house. "Oh, Abigail. I did some checking on the note you sent me before all of London came to a screeching halt."

His frown made my stomach hurt. "Please, Mr. Vaughn, tell me some good news."

As Stapleton and I stayed in place on the bottom stone step, Vaughn kept going. At the top, he turned to us. His full lips drooped more. "Can't be helped. Emperor Dessalines is dead. He was assassinated. That has been confirmed."

My heart stopped. My chest felt kicked in. Like he had when I started to faint, Stapleton stepped closer, supporting me. "My headache has returned."

"How, Mr. Vaughn?" Stapleton asked. "Who did it?"

"An ambush. They are saying his men conspired against him. Hayti, the young, free nation, is in chaos."

"His men? They murdered him?" I covered my eyes for a moment, then buried my face into the folds of Stapleton's greatcoat.

"Is she well? Did Abigail hurt herself like Florentina?"

"It's been a trying few days," Stapleton replied. "A bloody coup for a country she's had high hopes for is devastating."

With a shake of my head, I left the safety of the arms holding me and started up the steps. "If not for the past few days, I wouldn't believe it. The duplicity of those who are supposed to be close to you apparently knows no bounds."

"I can carry you, like the charismatic Mr. Shaw, if you need such assistance." Stapleton's whisper sounded humorous.

And I needed the moment of levity. "You just hurry back with Teacup. Maybe bring the greyhounds. My uncle's a dog person. These beautiful creatures make my aunt sneeze, but maybe they could come and stay in the mews."

"Or you could come home. They surely miss you."

Vaughn went inside. He'd started taking off his other glove when he did an about-face and stepped again over the threshold. "Oh, and I brought a surprise for you. It will be delivered soon,"

He disappeared inside the house once more

That sounded fun or ominous or both. Then I wasn't sure I was up for anything but a long bath and a fresh satin gown.

At the top of the steps, under the portico, Stapleton and I shared the best view of the quiet street, but it wasn't our street.

"I must be with you when the dogs get the special Christmas bacon. They must think it's from both of us," I said, "I'll pay you half for it."

"No need. I agree. They must love us equally, I suppose."

His chuckles were light, and his supporting arm stayed about me.

"Well, I should be going."

Didn't want that. Of the many things I was unsure of, he wasn't one of them.

Round woman full of pudding, my aunt came outside. "Here's the man who kept my girls safe."

"It was a . . ."

Before he could say another word, Aunt drew him into her loving arms. "Hurry back or simply stay. We have plenty of room."

Elegant as ever, with her chignon trimmed in pearls, my beautiful aunt finally released Stapleton. "I mean that."

His face reddened, and he began to step away.

My aunt then scooped me into a wonderful embrace that smelled of vanilla and ginger. If I closed my eyes, this scent would send me to past Christmases, but then Stapleton would be gone. And I didn't want that at all.

Aunt shivered but pointed up to the bright sun. "Oh, haven't seen that for days." She started inside. "You both need to decide what you're doing and not let out the heat. Coal is not cheap."

The door closed, and the two of us, the Greater Queen Street neighbors, remained under the portico.

"Abigail, after the holidays, we should have a long talk."

He probably wanted to speak about all the things we'd shared, from James to Nelson. "Yes. After. But today is for family and friends."

Stapleton grasped my hands. He kissed the bandaged one. "I will change this to a proper bandage when I return."

He put his lips to my other hand; his kiss hit my bare wrist before settling decently on my glove.

"Don't make it hurt. I think you've seen me squirm enough."

"You're a big girl, Abigail. Some things must hurt before they become better."

What his indigo eyes implied or meant would be a mystery if his words weren't a universal truth. They added to my resolve.

"Stapleton, would you still be my friend if I were a pariah?"

"I come from a family of pariahs and paragons. I think you fit somewhere in between. That's very keepable."

"I'm serious. What if I were disgraced and no longer Lady Worthing?"

The humor in his countenance faded. Some new inspiration lit his eyes. "What are you saying, Abigail?"

I took a breath and tried to order my rambling pile of thoughts. Then I said what was at the top of my mind. "A divorced woman will be a pariah. The ton may want nothing to do with me. I can't stay married to a man who wants me to live without truth. And I don't think I could want to be with a man willing to overlook it."

Stapleton let my fingers go. "You'd rather be without the security that marriage to Worthing brings?"

I dipped my chin in agreement. That was what James was now, security in a life I no longer wanted, not if it meant acting without principles. "Yes."

My voice sounded strong. I could do anything with friends, and I had both of my favorites.

"You're some kind of woman, Abigail Carrington Monroe. We're friends. I fought to be that. I won't let a simple thing like a fool named Worthing or my own stupidity stand in the way."

Stapleton blew heat on his hands and mine. "We shall remain friends, no matter your name or where you live. You shan't be rid of me."

He started down the steps. "I do prefer you close, somewhere where I and Santisma and Silvereye can get to you quickly. Teacup will agree."

"Please smuggle those dogs here. I can't stand how much I miss . . . them."

A carriage pulled up and parked behind Stapleton's. As large and stately, but with Vaughn's crest. Must be his surprise.

"I'll be back for dinner with the dogs," Stapleton said, "for a proper domesticated canine visit. With London reopening, I'll make a few inquiries to see if the secretary of war and the colonies have any plans to assist Hayti. Independence has made it easier for the nation to keep friends. Independence can be a good thing. Merry Christmas, Abigail. I don't think I have said that to you yet."

My stomach was in knots. "Merry Christmas and stay safe, Stapleton."

I folded my hands into my thick coat and watched his carriage leave.

The door to the second Berlin opened. A man offered a familiar wave, and I waited for him to respond.

Mr. Vaughn had outdone himself for my Christmas present. He'd returned to London my profligate husband, Lord Worthing.

Author's Note

My Thoughts on *Murder in Berkeley Square*

Vanessa here.

If you haven't guessed by now, I have a heart for military men from all eras. My husband, grandfather, father-in-law, and a lot of uncles all served with honor. Soldiers work incredibly hard. They rarely complain, and when their duties are done, they must assimilate back into society. I can't imagine how hard that is. Mr. Peters, Mr. Henderson, and even Mr. Holston—fictional characters—are ways to remember their service and the difficulties that can arise from being in combat. I salute them.

As a murder mystery fan, I adore Agatha Christie. I think she's one of the most brilliant minds of our time. Her stories are complex, witty, and drama filled. Nonetheless, I've always been a little uneasy about my favorite Agatha Christie novel, *And Then There Were None*. The novel was originally published in 1939 with the inflammatory title *Ten Little N—s*. The derogatory title was based on a minstrel song that has roots in a children's rhyme dictating what to do to runaway slaves.

Yep. A publisher okayed this book title in the year of our Lord 1939—seventy-four years after the end of the American Civil War, over a hundred years after enslavement ended in all British territories. The novel was not updated and retitled *Ten Little Indians* until 1964. This title is not much better, but at least I can mention it here in full. While I enjoy this Agatha Christie mystery, how does one ignore its origins? Personally, I've never been one to hide the good or the bad about history.

But when I objectively looked at what Christie does in the novel by isolating a group of privileged individuals—privileged in the sense that their very stature and connections in society allow each of them to get away with murder—on a postcolonial tropical island and systematically killing them, I realized that she is echoing what the grand-blancs, or owners of plantations (habitations), did when they trafficked in enslaved people and murdered the runaways.

Thus, my homage to Agatha Christie was born. I drew from the tradition of the chants used to rally the enslaved and incite rebellions in the colonies and created "The Rebel's Rhyme" as the basis of the murder plot.

General Comments on the Lady Worthing Series

Again, this series is my homage to all the things I love about murder mysteries and crime fiction, and even romance novels and thrillers, but it is set in the familiar world of the Regency era. As a junkie for the Old Bailey's criminal proceedings, I endeavor to portray the nuances of Regency-era crimes and bring you mystery solving conducted by an amateur detective who is trying to define her place in that world.

As each mystery unfolds, you are doing life with Abbie,

learning more about her backstory and some of the struggles this amateur detective faces as a progressive woman in Regency England. Abigail is bold. She wants her own space at a time when women, particularly women of color, struggle for agency.

Racial harmony and diversity are also a long struggle that cuts right through the Regency period. It feels as if this struggle has always been with us, like the original sin. My approach is to balance the good and bad of the era while showing a more inclusive side of history, one that matches the facts on the ground.

As always, I do a lot of research to build these inclusive narratives, and I've included some of my notes for you. For this mystery, I pulled facts straight from the headlines and stories of London newspapers.

So settle in and enjoy real places, true histories, and actual persons who lived during these times. Every element plays a part in these mysteries. And enjoy my *subtle* homage to *Murder, She Wrote*; *Matlock*; *Remington Steele*; *Dynasty*; *and Dallas*. This will be fun.

Want to learn more? Visit my website, VanessaRiley.com, to gain more insight. Make sure to join my newsletter, where I share travel notes, history, and a bit of background on my life writing historical fiction.

Cool Facts Related to *Murder in Berkeley Square*

The Battle of Valley Forge

General Wilhelm von Knyphausen led British troops on a raid of Valley Forge during the American Revolutionary War. American troops were storing supplies in Valley Forge, and on September 18, 1777, the British attacked the site and succeeded in burning a few buildings and stealing supplies. This minor clash became known as the Battle of Valley Forge.

The Enslaved Who Fought for the British

With the promise of being freed, it is estimated over twenty thousand enslaved men escaped their American masters and fought on the side of the British during the American Revolutionary War.

Laudanum

Laudanum is a tincture of opium. It was a pain relief drug of the Regency period. There is no single formulation for laudanum, and it is highly addictive.

Beestings

Austrian scientist and pediatrician Clemens von Pirquet did not coin the term *allergy* until 1906, but human's sensitivities and reactions to foreign substances were noted much earlier. For instance, in 1765 Ulrich Müller became the first to document a deadly reaction to a honeybee sting. A thirty-year-old man was stung on the eyelid, and after a short time, he collapsed and died.

Tyburn

Tyburn is a place in London where criminal executions (public hangings) were carried out from 1196 until 1783. After 1783 public hangings were held at Newgate Prison. Criminal executions in London were public spectacles. This was meant to deter crime. The process for these executions entailed placing convicts in carts, driving them through the streets, and often giving them a chance to talk to the crowd and confess to their crimes. Then they were hung.

The Assassination of Jean-Jacques Dessalines

When Saint-Domingue permanently abolished slavery and declared its independence in 1804 under the leadership of Jean-Jacques Dessalines, all the abolition movements in the world curtailed their efforts to achieve freedom. The fear of Black rule halted progress. On December 23, 1806, reports began to be printed in British newspapers that Emperor Jacques I, formerly General Jean-Jacques Dessalines, had been assassinated. As it turned out, the generals under his command were suspected of participating in the assassination. His men betrayed him.

Mary Edwards

Mary Edwards is considered the first human computer. She calculated positions of the sun, moon, and stars for the nautical almanacs of the British Navy. She was one of few women paid to do this work, and she received a man's salary. In the novel the fictional Florentina Sewell works for her.

Lord Nelson

Viscount Nelson was an admiral in the British Navy. One of Britain's greatest naval heroes, he led his forces to decisive naval victories against France and Spain in the French Revolutionary Wars and the Napoleonic Wars. The nation mourned his passing at a state funeral in 1806. The depiction of his death in *Murder in Westminster* is based on the records of the attending physicians and officers on Nelson's ship. In this series, the fictional Stapleton Henderson is one those physicians.

The Westminster Area of London

Westminster is in the central part of London and extends from the river Thames to Oxford Street and includes St. James's Park. It is the seat of the British government and Parliament and also contains Buckingham Palace, Westminster Abbey, and Westminster Cathedral.

The Park at Berkeley Square

London's Berkeley Square has a rich history. In 1696 it was originally part of a garden belonging to a large house, Berkeley

House, owned by the Duke of Cavendish. The land has some of the oldest plane trees in London.

While I couldn't pinpoint who lived at Nine Berkeley Square or Thirty-Seven Berkeley Square in 1806, I did find out that Sarah Child Villiers, Countess of Jersey (Lady Jersey), one of the famous patronesses of the exclusive London social club Almack's, lived at Thirty-Eight Berkeley Square.

Lansdowne House, which at the time was one of the largest residences in the square, was home to several prime ministers, including William Pitt the Younger, who would've been a neighbor to Lord Duncan until his death in January 1806.

Drury Lane Theatre

Drury Lane Theatre is one of the royal theaters in London and dates back to 1663. The original building was destroyed by fire in 1809. The old-scene store was a specific room behind the stage and housed props and old scenery canvasses. There were several other rooms, which housed costumes and more scenery items, things that were used nightly in current productions. The tunnels that went from Drury Lane to the Thames were filled in. The tunnels were part of a network built by kings to travel about the city sheltering their mistresses from public or wifely view. Sailors used to enter the tunnels during off times at the docks and would earn extra money working the rigging which was similar to what they used to lift and lower sails.

Mulattoes and Blackamoors During the Regency Era

The term *mulatto* is a social construct used to describe a person born to one parent who is Caucasian and one who is of African, Spanish, Latin, Indian, or Caribbean descent. Mulattoes during the Regency period often achieved greater social mobility than other racial minorities, particularly if their families had means. The term *Blackamoors* refers to racial minorities with darker complexions, and these include mulattoes, Africans, and West and East Indians living in England during the eighteenth and nineteenth centuries.

Mulattoes and Blackamoors numbered between ten thousand and twenty thousand in London and throughout England in the time of Jane Austen. Wealthy British with children born to native West Indies women brought them to London for schooling. In her last novel, entitled *Sanditon*, Jane Austen, a leading writer of her times, wrote of Miss Lambe, a mulatto from the West Indies, who possesses an immense fortune. Her wealth made her desirable to the ton.

Mulatto and Blackamoor children were often told to pass to achieve elevated positions within society. Wealthy plantation owners with mixed-race children and wealthy mulattoes, like Dorothea Thomas from the colony of Demerara, often sent their children abroad to secure an education and to marry. Read more about a woman who defies accepted notions of agency for Black women in Georgian and Regency times in *Island Queen*.